JACKSON'S DILEMMA

JACKSON'S DILEMMA

IRIS MURDOCH

Chatto & Windus
LONDON

First published in 1995

1 3 5 7 9 10 8 6 4 2
Copyright © Iris Murdoch 1995
Iris Murdoch has asserted her right under the Copyright,
Designs and Patents Act, 1988 to be identified as the author
of this work.

First published in Great Britain in 1995 by
Chatto & Windus Limited
Random House, 20 Vauxhall Bridge Road,
London SW1V 2SA

Random House Australia (Pty) Limited
20 Alfred Street, Milsons Point, Sydney
New South Wales 2061, Australia

Random House New Zealand Limited
18 Poland Road, Glenfield
Auckland 10, New Zealand

Random House South Africa (Pty) Limited
P O Box 337, Bergvlei, South Africa

Random House UK Limited Reg. No. 954009

Papers used by Random House UK Limited are natural, recyclable
products made from wood grown in sustainable forests.
The manufacturing processes conform to the environmental
regulations of the country of origin.

A CIP catalogue record for this book
is available from the British Library

ISBN 0 7011 6511 1

Typeset by Deltatype Ltd, Ellesmere Port, Cheshire
Printed in Great Britain by
Mackays of Chatham

CONTENTS

ONE

Edward Lannion was sitting at his desk in his pleasant house in
London in Notting Hill. The sun was shining. It was an early
morning in June, not quite midsummer. Edward was good-
looking. He was tall and slim and pale. He was very well
dressed. His hair, slightly curling, thickly tumbling down his
neck, was a dark golden brown. He had a long firm mouth, a
rather long hawkish nose, and long light brown eyes. He was
twenty-eight.

His beautiful mother had died of cancer when he was ten.
He had seen her die. When he heard his father's sobs he knew.
When he was eighteen, his younger brother was drowned. He
had no other siblings. He loved his mother and his brother
passionately. He had not got on with his father. His father,
who was rich and played at being an architect, wanted Edward
to be an architect too. Edward did not want to be an architect.
He studied mediaeval history at Cambridge. Informed by his
father that he should now earn his living somehow, he joined a
small academic publishing house which dealt with the kind of
books Edward liked. Unknown to his father he employed
himself at publishing for only two mornings a week, devoting
the rest to reading, and attempting to write historical novels,
even poems. When Edward's father died Edward shed tears
and wished he had behaved better to his father, who had left
him the house in Notting Hill, and the estate, and the
handsome house in the country. The name of the house was

I

Hatting Hall, a name regarded as ridiculous by Edward and his brother Randall when they were children.

Hatting Hall, half Tudor half Georgian, having by now lost some of its larger property, was now content to own big beautiful gardens and some miles of adjacent meadows. Through these meadows ran the narrow stream of the river Lip, passing through the village known as Lipcot. Lipcot, high up upon the far side from Hatting, after giving its name to the river, was now becoming nothing more than a hamlet, consisting of a few small houses, some smaller genuine cottages, a few shops, and a pub. Upstream, recently restored, was a sturdy bridge, leading to what the villagers called 'civilisation'. The Hall owned the land on its own side down to the river, together with half of a much disputed fragile bridge, the land on the other side, for a considerable distance, being the property of the only other 'grand house' in the vicinity. Farther down the river, on the Hatting side, reached by an ancient stone bridge, upon a little hill (land owned by Hatting) was a fourteenth-century church, complete with a little rectory and a tiny congregation. The other 'grand house', up from the river and among many trees, was called Penndean after the Quaker family which had owned it, and still owned it since the days of William Penn. In fact Penndean was older still, its original name being lost. It had thereafter been diminished by fire as well as being (as Edward's father said) 'messed about by the Victorians'. Edward's grandfather had had some feud with the inhabitants of the 'other House' (their family name was Barnell). Edward's father had been polite. Edward was polite.

Edward's ancestors had not perpetually possessed Hatting Hall, being by descent Cornishmen, and having only acquired Hatting late in the eighteenth century, the previous owners being obligingly bankrupt. This Cornish legend pleased Edward and Randall, but displeased their father, who did not care for piratical ancestors feasting on myths. He preferred to 'take up' the line of the unfortunate but titled gentry from whom the Lannions seized the charming and romantic residence. Even before the chaotic troubles of his grown-up life Edward had been aware of his *odd* aspect, his being rather *fey*, even as being, perhaps because of the Cornish past, under a curse. This withdrawal had also, at school and much later, led to his being called a prig, a prude, a puritan, even a 'weirdo'. He did not greatly mind such treatment, or even being lonely and secluded – but he found himself at times mysteriously frightened. He sometimes had a sensation of being followed. He even pictured himself as a criminal, perhaps a terrorist, who had been reformed, but knew that his erstwhile comrades were on his track and would certainly kill him. He seemed to remember that when a child he had played some sort of game like that with Randall. Later, when he was over twenty, he had another very remarkable and puzzling experience; but of these matters he did not speak to anybody. Edward's father had never recovered from Randall's death, Randall had always been his favourite. Randall was merry, Edward was taciturn. With surprise, moreover, he now found himself the master of Hatting Hall. This discovery which in itself might have cheered him up, filled him at first with alarm, though later he found that things 'went on much as before'. The staff, the 'people' as his father had called them, the butler and gardener Montague, his wife the maid Millie, continued as before, perhaps almost as before, since Edward's father (Gerald Lannion) had been more self-assertive and explicit than the kinder and vaguer 'young master'. Edward continued to stay much of the week in London, abandoning the publishing house, attempting another historical novel and trying to write poetry.

Then, when he was settling down and assuming that now nothing would ever happen, there was a change, a bright light, a fresh wind. He had a little earlier, partly in connection with his father's death, made some sort of mild relationship or 'reconciliation' with the inhabitants of Penndean. At that time these had consisted only of an elderly man, known as 'Uncle Tim', somehow connected with India, and a younger but over forty man, his nephew called Benet. Meeting him in the village, Benet had asked Edward if he would come to lunch. Edward, just returning to London, had said sorry, he could not. A little later Edward, again in London, learnt from Montague by telephone that the 'old man' at Penndean had just died. Edward felt sorry, he realised now that he would have liked to have met him. He sent a letter of condolence to Benet. A little later still he accepted an invitation to lunch. He liked Benet, and was able to glimpse the gardens of the house not visible from the road, but he did not get on with Benet's friends and refused a subsequent visit. The time was now late autumn. Invited yet again a little later he accepted, finding that the party consisted of Benet, the local Rector on visit, a handsome middle-aged woman with a great deal of glossy brown hair (Edward recognised her from the last occasion), another good-looking woman evidently 'from Canada', and her daughters, two pretty young girls, one nineteen, one twenty-one, one called Rosalind, the other Marian. Benet explained to Edward that the girls' surname was that of the (now dead) father, Berran, while their mother, subsequently married to a Canadian whom she later left, was called Ada Fox, that the girls had been to, and now left, a girls' boarding school, and that they had all rented a cottage in Lipcot for holidays. During lunch the girls reminded Edward that they had met him more than once in the street when they were inhabiting their cottage. Ada, sitting next to Edward, told him that the girls had just completed a trip with her to Scotland, after which she would return to Canada leaving them with their new flat in London to amuse and educate themselves. 'London is itself an education,' she said, and Edward, sitting next to Marian on his other side, nodded sagely.

Contrary to his expectations Edward did not see very much of the girls even after the delayed departure of their mother shortly before Christmas, after which the girls went to Paris, returning to London and reappearing in early spring in Lipcot and again meeting Edward in the street, when they told him they had again rented the same cottage. After that – well, after that – the girls now staying on at their cottage wanted to play tennis. Edward hastily refurbished the tennis court at Hatting. They wanted to ride. Edward did not ride, but he arranged for them to have ponies. Edward did not like long walks, but the girls did and they all went on long walks and Edward read the map. The girls wanted a swimming pool and Edward told Benet that there must be a swimming pool. The girls teased Edward, they made fun of him, they called him solemn. They were often with Benet and with Benet's friends, some of whom

Edward began to tolerate. In all this time however they had not set foot in Hatting Hall. At last Edward, who was absolutely averse to entertaining, noticed the now continual hints, and gave a lunch party. Indeed it took Edward himself some time before he became thoroughly aware of what was going on, what it was all about, that he was falling madly in love with Marian, who was madly in love with him. Only later did he discover that everyone at Penndean, and at Hatting, was 'in on it', not of course excluding the inhabitants of the village who were taking bets in the pub.

How had it all so gently, so quietly, so inevitably come about? *Can* I be happy, Edward wondered to himself, can my dark soul see the light at last? There he was now, early in the morning, sitting upright at his desk on the first-floor drawing room of his house in Notting Hill. He was breathing deeply and expelling his breath in long gasps. He could feel his heart hitting his ribs violently. He put his hand to his chest, the palm of his hand feeling the force of the blows. He sat there quietly, silently. Tomorrow he was to be married in the little four-teenth-century church upon the hill near Hatting Hall.

Suddenly something terrible and unexpected occurred. The window pane had cracked and fallen inward, showering the carpet with little diamonds of broken glass. The sound of the report seemed to come a second later. A pistol shot? He leapt to his feet, crying out, as he remembered later. An assault, an attempted assassination, a nearby bomb? Then he thought, someone has thrown a stone through the window. He stepped quickly across, grinding the glass under foot, and looking down into the street. He could see no one. He thought of rushing down but decided not to. He turned back into the room and began to pick up the gleaming fragments of glass, looking about him as he did so, at first putting them into his pocket then into the waste paper basket. Yes, it was a stone. He picked up the stone and held it, then dusted it with his other hand to remove the specks of glass. He put the stone carefully upon the mantelpiece. After that he drove in his beautiful red car to Hatting Hall.

On the afternoon of the same day Benet was, or had been, busy making arrangements for the evening dinner party. Arrangements for tomorrow's wedding were, so far as he knew, complete. He had discussed every detail with the Rector, Oliver Caxton. The wedding was to be at twelve o'clock. The service would be the usual Anglican wedding service. The church was normally visited by the Rector, who was in charge of other parishes, once or twice a month, and on special occasions such as weddings, funerals, Christmas, and Easter. Curates just now were hard to come by. The congregations on ordinary occasions (Sunday and matins only) consisted sometimes and at most of Benet, Benet's visitors, Clun the Penndean gardener, his daughter Sylvia, three or four women from the village, in summer perhaps two or three tourists. Uncle Tim, Benet's late uncle, had regularly read the lessons. Benet also used to read the lessons. Now Clun sometimes did. Benet had now given up except for special occasions. Sometimes in winter the Rector conducted the service in the otherwise empty church. Of course the Barnells were Quakers, but there was no Meeting near Lipcot, and the plain Anglican service contained, in accord with wishes from Penndean, periods of silence. There was at present no piano. Benet did not object. As for the two beautiful young people, the radiant hero and heroine of the scene, they had at first demanded a scrappy civil wedding, but had been overruled by the bride's mother, Ada Fox, who unfortunately was unable to be present, and by Mildred Smalden, a holy lady, friend of the Barnells. Benet had wanted a 'proper show', as he thought Uncle Tim would have wished. How very sad that Uncle Tim was no longer with them. Concerning the number of the guests, the young pair had prevailed, there were to be *very few*. There was to be champagne and various wines (Benet did not like champagne) and all sorts of delicious things to eat, sitting, or standing, or walking about, at Penn after the wedding, immediately after which the two children (as Mildred called them) were to depart for an undisclosed destination in Edward's Jaguar.

A small number of wedding guests were to be present at Benet's dinner table that final evening. Benet knew Ada well and her daughters very well, having become recently something of a ward to the girls and thus a convenience to their flighty mother. Marian, who loved 'creating' things, was spending the last day and night in London completing some secret 'surprise', and would drive down very early on the wedding day. Edward, in spite of protests, was to return to Hatting on the morning before. Rosalind, who was of course to be her sister's bridesmaid, was also coming 'on the day before', with Mildred. Two other guests, friends of Benet, were Owen Silbery, an eccentric painter, and a young man who worked in a bookshop called Thomas Abelson, a friend of Owen, nicknamed 'Tuan' by Uncle Tim, and likely to arrive by taxi from the distant railway station. Rosalind and Mildred were to stay in the house, in the 'old part', usually closed up, supposed to be haunted, bitterly cold in winter, but now delightfully opened up and prettified by the maid Sylvia. Tuan was to stay in the guest bedroom in the main part. Owen stayed in the village pub, as he always insisted on doing, being a special friend of the proprietor. The pub was called the Sea Kings, with a sign of a pirate ship painted by Owen. In fact Lipcot was not near the sea, but the pub had borne that name for a long time, centuries it was said.

Benet was alone in the library. In the library there was silence, as of a huge motionless presence. The books, many of them, were Uncle Tim's books, they had been in their places since Benet was young. Many of the books still glowed, faded a fainter red, a fainter blue, the gold of their titles dusted away, emanating a comforting noiseless breath. Most of Benet's books were still in London. (Why still? Were they planning a sortie to take over the library at Penndean?) Benet's uncle had died leaving Benet so suddenly in absolute possession, here where from childhood he had lived more as a guest or a pilgrim, a seeker for healing. But even when Uncle Tim was

7

away in India some pure profound gentle magic remained. The books did not know yet, but they would *find out* that Tim had gone, really gone away for ever.

Benet's father, now long deceased, had been Uncle Tim's younger brother. Benet's paternal grandfather, a lover of the classics, had named his elder son Timaeus and his younger son Patroclus; appellations which were promptly altered by their owners to Tim and Pat. Benet (who narrowly escaped being called Achilles) called his father Pat and of course his mother Mat. Benet's full name was William (after William Penn) Benet Barnell. He had early suppressed the William and of course rejected Ben. The origin of Benet, passionately clung to by its owner, was not clear, except that it had something to do with his mother and with Spain. Pat always claimed that he, Pat, was unlucky and 'put down'. However he made what seemed to be a sensible, even happy, marriage with sweet Eleanor Morton, daughter of an amicable solicitor, and training to be a singer. However Pat did not like music. He was also, as Benet soon found out, dissatisfied with his son. He wanted a daughter. He once asked Benet if he would like a little sister, to which Benet shouted 'No, no, no!' In any case no more children came. Pat's ill luck continued. Eleanor died quite early on in a car crash, Pat driving. Pat himself, a dedicated smoker, died of lung cancer, by which time Benet had grown up, had left the university, where he had studied philosophy, and followed his father into the Civil Service. Benet had loved his parents and regretted later that he had not revealed his love more openly. Remorse.

Uncle Tim (he did not marry, neither did Benet) was for Benet, and indeed for others, a romantic and somewhat mysterious figure. He had been involved in 'various wars'. He had left the university without a degree but had been (this much was known) a talented mathematician. He became, using this talent no doubt, an engineer, and somehow thereby came in contact with India, where he then spent much of his life, returning at intervals to England. During his absences Pat 'took over' Penndean, but more often, to Benet's chagrin, rented it.

Nobody quite discovered what Uncle Tim did in India, after

his war, except perhaps building bridges. Perhaps they simply did not ask him; even Benet, who adored him, did not ask him until late in his life when Tim gave him what sometimes seemed to Benet strange answers. Pat used to say that his brother had 'gone native'. Uncle Tim more than once asked his family to visit India and to see the Himalayas. Benet longed to go but Pat always refused. Late and at last Uncle Tim started spending longer and longer times at Penndean and then settled down there altogether.

Thinking of the books, Benet recalled how Tim, who, though no scholar, loved reading, used to utter, again and again, his 'quotes' or 'sayings', 'Tim's tags', lines out of Shakespeare, sentences out of Conrad, Dostoevsky, Dickens, *Alice in Wonderland*, *Wind in the Willows*, Kipling, Robert Louis Stevenson. 'Another step Mr Hands, and I'll blow your brains out.' When he was dying Benet heard him murmur, 'Keep up your bright swords, for the dew will rust them.' Of course Benet had had his classical education, but had inclined to the philosophical side. His sense of the Greeks had come to him later, distantly from memories of his grandfather, and from Tim and Tim's books. In a strange way the books, which were indeed not all 'classics', were somehow deeply soaked in some spirit of the Ancient World. Benet had sometimes tried to analyse this atmosphere, this rich aroma, this trembling resonance, this *wisdom*, but it eluded him, leaving him simply to bask within it. He recalled now, something which Tim liked to picture again and again, the moment when Caesar, angry with the Tenth Legion, addressed them as *Quirites* (citizens), not as *Commilitones* (fellow soldiers)! Benet, even as a child, instantly shared the grief of those devoted men as they hung their heads. There were some magic things which these books and utterances had in common. A favourite inner circle, *The Seven Pillars of Wisdom*, *Lord Jim*, *Treasure Island*, *Alice in Wonderland*, *Kim*. Tim also liked Kafka, which might have seemed strange, but on reflection Benet understood that too.

Pat used to say of Tim that he remained 'absolutely childish'. This was perhaps an aspect of his character which Benet saw rather as a heroic romanticism. Some years ago Benet, accidentally talking to an Indian diplomat at a Whitehall party, mentioned casually that his uncle worked in India, and was amazed to find that the diplomat had heard of Tim. He said of him, 'Dotty, crazy, but brave as a lion.' Benet was sorry that he had then lost track of the diplomat, not having even discovered his name. Tim's books were indeed adventure stories, as Benet saw them in his own childhood; but as he grew up he saw more in his uncle and his tales, a sort of warm ringing undertone, a gentle compassionate light or sound, an awareness of the tragedy of human life, good and evil, crime and punishment, *remorse*. Tim must have seen terrible things in India; perhaps done terrible things, which he might or might not have regretted, but which, in the sunny peace of Penndean, were never spoken of. The strange sound was then a sort of silent pain, which he rehearsed again and again among his broken heroes – Macbeth with bloody hands, Othello having killed his wife, the bizarre devastation of Kafka's people, T.E. Lawrence, Jim jumping from the ship. For consolation, Kim and the Lama. Another thing which Pat said of Tim was that he was covered all over in sugar. Benet (then adult) objected. It was not sugar. It was a sort of faintly beautiful profound grief. Alice listening to the Mock Turtle weeping. When Tim was dying he was reading *Through the Looking Glass*. This was a strange point at which Benet often paused. Well, why not? Was not Lewis Carroll a mathematician? Tim did not display his mathematical mind to his family, though he did once try to explain Gödel's theorem to Benet. Building bridges? Pat, and Benet when young, thought of Tim's Indian activities as those of some simple labourer; then, after he had (as Pat said) 'gone native', as a descent into some sort of occult necromancy. A regular joke was to ask Tim if he could perform the Indian Rope Trick, then laugh when Tim took this seriously and started to explain. To Benet alone, in later years, Tim, now old (confused some said, but Benet never accepted that) spoke of the magic of mathematics, of calculating prodigies, of the deep reality of human intelligence, beyond words and outside logic. Many people in India, he said, could easily master contrivances beyond the comprehension of the brightest Cambridge scholars. It only dawned later on Benet why Tim tenderly avoided playing chess.

Leaving at last the silence of the library, Benet moved towards the drawing room, pausing in the hall to survey himself in the long mirror. The hall was large and rather dim, deprived of the sunlight of the summer afternoon; it contained an old Sheraton writing desk, never opened, and was the only part of the house to have parquet flooring. The mirror was also dim, a little smudged at the sides. Ever since childhood Benet had wondered what he looked like. This wonder was connected with 'Who am I?' or '*What* am I?' Benet had discovered quite early in life that Uncle Tim shared this lack of identity. They sometimes discussed it. Does everyone feel like this, Benet had wondered. Tim had said that no, not everyone did, adding that it was a gift, an intimation of a deep truth: 'I am nothing.' This was, it seemed, one of those states, achieved usually by many years of intense meditation, which may be offered by the gods 'free of charge' to certain individuals. Benet laughed at this joke. Later he took the matter more seriously, wondering whether this 'gift' were not more likely to precede a quiet descent into insanity. Later still he decided that, after all, 'I am nothing', far from indicating a selfless mystical condition, was a vague state of self-satisfaction experienced at some time by almost anyone. Yet more profoundly he wondered whether Tim, thought by so many of his friends and acquaintances to be 'rather dotty', were not really a receiver of presents from the gods.

Benet now, looking at himself in the mirror, experienced a usual surprise. He still looked so remarkably young. He also, when thus caught, always seemed to have his mouth open. (Did he always go about with his mouth open?) He was of medium height, about the height of Uncle Tim, though shorter than Pat. He was lean and slender, always neatly dressed even when gardening. He had thick ruffled hair, copious red and brown, flowing down over his ears, without any streaks of grey, a broad calm face, a high bland brow, dark blue eyes, a neat straight nose, full lips which often smiled though their owner was now often sad. Ever since he had left the Civil Service he had had troubles. Tim of course – his unsuccessful return to philosophy – his having never been in love – was that a trouble? What am I to do next? Of course this business with the girls had been a happy distraction.

The drawing room was a big room with glass doors opening on to the main lawn. There were books here too, in low wooden bookcases, all sorts of books, atlases, cookery books, guides to English Counties, to London, France, Italy, big books on famous painters, books about games, books about animals, trees, the sea, books about machines, about science and scientists, books about poetry, about music. Of these books Benet had read only a few. Benet's numerous philosophy books were beyond in the study, a room which opened off the drawing room. The drawing room floor was covered with a huge dark, dark-blue almost black, now very worn, carpet covered with minute trees and flowers and birds and animals, brought back from India by Uncle Tim when he was still young. There was a fine open fireplace surrounded by a heavy curly mahogany Victorian surround, numerous pictures on the walls, some of Quaker ancestors with dogs, more recent water colours with various views of the house, and of the river Lip. Uncle Tim had donated some Indian miniatures, said to be very valuable. There were numerous old armchairs with embroidered cushions, and a (not valuable) piano introduced into the house by Benet's sweet short-lived lovely mother, Eleanor Morton. Benet recalled the happy childhood evenings when she played and they all sang. She soon set her opera music aside. Tim and Pat and indeed Benet preferred '*Jeanie with the Light Brown Hair*', and (a song which brought tears to Tim's eyes) 'The Road to Mandalay'.

Benet surveyed the room, re-arranging upon the mantel-piece, which still subsisted inside the Victorian surround, the netsuke which Owen Silbery had given him long ago; then he went through into his study. This also looked upon the terrace, and the immense lawn which had been dotted here and there with various tall and bushy trees by Benet's great-grandfather and other far more remote ancestors, even beyond the Quaker time. A little farther off there was a small copse of dainty birch trees, and beyond that the dark forest of huge Wellingtonias. Somewhere else, beyond the fountain and the rose garden,

Benet had vaguely dreamed of erecting some little Grecian building with marble columns; within which, the girls had insisted, there might one day be a warm indoor all-the-year-round swimming pool! Had the girls convinced him at last about that pool? Smiling, he opened the window which Sylvia was always shutting, and let in a thick warm pressure of air, filled with the odours of flowers and mown grass and mingled with the music of blackbirds, thrushes, larks, finches, sparrows, robins, collared doves and a distant cuckoo. He thought for a delicious moment how lucky he was – then he turned to worrying about his guests, about tomorrow and the wedding.

After that, and when he was about to leave the room, he looked down at what he had been writing earlier in the day, not upon a typewriter or word-processor, machines which he despised, but upon the inky foolscap pages of his book on Heidegger. Benet had intended for some time to write, or attempt to write, that book. However, he found it difficult to plan the work and to decide what he really, in his heart, *thought* of his huge ambiguous subject. He had made a great many notes, with question marks, in fact his book so far consisted largely of notes, unconnected and unexplained. Benet found himself accusing himself of being fascinated by a certain dangerous aspect of Heidegger which was in fact so deeply buried in his own, Benet's, soul that he could not scrutinise or even dislodge it. Of course Benet admired *Sein und Zeit* and loved (perhaps *this* was the point) the attractive image of Man as the *Shepherd of Being*. Later Heidegger he detested; Heidegger's sickening acceptance of Hitler, his misuse of the Pre-Socratic Greeks, his betrayal of his early religious picture of man opening the door to Being, his transformation of Being into a cruel ruthless fate, his appropriation of poor innocent Hölderlin, his poeticisation of philosophy, discarding truth, goodness, freedom, love, the individual, everything which the philosopher ought to explain and defend. Or was the era of the philosopher nearly over, as Pat used mockingly to tell him? Benet wished now that he had talked more with Uncle Tim about the Indian gods. How close had

Tim come to those gods whom Benet himself knew only through Kipling and Tim's rambling talk? Was it too late to learn the Hindu scriptures – was it *all* too late? A big bronze dancing Shiva, dancing within his ring of fire, forever destroying the cosmos and re-creating it, had stood upon Tim's desk, which now was Benet's desk. I wish I had started all this up earlier, thought Benet, I kept putting it off until I retired, I should have *held on* to philosophy, instead of going into the Civil Service, as Pat insisted. Of course Benet had never believed in God, but he had somehow believed in Christ, and in Plato, a Platonic Christ, an icon of goodness. Pat had not believed in God, indeed he hated Christianity. Eleanor had been a silent Christian. He recalled now how he had intuited her Christianity. Of course he never thought of such things then. And now – well, Heidegger, the greatest philosopher of the century? But what was Benet thinking somehow so deeply about when he turned his mind to that remarkable thinker? It seemed to him that after all his philosophical reflections, there was a sound which rang some deeper tremor of the imagination. Perhaps it was his more profound desire to lay out before him the *history* of Heidegger's *inner life*, the nature of his *sufferings*: the man who began as a divinity student and became a follower of Hitler, and then –? Remorse? Was that the very concept which sounded the bell? What had Heidegger said to Hannah Arendt after it was all over? What had *that* pain been like – what had those millions of pains been like? A huge tormented life? Was Heidegger really Anti-Christ? 'The darkness, oh the darkness,' Benet said aloud.

He rose and left the study and crossed the great carpet to the glass doors and walked out onto the lawn. Here he listened again to the sounds, which he had failed to hear when he was so strangely struggling with that mysterious demon. The sweet sounds of the garden birds, and now, coming from the river, the geese flying overhead uttering their strange tragic gabble. Damn it, he said to himself, I am supposed to be *organising* this evening, *and* tomorrow! Oh I wish it was over and all well. Of course nothing will go wrong, they themselves will orchestrate everything!

Benet was now checking the dining table. The dining room, adjacent to the hall and the front door, looked upon the drive where, emerging from among the trees, cars were soon to be expected. Sylvia, who loved Benet dearly, almost as much as she had loved Uncle Tim, smiled tolerantly across the table as he intently pushed things about, then she quietly left the room. The *placement* was proving difficult as usual. There were few guests, only from the 'inner circle'. Strictly Benet should have Mildred on his right and Rosalind on his left. However, actually, Benet wanted to have Edward on his right, he wanted very much to talk to Edward, he felt that Edward needed *protecting* and he wanted to be *fatherly* to him. So then Edward would have Mildred on his right. Then there were Owen, and Tuan *alias* Thomas Abelson. But would that do? Owen was always difficult and should not sit next to Mildred whom he knew so well, nor to Rosalind whom he sometimes reduced to tears. Was Tuan, so called by Tim after Conrad's novel, a solution? Hardly, put anywhere he was rather inarticulate. Suppose Benet took him on, upon his left? Benet was shy of this, and would feel bound to talk a lot to him, thus reducing his time to Edward. At last he decided to keep Rosalind on his left, Owen between Rosalind and Tuan, and Tuan thus next to Mildred, who was next to Edward who was next to Benet. Rosalind would have to look after herself, and Tuan would be at the far end of the table facing Benet. He must remember to put out the cards. It was a small table where they would all hear each other, of course it could be lengthened by leaves. Benet reflected upon how rarely he had done that since Tim died. A moth appeared and fluttered quietly across the room. Benet blew it gently away, not wanting to damage its frail antlers. Sylvia was the one who made war on moths.

A small dark car appeared out of the wood and slewed round noisily upon the beautifully raked and weeded gravel. Benet hurried out into the hall and opened the front door. Mildred and Rosalind emerged, waved, then began to unpack various boxes. Benet went forward to help. He had known Rosalind and her sister and their mother, on and off, through summers when they had come back to the cottage in Lipcot. Rosalind had grown up almost as beautiful as Marian, and, following Shakespeare's heroine, persistently dressed as a boy, not in jeans, but as a real trousered well-dressed boy, even with waistcoat. Her bright straight golden hair, falling beyond her shoulders, was allowed as boyish. Mildred was an old friend. Long ago Benet, or so he claimed, had dissuaded her from becoming a nun. Later, for a while, she was a member of the Salvation Army. However, she remained nun-like. Owen who had known her longer than Benet, often painted her, spoke of her pale wistful pre-Raphaelite look. She wore long dark brown dresses and her long thick dark brown hair was supported by big tortoiseshell combs. She lived austerely in a small flat, worked as a dress-maker, caring for the poor, visiting the sick, assisting the homeless. She also frequented the British Museum; 'her gods are there,' Owen used to say. Apparently or perhaps she had some sort of small pension. She had, some time ago, entered the lives of Owen and Benet through Uncle Tim, who said he had found her wandering late at night near Saint Paul's. What Tim, or Mildred, was doing there was never made clear. She spoke in what some called an 'aristocratic voice'. Others said 'like a head mistress'. She too, through Benet, had met the girls some time ago. She quite often went to church and was prepared to be called 'some sort of Christian'.

'Hello, Sylvia,' said Mildred, ignoring Benet, to the pretty girl who had run out too.

Benet kissed Rosalind, Rosalind hugged Sylvia, talking they moved toward the house carrying the bags and boxes. At that moment, out of the trees, more than ever like the Green Man, silent Clun the gardener, Sylvia's father, with a gesture, got into the car and drove it away.

Rosalind went upstairs with Sylvia, and into the rarely used 'old part' of the house. Mildred had 'her own room' there too, though often when visiting she preferred to stay in the inn. Now she followed Benet into the drawing room. They sat down on the sofa and looked at each other. Benet reached out and took her hand.

'Now look here,' said Mildred (a well-known formula), withdrawing her hand, 'how are you going to manage? Will you be able to feed them all after the wedding? Half the village will want to join in, you know. I've hired this car, by the way, Rosalind still hasn't got one.'

Benet, who had not thought too clearly about all this, said, 'Oh, it will be all right. They'll stay at the gate. Only the three or four old faithfuls may decide to come into the church. And afterwards it's just our lot up at Penn.'

'Hmmm. How many guests have you invited to the wedding, not just tonight of course – ? Is Anna coming tonight, by the way?'

'No, she is coming tomorrow. Very few guests. *They* wanted a three-minute wedding with a Registrar!'

'I suppose Ada ditched that. But why isn't she coming?'

'Marian says she has just found another man! I don't know. My God, Mildred, I shall be so glad when this is over!'

'Nonsense, you'll enjoy it. Anyway I will. Any friends of Edward's?'

'No. He doesn't want any. He says he hasn't got any!'

'Typical Edward. I'm so glad he is marrying at last, such hawkish looks, but he is pure in heart. So Marian is coming down very early tomorrow morning, upon the *day itself*! She always liked treats and surprises. That's typical too. Oh look!'

Rosalind, now wearing her bridesmaid's dress, had quietly entered the room carrying her bouquet.

When all were assembled and the parade to the dining room began, Benet was delayed by Rosalind. (Had Edward got a best man? No, Edward had *not* got a best man!) Thus Mildred, entering the room first, sat down in her frequent place on Benet's right, and thereafter seeing Edward, standing helpless, signalled him to her other side. Owen, who was longing to talk to Edward, at once sat down beside him, at the same time capturing, by gripping his sleeve, the timid wandering Tuan who was shy and often silent. Rosalind, then entering alone, placed herself on Benet's left, finding herself thus next to the harmless Tuan on the other side. Benet, who had just realised that he had forgotten his instructions, entered last, thus placed, silently cursing, between the two women. Before dinner Mildred and Rosalind had hoped for some music and singing, but Benet had quietly and hastily informed them that Edward would not like it.

The guests, now at table, knew each other in some cases very well, in other cases just fairly well. Mildred and Owen, both 'oddities', were close friends, by some deemed a 'strange couple'. Benet had met them years ago through Uncle Tim, who had discovered Owen in an exhibition of Indian pictures. Tuan was a later acquisition, allegedly 'picked up' by Uncle Tim in a train from Edinburgh. He was extremely slim, even thin, with a long neck and a dark complexion, straight black hair, dark brown eyes, a thin mouth and a shy smile. Tim called him (without any visible evidence) 'the Theology Student', and conjectured that he must have had some sort of awful shock in the past. In any case Tuan said little of his past and nothing of his family. He had been at Edinburgh University, even taught at a London university, and now worked in a bookshop. He had been devoted to Tim and shed many tears at his death. He was also now attached to Benet and to Owen Silbery. He was deemed not to be gay. Owen was a painter, in fact a distinguished and well-known painter. He announced himself sometimes as 'in the style of Goya', and moreover, it was said, painted horrific pornographic pictures which he sold secretly. He was in fact well known as a portrait painter, and one who could satisfy his clients. His pictures were bought at high prices. He was tall, becoming stout, but remained handsome, even 'dashing', a big head, a high and constantly lined brow, a large sturdy nose, watery pale blue eyes and thick lips, and long black straggling hair, said to be dyed. He could smile and laugh a lot and was much addicted to drink, only saved (it was said) by the attentions of the saintly Mildred.

'Are you thinking of opening your house to the public now?'
Owen was saying to Edward. 'You thought of doing that,
didn't you?'

'I didn't actually,' said Edward. 'My father mentioned it, but
he never really wanted to. I certainly don't.'

'I don't blame you,' said Owen. 'After all you don't need the
money, and showing the place would be a burden and a
nuisance. Yes, I can see, absolutely a nightmare.'

'Quite.'

'Have you still got that Turner, the Pink One it was called?'

'Yes. How did you know about the Turner?'

'It was lent for the Turner exhibition. Your ancestors had
very good taste. Of course I am not implying that you and your
father lacked it.'

'That is just as well.'

'Of course you have the latest burglar alarms I assume. Are
you writing a novel?'

'No. Why should I be writing a novel?'

'Everyone writes novels nowadays. Someone told me you
were. I feel that you have much to write about.'

'And you are a painter.'

'Yes, I am a painter. One day soon I shall paint you.'

'How is your swimming pool getting on?' Mildred asked
Benet.

'Oh, it's rather at a standstill, actually I'm still just planning
it.'

'All those marble columns? The girls are longing for it to be
ready! Isn't it good news about Anna, pity she isn't here
tonight.'

'She's coming tomorrow.'

'It's time they came back from France. It's so sad that Lewen
didn't live to see – '

'So you're going into the Courtauld?' Tuan was saying to
Rosalind.

'No, not yet anyway, I'm just taking a course – '

'But you are a painter!'

'I have tried painting, but I've given it up for the moment.'

'You must feel so happy about Marian.'

'Yes, but I'm rather worried about myself.'

'What about?'

'About tomorrow. I've never been a bridesmaid before and I'm afraid I shall fall or drop the bouquet or start to cry.'

Sylvia had gone home. The sequence of her beautiful dishes was nearing its end. She never forgot that Mildred was a vegetarian. The first dish was vegetarian anyway, consisting of salads of all kinds of fresh green leaves with a cheese *soufflé*. From here Mildred went on to spinach and leek pie, the others to a delicate leg of lamb. The pudding was of course summer pudding, but special. Bottles of Uncle Tim's claret were consumed. Mildred was not against this, if not taken in excess. They had now been arguing for some time about politics, Owen dominating as usual.

'What we need is a return to Marxism, early Marx of course, Marxism was created when Marx and Engels saw the starving poor of Manchester. We've got to get rid of our vile, stupid, rapacious bourgeois civilisation, capitalism must go, just look at it now, what a senseless government – '

'I agree with you about the poor people,' said Mildred, 'and our unhappy leaders may be in difficulties, but we must hold on to our morals, we must civilise and spiritualise politics, and most of all we must develop a believable form of Christianity before it is too late.'

'It is already too late. You are a disciple of Uncle Tim, you worship T.E. Lawrence, Simone Weil worshipped him too, at least the poor girl never knew he was a liar and a cheat – '

'He wasn't,' said Mildred, 'he was cheated, he didn't know that he would not be able to help the Arabs – '

'Can you believe a single word of what he said happened at Deraa?'

'I believe it,' said Benet. This was a touchstone often skirmished around.

'It was a fantasy, he was after his own glory, then he spent the rest of his life punishing himself, and then he committed suicide – '

20

'He didn't commit suicide,' said Benet, 'it was an accident.'

Mildred said, 'Of course there is such a thing as redemptive suffering, but – '

'There is no redemptive suffering,' said Owen, 'only remorse – remorse is what is real – Uncle Tim knew it all right – and your philosopher friend Heidegger, Benet, except of course he's Anti-Christ – '

'He's not my friend,' said Benet. 'I daresay he is Anti-Christ.'

'You love him,' said Owen. 'You are sinking into his evil!'

Benet smiled.

Mildred said, 'I think it is time for a rapprochement of philosophy and theology, and Christianity must learn from the religions of the east, and they must learn – '

'In that case,' said Owen, 'there will be only two world religions, your oriental Christianity, and Islam. Don't you agree, Tuan?'

'And Judaism,' said Tuan. I believe – '

'Judaism of course,' said Owen. 'Our future will be total destruction, Heraclitus was right, war is the king of all things, war is necessity, it brings everything about. Kafka was right too, we are in the Penal Colony, behind our rotten bourgeois civilisation is a world of indescribable pain and horror and sin which alone is real.'

'I'm glad you mention sin,' murmured Mildred.

'Is that what you really believe?' said Edward to Owen.

'He believes in romantic heroism and *discuter les idées générales avec les femmes supérieures*,' said Benet.

'It isn't all play!' said Mildred, defending Owen.

'Well, I think we are now drunk enough,' said Benet, 'we must not go on to get cross! Let us now go out into the garden and breathe deeply and admire the marvels of nature. I suggest we rise and give our usual toast, and another very special toast as well.'

The diners were now rising and moving their chairs.

'First to dear Uncle Tim, whom we love and whose spirit is still with us.'

'Uncle Tim!' Glasses were raised and everyone was solemn. After which all remained standing, expectant, during a brief silence. 'And now let us all drink the health of our dear friend and neighbour, Edward Lannion, and his absent bride, Marian Berran, who this time tomorrow will be Mrs Lannion! May these two lovely young people have long and happy lives, may they have happy children and may all of us here be privileged to share in their joy and goodness. Marian and Edward!'

'Marian and Edward!' During the toast, Edward, pale, almost alarmed, looking suddenly very young, having hesitated about sitting down, stood, first lowering his head, then lifting it, and looked about upon the company with an air of frightened gratitude. Benet now moved quickly in case Edward should feel that he must now make a speech.

'Come on now, all of you, out into the garden!'

They all crowded out into the garden, passing back from the dining room into the drawing room whose glass doors opened onto the paved terrace and the grass. There was a light on the terrace, revealing the brilliant colours of flowers in big mossy stone urns. Beyond was what at first seemed like darkness, but was in a few moments seen to be starlight. The moon was not present, being elsewhere. But a dense light came to them from the innumerable crowding stars of the Milky Way. Upon the grass, already damp with dew, they stopped at first, looking up with silent awe, then talking to each other in soft voices, gradually separating, never going too far away as if, though exalted, they were also afraid.

Owen, taking Tuan's arm, led the youth away from the house, past the scattering of bushy shrubs and past the dainty birch copse, towards the Wellingtonias. The great silent trees, faintly visible, were outlined against the starry sky whose crowded curtain reached down to the darkened horizon of the garden. The air was thick with moisture and the smell of dewy earth and the faint perfumes of leaves and flowers and the fresh breathing of the huge tall trees.

Owen led Tuan into a sudden darkness, a great soundless presence. The starry dome was taken from them and they moved upon a different carpet. Owen stopped, releasing Tuan's arm and taking hold of his hand. He turned the boy gently to face him and sighed, now touching his head, his hair, drawing his fingers gently down over Tuan's brow, his nose and mouth. Things like this had happened before. Tuan, who did not share Owen's inclinations, but loved him, stood quietly dreamily smiling, now leaning back against one of the trees. Owen kissed him.

Mildred and Rosalind had crossed the lawn in another direction towards the stone steps, now faintly visible, which led down to the rose garden. There was, now just visible, the lucid wet sound of a fountain, which they approached, and sat down upon the stone rim of the round pool into which the starlit water was murmurously falling. Velvety bats passed noiselessly by, a distant owl fluted.

They dabbled their hands gratefully in the cool water. They spoke softly.

Mildred said, 'How moving – how happy Tim would be – Edward and Marian together – it's perfect – '

'Yes, yes, indeed –,' said Rosalind. 'Do you know, I think I foresaw it in a dream – they were the King and the Queen – I've just remembered the dream.'

'How beautiful! Marian kept looking about, then she found what she wanted suddenly so close. Or do you think she really fixed on Edward long ago?'

'I think she did – or fate did. Of course when we were with Mama we didn't see much of Edward – '

'I think it's better she comes later on, you know what a fuss she always makes! Are you still determined not to marry? Of course I know it's a joke, and anyway you'll change your mind!'

'My mind is fixed on art history at present!'

Benet had firmly laid hold of Edward, seizing his sleeve, as they moved out onto the lawn, stopping just a little way away from the lights of the drawing room. Benet for a moment, and such strange moments sometimes came, felt the spirit of Uncle Tim descending upon him, *clothing* him as it were, and breathing his breath. Edward, pale and tall, loomed over him.

'Edward, if only Tim were here we would really be in heaven. Well, of course now we *are* in heaven anyway! I've longed for you to marry that girl. I didn't make any tiresome hints to either of you – I just prayed! You're a wonderful chap, she's a wonderful girl – forgive me for being slightly drunk – '

'I'm drunk too,' said Edward. 'I think the Grand Marnier was final.'

'Dear me, it's so late, I should have sent you all away long ago! I do hope you'll spend lots of time down here together, you could be in peace writing your historical novel – '

'I'm not writing a historical novel – '

'You do love Hatting Hall, don't you?'

'Yes I do – I increasingly do – and Penndean – '

'I hope you'll have lots of children, I hope you don't mind my saying so, a boy first of course – '

Edward sighed, then laughed as Benet seized hold of the collar of his coat.

Gradually the others came back to the terrace and stood looking up at the Milky Way where the stars were continually falling, tumbling and disappearing.

'It's like the end of the *Paradiso*,' said Tuan.

'You mean in Dante,' said Mildred.

'For us, it is not the end of the *Paradiso*,' said Benet, 'it is the beginning.'

They moved back into the house.

After that there was a lot of fussing about in the drawing room, making sure that everyone knew what they were to do tomorrow. They exclaimed about how few they were, and what a charming little wedding it was going to be. The Rector was coming over early in the morning, otherwise Benet would have had to invite him to dinner! All the flowers had already been done by Sylvia, who had also arranged most of the eats and drinks. 'How dull we shall be when they've *gone*,' said Rosalind. 'Edward would not tell where they were going, but I guess it *must* be in France!' Benet was hustling them now through the drawing room and out into the hall. Rosalind and Mildred were to betake themselves to the old part of the house, where the ghosts were. Tuan was to sleep in a small guest room in the main house. Owen was to return to the Sea Kings where he had always stayed and had done so for far back in history. Edward at home was to sleep by himself for the last time! Jokes were being made. Rosalind was said to be falling asleep in the library. Mildred was trying to hustle them all like sheep out into the hall. There was hugging and kissing and holding of hands and picking up of coats and wraps.

'Be careful, for heaven's sake,' Benet was saying to the drivers. 'Some police may be hanging around, we don't want you to spoil it all by being arrested!'

Rosalind had moved forward and opened the front door. The lights shone brightly upon the two faithful cars, patiently waiting, Edward's red Jaguar and Owen's blue Volvo. She stepped back again into the hall.

'You're stepping on something,' said Mildred, 'it looks like an envelope.'

Rosalind picked it up. 'Someone must have delivered it when we were talking – '

'We were always talking!' said Mildred.

'It must be for me,' said Benet, 'it's probably a circular or an overdue bill!'

Rosalind gave it to him. He looked at the envelope, tore it open, then pulled out a piece of paper and looked at it.

Benet sat down abruptly upon a chair. For a moment or two the others were talking to each other, then one by one they fell silent, looking at him.

Mildred spoke first. 'Are you all right, Benet? What's the matter?'

Benet had flushed violently, then become pale, his breath, coming in gasps, was loudly audible, his face, anguished, scarcely recognisable.

Mildred said, 'It's a fit, or a heart attack – are you all right?'

Rosalind said, 'It's the letter – someone is – '

They stood about him helplessly. Benet had now bent forward still holding the paper, his head in his hand, he seemed to be gasping for breath. Rosalind cried out, 'Oh he is ill – what is it, what is it?'

Benet stood up suddenly, staggering slightly, his mouth open. Then, as gathering himself, closed his mouth and looked at Edward, who was standing back near the drawing room door. Benet moved towards Edward, the others parting to let him pass. He turned slightly and said, 'Could you wait outside – somewhere else – please?' then to Edward, 'Please come into

25

the drawing room.' Edward moved before him into the drawing room. Benet entered the room and closed the door behind him. The others stood helpless, then moved into the dining room where the remains of the dinner were still in place. Rosalind and Mildred sat down, holding hands. Tuan was standing, his hands at his throat. He undid his tie. Owen poured himself out a glass of wine.

Inside the drawing room, Benet went over to the large settee and sat down. Edward picked up a chair and sat down opposite to him. Edward was trembling. Benet said, 'The message is for you.' He handed Edward the piece of paper. Edward read it. It ran:

'Forgive me, I am very sorry, I cannot marry you. Marian.'

Benet was dragging off his tie and undoing the neck of his shirt. Turning away from Edward he uttered a stifled sob, then controlling his breathing he turned towards Edward again.

Edward was (as Benet recalled and even retailed later) made of steel. He had ceased to tremble. He was no longer pale, but somewhat flushed. He sat silently, very still, frowning and looking down at the paper. Then he handed it back to Benet, and speaking in his ordinary voice, he said, 'So be it.' Then he said, 'We must put off the wedding guests. Is it too late to ring them?'

Benet, now more collected, said, 'That is her writing, isn't it? It could be a hoax – '

'It is her writing – rather hasty – but yes, hers.'

'Perhaps she has been kidnapped, it may be – oh – '

'It is her writing. Anyway now we must tell the others. I'll go and fetch them.'

Edward marched to the door, opened it, and called out 'Come in here, please' to the group in the dining room. They hurried forward and followed Edward back into the drawing room. Edward, removing the chair he had been sitting on, sat down beside Benet. He said, 'Please sit down.' They sat down. Mildred began to say something, then fell silent. Edward said, 'This letter has come. I shall read it.' He read it out, then held it out to Owen who passed it round.

Rosalind sobbed, Mildred moaned, Tuan hid his face, Owen looked grim. He said, 'Is it her writing?'

'Yes.'

'Perhaps written under duress?'

'Perhaps, but I do not think so,' said Edward. 'Anyway, our problem now is to cancel tomorrow's, that is today's, engagements.'

'Who brought the message,' said Owen, 'and when? How long has it been here?'

'That could have been anyone at any time,' said Edward.

'Could it have been *her*? Well, I suppose she wouldn't have – someone might have seen her. But do you know anyone?'

'No. No one. Now please – '

'But *where is she*?' said Mildred. 'We must find her, she might have had an accident and become deranged or something – when did you last see her?'

'Quite recently, I – '

'Let us at least ring her telephone number – she may have changed her mind or – '

'Try if you like, but it will be useless.'

Mildred ran to the telephone and rang the familiar number, but there was no reply.

'Nothing on the envelope?' said Owen. 'No?'

Benet watching Edward was amazed by his coolness, indeed his coldness. He is just preventing himself from breaking down, he thought. Steel, yes, *steel*. He said, 'Edward, did you expect this?'

'No.' He added, 'She means what she said, and that is all.'

'You're *sure* it's her writing?' said Owen.

'Yes. Look.'

It was passed around. Tuan restored it to Edward, who passed it back to Benet. 'You keep it please.'

'How *can* she,' said Mildred. 'Surely she has had some fit, she has given way under the strain, we have all tried her too much, we must *find* her, *go* to her, – Edward, listen, you must *forgive* her, I see it all, it's all our fault, it's having the grand wedding, in a little while she'll marry you quietly in a Register Office. *Please* don't leave her just for this – '

Edward stood up. 'Of course I shall drive to London now,

and yes I have the keys of her flat. I shall come straight back before six. After six will you please telephone all the guests. I think you have a list.'

Edward made rapidly for the door. Benet, catching him up as he was getting into the Jaguar, seized Edward's arm, then his hand. Edward gripped Benet's hand for a moment, and Benet saw in the bright lights Edward's distorted face.

The sun, which had scarcely been away, returned to Lipcot, the birds who had scarcely been asleep, were all singing together. The huge sky was radiant with its empty blue light. Benet sat up and thought what a lovely day for a wedding! Then a black veil fell upon him and he could scarcely breathe. He moaned, bowing his head. He had been lying upon the sofa. How *could* he have been asleep, he had no *right* to sleep, he had thought that sleep was now impossible.

He sat up and looked around as if for his clothes, then found that they were still on. He looked at his watch, it was six o'clock. He got up, still quietly moaning. He could hear that other inhabitants of the house were up already. He went out into the hall.

Mildred was hurrying down the stairs. 'Benet, what can we do, what can we say – I still think – '

'We must ring up all the guests and say it's off, that's all. I've still got the message – '

'But we don't know what has happened, what has *really* happened, she may suddenly turn up and – '

'We must *ring up* – '

'That note was just a protective cry when she realised she'd be married, I could feel like that myself, she may come running back, she may even suddenly turn up here, we don't have to say it's all over – '

'Mildred, return to *reality*, we can't make up stories, we can only give them the facts, we owe it to Edward – '

'Exactly, we owe it to Edward, we don't know whether it's the end of the world, oh can't you see – '

'I think that's his car now.'

Benet ran towards the door followed by Mildred. He passed Tuan standing in the doorway of the dining room. He opened the front door which he had deliberately left unlocked. The door opened to the pale blue radiant sky making a halo round the tall figure on the doorstep. Edward came in.

Mildred said over Benet's shoulder, 'Oh Edward, I've rung her flat. There's no reply, of course you have too, we don't really know what's happened, we don't know what to say, do we – '

Ignoring Mildred, Edward, closing the front door behind him, said to Benet, 'I've got my list here, I expect you have yours. It's a very short list. Now it is after six, I think that's early enough to start ringing round. Could you do the talking please?'

'Yes, yes,' said Benet, 'I imagine you've already tried – '

'Of course.'

Benet led the way back into the drawing room.

'We *must find her*,' said Mildred to Edward, 'she may have terribly regretted that note, she may now be simply *afraid* to say so, *afraid* to come to you – or she may intend to do something awful – '

'Like throwing herself into the Thames. Yes.'

Mildred, who never got on very well with Edward, stepped back, putting her hand to her mouth.

Meanwhile Benet had already reached one of the guests by telephone, a former college friend of Edward, and was telling him that the wedding was cancelled. Why? Well, he was not sure, unfortunately it was just not on – postponed, yes perhaps – no, Edward wasn't at Hatting he was here at Penndean – 'I don't know whether Edward would like to have a word – '

Edward, grimacing with exasperation shook his head violently.

'Well, he's not available just now actually – I expect later –

yes, yes – I'm so sorry we've had to postpone – ' Benet put the phone down. 'Sorry, Edward – if it's going to be like this – '

'I'm going back to London,' said Edward. 'Here's my list. No, keep the message. You can do what you like.'

'Should we alert the police? And there's her mother, only Rosalind doesn't know where she is now – '

Edward strode across the room and across the hall. He banged the front door behind him. Benet prevented Mildred from following him. When he reached the door the car was already vanishing.

'Mildred dear, do sit down, do lie down on the sofa, do, go and lie down *somewhere*, please – I'm just going to ring the Rector.'

Upstairs Rosalind, who had been awake for some time, was up and dressed and sitting on her bed. She was looking at her bridesmaid's dress, laid over a chair, and her bouquet of flowers, which Clun had made up for her so carefully and placed in a jug. Tears were slowly moving down her hot cheeks. She closed her eyes and lowered her head and wailed silently. Where was Marian, oh where, *where*?

Not far away, in the Sea Kings pub, Owen Silbery was still asleep, dreaming that he was sitting at a table in a candlelit room alone with Caravaggio.

The wedding had been arranged for twelve o'clock, but in the bright sunshine some villagers had begun to assemble much earlier. The Rector, Oliver Caxton, alerted early by Benet, had sent out one of his older choristers (there was to be a little choir) to inform these outsiders that the wedding was off. When Caxton, later, came down to address them, they pretended not to believe him. At any rate they had come for a show, and felt sure that there would, somehow or other, be one. They were in fact right, since Benet had been unable to reach all the invited guests by telephone. He had, for instance, not been able to warn Anna Dunarven. In any case he and Mildred had agreed they and the others would be on guard to accost any persons who attempted to enter the church under the impression of attending a marriage. After all, various friends of Marian, whom she had invited but forgotten to mention, might have decided to turn up. 'The others' officially in fact comprised only Benet, Mildred, Rosalind, and Tuan. Owen, whom they reached at last, had said he would come along later. Mildred said that was just as well. Edward was an unknown quantity. Would he come back again? Telephone calls were in vain. They had decided to set out for the church soon after nine.

The enormity of the outrage, or rather the tragedy, seemed in daylight even greater. Why didn't she say it earlier, they kept on repeating. It was so terribly cruel to spring it on him like that. Though, Mildred said, at least it needed enormous courage to do it at the last moment. The sealed envelope and the messenger remained mysterious. Had *Marian herself* brought the message, dropping it in quietly while they were all shouting and laughing over dinner? The thought of this, the picture of Marian standing in silence outside, crying perhaps, and wondering whether she should leave the terrible missive, or take it away or destroy it, was heartrending. It was, it was agreed, equally likely that it was delivered by someone else – someone who *knew* – or else some hired person, working for some official firm, arriving in the dark, told not to knock? Over and over they made themselves wonder if it were a vile joke, a hoax – but then, it was agreed, the writing was certainly Marian's. Poor Edward, brave Edward, they kept on saying, and wondering whether after all Marian would come rushing back to him and he would take her in his arms. That would be best, wonderful. Perhaps when the time of the wedding came, the pair would suddenly appear together smiling. Mildred kept

31

wishing and dreaming this. 'And we shall forgive them instantly.' At any rate Edward has not cursed her. A reconciliation later on, or indeed soon, was not at all impossible – and then they might look back upon their present emotions with amused relief. In fact, for each one of them, it was an agonising shock, from which it would take them a long time to recover.

As they set off to the church in Benet's car, each pain was deep. They talked of hopes, but really without hopes. And in each of them there were very private griefs, losses, regrets, and disappointments, even feelings of shame. Benet was reflecting that really, profoundly, it was all his fault. He had imagined how wonderful that particular union would be, how absolutely made for each other they were. In fact this idea (obvious enough once thought of) had been put into Benet's head by Uncle Tim a long time ago. How sad Uncle Tim would be now! Or, another thought struck him, if Uncle Tim had been alive now of course all would be well – or it would have much earlier been found to be impossible. I have messed it up, Benet thought, I hustled the two of them together, I was always arranging that *they* should pair off, *they* should go walking together, *they* should sit next to each other at dinner! It had all seemed to sail along! Other selfish personal worries now crowded into Benet's head. Suppose Edward were now to marry some awful girl who was hostile to Penndean, or else that Edward would never marry at all, sell Hatting, let it pass into the hands of vile cousins or strangers? Benet had no children. Marian and Rosalind had become his children, I saw them as so happy, he thought, he had pictured himself playing with *their children*! But I was pressing her into a match which she increasingly felt to be impossible – at any rate she had the courage to say so at the last moment. And this at least could seem a consoling thought. Mildred, restraining her tears, was thinking it's all our fault, we had not been deep and loving enough to see what the difficulties were, we had not *tried*, we had thought selfishly of our own satisfaction, really we didn't *know* Edward enough, we built up some solemn ideal Edward, and now it's somehow really Edward's fault, he should have seen it coming, he should have been brave enough to have it out with her. Rosalind, restraining her tears, was crying out in her heart, Oh Marian, Marian, what terrible pain you must be in, oh let me find you, let me come to you, oh I love you so much and you are so terribly wounded.

The church, which was dedicated to Saint Michael and All Angels, was strikingly situated upon a grassy hillock on the (from Penndean) far side of the river Lip, reached by an ancient stone bridge. Continuing from the bridge a little lane, just viable for cars, led up the hill, ceasing at the church gate. The church was built out of the local grey stone which often gleamed and sparkled. It had a sturdy square tower, and a statue of the saint, battered it was said by Cromwell's men, over the doorway. The interior was dark, the five windows, mostly decorated, being filled with Victorian stained glass. The east window presented the soldier saint triumphant, leaning upon his sword, the side windows Christ healing and teaching. The crucifixion was represented only by a wooden gilded image, nineteenth century, hanging in the chancel arch. The elaborately carved pulpit was Jacobean, made to glow by many hands which had stroked the saints who were portrayed upon it, the big solid fourteenth-century font was carved with interlaced arches with stars and crosses, there was a kneeling female figure in an alcove, and an alabaster reclining figure of a knight in armour, open-eyed and praying, with his dog at his feet. Tablets remained on the walls, but not in great numbers since some cleansing Rector at the beginning of the century had stripped away many of these. Two memorials, beautifully lettered in slate, commemorated the village victims of two wars, forty-five in the First World War (including a relative of Edward's) and four in the second. The handsome church had contained in its long past many more embellishments and trimmings, only time, warfare, thieves and loss of congregations had dimmed it.

They parked the car over the bridge, on the church side, deciding to walk the rest. Here Benet felt his guilt at having abandoned the attentions which had bound him to the people of the village. Beyond the church, close to it served by little lanes on the other side, was the small but serviceable eighteenth-century Rectory, opened for Oliver Caxton's regular visits. The sun was shining from an almost cloudless sky. Benet and his party neared the church gate.

A large crowd had now gathered outside the gate. Benet was thinking, why on earth have I brought Rosalind, she just insisted on coming, and now this mob will see her tears. The news has got round already! Oliver must have been busy. They look threatening, we shall have to elbow our way. However, as they approached, there were some friendly and courteous faces, and Benet quickly led his party through. Only a few stared with amusement, most lowered their eyes, some bowed their heads, and there were a few incoherent murmurs of sympathy. One youth (on holiday) who said loudly, 'Too bad, chum, she's bolted!' was hushed up by others. Rosalind was not crying. They mounted the little grassy path, Oliver Caxton, standing at the door of the church, ushered them into the cool dark interior. There was a strong scent of innumerable flowers. Mildred and Rosalind sat down near the front. After a moment or two Mildred pulled out one of the kneelers, finely embroidered long ago by ladies of the parish, and knelt down, gazing up at the gilded figure of Christ which, in the sudden dark, seemed to be poised alone in mid-air above the chancel. Benet stood with Oliver in the aisle. The church was otherwise empty.

'Has anyone arrived yet?'

'Benet, I am so sorry – '

'Has anyone –?'

'No. I've put sentinels out in all the lanes. There'll be some cars I suppose.'

'Yes, we couldn't get hold of all of them by telephone. We – I – have got to collect them and talk with them. We can't just say "go home, the thing is off!" '

'Should we direct them up to Penndean?'

34

'No, for heaven's sake! I don't want them up there! We can't make it into a kind of muted feast. Have you seen Edward?'

'I was going to ask you that. I've telephoned Hatting – '

'So have I. He has gone to London, I think, only he doesn't answer the phone.'

'Oh dear, what a very tragic business! Look, I've been thinking, let me deal, at least we can give them sandwiches in the Rectory – I've already – '

'Oh *hell*,' said Benet, 'I haven't thought it out – '

'It's remarkable you can think at all. Oh how dreadful for both of them – '

Now Mildred was standing beside them. 'Benet, we must be outside where they'll be parking their cars, we must field them at once – '

'Oliver says sandwiches in the Rectory. I suppose I should have brought the bridal cake down! At least we can give away the flowers!'

'I think they will want to go away at once,' said Mildred. 'They'll respect our misery – they'll realise we don't want to chat – now look here – '

'Oliver says he's posted sentinels, but *we* must speak – '

'Make a speech?'

'No, to each of them individually – '

'Perhaps they'll tell each other and go away.'

'No, they'll want to see *us*, to *find out* what's happened – '

'But if *we* don't know –! It's just as well Edward has disappeared, he'll be in London by now!'

In fact the problem did not turn out to be so insoluble. Oliver Caxton's sentinels, standing in the lanes, stopped the guests and informed them that the wedding was cancelled. If the guests desired more information or wished for some reason to stay they were directed to the Rectory, where by now sandwiches, and later drinks, it was said, were available. A few who, since it was such a lovely day, had left their cars earlier at a distance and walked, arriving through the meadows, were also dealt with by sentinels. There were, as Benet had said, not all that many. Some tactfully went away at once, back, usually to London, others it was later known returned as far as the Sea

Kings, looking for lunch and rumours. The rest stayed politely at the Rectory for what Benet had called a muted feast.

Rosalind had remained alone in the church. Of course she knew it well, though she had not often been to services there. Of course all churches were magical places. But this one seemed to her, especially in her present state of shock, something more absolutely amazing. She began to walk about in the heavy silence. She felt an impulse to touch things and thereby make them, in her terrible distress, her own. She walked quietly upon the brown encaustic tiles towards the altar, passing beneath the gilded Christ, up the steps into the chancel. She looked up at the soldier saint, pale and young, in armour, with golden hair, leaning gracefully, pensively, upon his long sword, gazing over her head into the interior of the church. Rosalind turned round – he was reckoning up his countless angelic host – and in that moment there was a strange pressure of beings surging up out of the dark. She turned back again, touching hastily the small wooden cross upon the altar, it seemed strangely damp as if it were clinging to her hand, like a poor little animal. She let go quickly and walked away backwards, slipping over the step down from the chancel. Looking at the saint from there she noticed between his feet the decapitated head of the immense reptile, opening its mouth piteously, showing its white teeth and terrified anguished eyes. She thought, poor innocent serpent. Of course she had seen it before. She turned now hastily toward the door. Out of the dimness a human form, recumbent, was taking shape. Of course it was the lonely alabaster knight, also in armour, deep in his alcove, whom someone had shown to her long ago, pointing out the little dog which lay at his feet. Rosalind stroked the dog, feeling his head, his pricked-up ears, and the tossed locks of his fur. Then, breathing deeply, she gently touched the serene and ancient face of the warrior, worn away by time and the caresses of innumerable pilgrims. Her fingers touched his lips and it was as if his lips moved. She went quickly away and made for the door.

Outside the sun was shining as brightly and hotly as before. Rosalind stood for a moment in the doorway covering her eyes. She gave a sudden cry, like a bird's cry, as she emerged from the dark. She moved forward into the open. From here the Rectory was well visible, and she could see people emerging from it, whom she recognised. Benet was standing there, saying farewell evidently to Charles and Jennie Moxon. Oh how *weird* it was, and *terrible*, what an *extraordinary* scene as if some great ceremony were being performed. She thought, they will never forget it, *I* shall never forget it. And – they will never forgive it. Afraid that someone, even at this distance, might see her and call to her, Rosalind turned away, passing behind the church towards, on a higher level, the churchyard, and, among the grave stones, the immense dark centuries-old yew trees. She thought she would hide among those trees. Then she saw something, somebody, just visible from where she stood now, dark before the sweeping lower boughs of one of the trees, a man, sitting upon the flat top of a tombstone and looking down. Rosalind stopped and once more walked backward, then ran. The man was Edward. He had not seen her. She thought, oh poor poor Edward – he is waiting there in case Marian should come after all!

'I hope that's the lot,' said Benet to Mildred.

'I hope so, I think so.'

'Owen didn't turn up.'

'Oh yes he did! I saw him with one of the sentinels in the meadow and then – '

'Those sentinels deserve some food and drink – '

'They're here in the kitchen, and Owen too!'

'What a weird business. You know, some of them enjoyed it!'

'Of course! The Moxons patently did, and the children – '

'Well, Elizabeth was in tears.'

'Yes. She loves Marian. I think she's gone back to London now – '

'We should have detained her – '

'Impossible.'

'At any rate we've made contact with Anna. She's gone now too, hasn't she? I hope she won't skip back to France.'

'Oh dear, listen to all those roars of laughter in the kitchen!'

'Surely they wouldn't laugh *now* and in front of Oliver!'

'He's upstairs, oh here he is, Oliver, thank you so much. Did you ring Alexander?'

'Yes. I'm afraid he found it rather amusing.'

'Oh hell. I suppose now everyone knows – what she did – how she ditched him at the last moment – '

'Well, yes, that's what you told me, I thought you wanted it to be public – '

'Don't worry, Oliver, you've been a brick. We've caused you a lot of trouble. We're going back to Penndean. Do come later, well, some of us will be gone – '

Back at Penndean there was no enthusiasm for lunch. Owen arrived on foot rather drunk and fell asleep in the drawing room. Rosalind had gone upstairs to lie down. Mildred was anxious to get back to London and be 'on the track' as she put it. Marian *must be found*, some of the people whom they had 'caught' this morning might already have found her. There was no point in staying longer at Penn.

After some discussion Benet agreed that Mildred should go at once, with Owen. Rosalind was nowhere to be found. Owen woke up and said of course he would drive Mildred to London, only his car was down at the Sea Kings, since he had walked from there to the church. Though they had already declared that a walk down to the pub would do them good, Benet pointed out that they would have to carry all Mildred's luggage, and in the end he drove them down himself. When he got back to the house there was still no sign of Rosalind.

Soon after her return to Penndean, Rosalind had left again with one view in her mind. She *must see* Edward. She had kept secret that glimpse of him sitting upon the tombstone beneath the yew trees. Of course he had not gone to London, he had just stayed hidden at Hatting, like a secretive animal fading into the landscape. He had not been able to resist emerging to see the arrivals, perhaps thinking desperately that Marian would come after all, materialising at the church, surprised to find them all confounded, taken in by the awful evil false message. After changing into her male attire, Rosalind left Penndean, not by the drive, but by a gate in the wall farther down the road, reached by a little path through the trees. The gate, sometimes locked, was now fortunately not locked. She crossed the road and followed through tall grass a scarcely perceptible right of way running steeply down to the River Lip at a place where there was a shaky little wooden bridge, always said to be likely to fall down. Crossing swiftly, lightly, she glimpsed below her the dark little river enclosed by the many wild flowers, whose names she could not remember. After the river, she had left Benet's territory, and entered Edward's territory. (They still feuded about the bridge.) She climbed over a stile and slowed down in a field which showed evidence of cultivation. Here she paused to greet a dear friend, a horse called Spencer, once a hunter, a very old horse now, Edward had told the girls about him some time ago. Spencer, who knew her well, advanced slowly moving his big gentle brown head to and fro. Rosalind hugged his head, and tears which she had been checking came again, and her wet tears smeared his brown glossy cheek and coat. 'Oh Spencer, dear dear Spencer – ' She kissed him near to his soft mouth, then hurried on, down a hill, over a five-barred gate and another meadow, walking breathlessly. Hatting Hall was by now well in sight. Rosalind, now passing another gate, which was open, crossed a narrow tarmac road, and, over mown grass, approached the gates, always open by day, of the handsome building. The drive was short, passing between two huge and very old mulberry trees. Steps led up to the large ornate door, beside and above which the tall Elizabethan windows glittered in the sunshine and the turrets rose high above the doorway and above the battlemented roof which supported also the magnificent twirling chimneys, each one different. The sun shone upon the warm soft powdery red-brown brickwork. This external glory of Hatting however was mainly limited to its façade, since Cromwell's troops who had battered Saint Michael had also occupied and devastated the interior and, perhaps accidentally, set fire to it. Marks of the fire could still be found in places upon the frontal bricks. The rather ramshackle and unattractive house which had been hastily put up behind the façade had happily fallen down in the early eighteenth-century, when a large elegant Georgian house was at last firmly fitted behind the Tudor front. Edward's family, who had lived, 'forever' they said, in Cornwall and had come to own valuable lead mines, bought Hatting early in the eighteenth century. The huge beautiful garden, invisible from the front, was said to have been designed by Capability Brown.

Rosalind was running now, the coat-tails of her jacket flying behind her. She could see, as she passed between the mulberry trees, the steps, and the front door which was open. She ran up the steps, paused gasping at the top, then cautiously pushed the open door a little farther, and entered the hall. There was silence now, except for her slowly calming breath. Neither the butler, Montague nor his wife Millie, were in evidence. She looked about, blinking her eyes after the bright sun, gazing in, what for a time seemed a twilight, at the big hall and, through open doors, the drawing room and farther off the billiard room where they used to play 'Freda'.

Edward appeared upon the stairs. He stopped. For a second Rosalind thought that he had taken her to be her sister. Then he said, 'Is there any news?'

'No. I'm sorry. I mean not that I know. I – I just thought I'd come to you in case, before you went to London – I could help somehow – I'm so sorry, I'm so *terribly* sorry – '

Edward, who had been grasping the banisters, came slowly down, then stood near Rosalind looking away as if he had forgotten her. Then he said, 'Could you close the door?'

Rosalind, who was standing nearest to it, closed it. She was thinking about what to say next.

'Would you like a cup of coffee?'

'Yes,' she said, 'Oh yes, thanks – I hope I'm not in the way – '

Edward turned, moving promptly upon his heel, and marched fast further down the hall into a dark corridor. Rosalind ran after him, mopping her eyes to remove the sunlight and the sudden tears with the back of her hands, she had no handkerchief. She emerged from the corridor into a large airy sunny kitchen.

Edward had put the kettle on. Frowning, he was spooning coffee powder into mugs. His hand was trembling. Rosalind came nearer to the big well-scrubbed wooden table. She looked at his long hands and pale slim fingers. 'Can I help?'

'No.' He put down the mugs and gazed at the kettle.

Rosalind, suddenly feeling rather faint, said 'Oh dear – ' and sat down on a chair.

'Are you all right?'

'Yes, yes. Oh Edward – I'm so – terribly sorry – ' She put a hand up to her throat.

With a kind of military precision Edward was pouring the boiling water into the mugs. He said, 'Milk and sugar?' Rosalind nodded. He said, 'Let's go upstairs. Would you like to look at the pictures?' He gave her a mug and left the kitchen carrying his own.

Rosalind, holding her mug carefully, followed him up the stairs. She did not want to look at the pictures. She wanted to sit quietly beside Edward and talk to him. Pausing to sip the coffee she found it burning hot, and without milk and sugar.

The gallery, established in the late eighteenth century, was a very long room with a shining parquet floor overlooking the garden. It contained a medley of pictures collected by various owners with various tastes. Edward had only lately, since the death of his father, been able to indulge his own taste. Rosalind put down her mug carefully on a window ledge behind a bowl of flowers. *Flowers*, which had been picked yesterday for the bride! She looked out at the sunlit garden, so immobile, so still, near to the house the big clipped box, a line of sentinels, the laburnum walk, then the great trees, receding into the distance, very old trees, oak and beech and chestnut and deodar, some of them four hundred years old or more. The absolute silence in the sunshine. Rosalind, her eyes dazzled, turned back to the room, picking up her mug and spilling some coffee on the glowing parquet. Hastily, looking about her, she mopped it up with her sleeve. Edward had gone, no he was a little way away down the room. Once again she felt faint. What was it now, that sudden startling pain: *Marian could have owned all this, all of it, this garden, this house, these pictures, Edward.*

Edward, who had put his coffee down somewhere, was now returning towards her. She saw his face clearly, it was pale, almost white, gathered into a steel mask, his grim mouth, his lips pale, his eyelids, his hawkish nose. She tried to think quickly of something to say to him, and sudden words were put into her mouth.

'I met Spencer in the meadow on the way.'

Edward's face changed. He said, 'Yes, Spencer, that dear old chap.' Then he said, 'I bought a picture lately, a modern one, it's down there.'

She followed him, passing a brilliant Goya on the way. She only once had been in this gallery. Why? Perhaps because Marian was not interested in paintings.

There was a sound. Someone had entered at the far end. It was Benet.

Edward turned to go towards him. Rosalind paused then followed. She could see at once that Benet was displeased with her. The impression was momentary, but connected in some way with the pain she had felt by the window. Benet reached out his hand towards Edward. Edward with a slight hesitation took Benet's hand. Benet with his other hand gripped Edward's shoulder for a moment. Then they both drew apart.

Benet said, 'There's no one downstairs. I thought you might be here. I didn't like to come earlier. At least I thought at first you must have gone to London. Then I – '

'I'm glad to see you.'

Rosalind moved past them. She said, 'Goodbye, Edward – I'm so glad Benet has come – I – ' She felt at once this was the wrong thing to say. She hesitated. She thought, I should say something about Marian –

Edward said, 'Thank you for coming, Rosalind.' He made a vague gesture. She turned and went away.

Benet said, 'Oh dear boy – ' He had not said this to Edward before. He found himself thinking of Uncle Tim. He said, 'Let's sit down somewhere.'

'Let's go downstairs,' said Edward.

Benet followed him down the stairs and into the drawing room. It was dark, the blinds had been drawn against the sun. Edward put up one of the blinds. He sat down upon the big settee which faced the huge fireplace and Benet sat beside him. Edward moved away, leaning upon the arm of the settee. He uttered a deep sigh. Benet thought, how pale he is, well he has always been pale and thin, now suddenly he looks gaunt like his father, and has he, since yesterday, cut off some of his hair?

Edward, now wrinkling up his face and half closing his light-brown eyes said, looking down at his feet, 'You must blame me.'

'My dear, blame *you*, of course not!'

'I think many people will blame me. After all, she may have decided, and had her reasons, and at the last moment – it was a great act of courage – '

'You have a noble heart,' said Benet.

'She must have had reasons, I must have heard, seen – *I* should have checked it at the last moment – perhaps she wanted me to – I should have done it, only I was so anxious – '

Benet, not sure what Edward was saying, and feeling his own anguish said, 'You are both young and you just don't want to be hasty. Later you may both see – other things will come – and anyway nothing that has happened means that you cannot put things together again later on – '

'No, no, it's just another thing, another wound in my life, or not a wound, wounds can heal, damage, my fault – anyway I mustn't detain you.'

He stood up. Benet stood up too, trying desperately to think of some right thing to say. Awkwardly he said, 'You know how much I have wanted you to be – that you should marry – and happiness – you know how much I care and will care. Are you staying here tonight or going to London?'

'I don't know.'

'I shall stay at Penn – would you like to come over for lunch, or well now, for dinner?'

'No, no. I may go to London. Thank you for your visit.'

Benet drove his car, a rather elderly Rover, back to Penndean. The sunshine, the quietness of the countryside, the beauty of

43

trees and flowers made him ready to weep. He had done nothing for Edward, he had come to him simply to pour out his own anguish. He had so passionately wanted Edward to be, as it were, his son-in-law, as Marian was, as it were, his daughter. Now, it came to him more and more clearly, he had *lost both* of them, and *for ever*. And nothing at Penn would ever be the same again.

When he reached the house he found a car before the front door, Owen's glossy blue Volvo. As he opened the door he heard voices in the drawing room.

'Oh *here* he is! Benet, I'm carrying off Mildred – we were waiting for you – where have you been?'

Owen and Rosalind had emerged into the hall.

'Won't you stay for lunch,' said Benet, 'won't you stay the night –?'

'Well, no, sorry – we thought you would be going to London, back to – '

Mildred was coming down the stairs carrying a suitcase. 'Benet dear, will you be all right? Shall we stay? The house is – '

'I'll be all right,' said Benet. 'I'll probably come back to town tomorrow. Let me help you with the luggage.'

'It's all packed now I think,' said Owen, taking the case from Mildred. They were anxious to go. Benet followed them out into the sunshine.

'Where's Tuan?' said Benet. He had forgotten the young fellow's existence.

'He ordered a taxi to take him to the station – '

'That's *miles* away – '

'We offered but he was in a terrible hurry, and we weren't ready – '

'Well, see you soon – I'm sorry – that you have had this dismal – '

'We are all in the same grief,' said Mildred. 'Perhaps we shall suddenly find her running back.'

'I doubt it,' said Owen. 'Thank you, dear Benet, for – well, thank you – '

Mildred put her suitcase into the boot and after Owen climbed into the big car, she wound down the window.

'Where's Rosalind? Yes, the hired car, she'll drive it back, she's gone into the house, she wants to stay with you – you can console her better than we can – dear dear Benet – ' She stretched out her hand. Benet kissed it. The big car disappeared among the trees, Mildred's hand fluttering.

Benet, returning, found Rosalind sitting on a chair in the hall. He brought up a chair and sat down beside her. He was about to speak, but she spoke first.

'I'm so sorry, I know you didn't want me to run to see Edward, I oughtn't to have done – and I couldn't say anything good to him, I just disturbed him, I'm so sorry, I know I shouldn't have been – '

Benet, who had now recalled his faint annoyance, said, 'But, dear Rosalind, I didn't mind your going to see him, why should I. I am sure he was glad to see you, he took you to see the pictures – it was I who interrupted – '

Rosalind, shaking her head and screwing up her eyes, said, 'Oh, never mind – Benet, I'm sorry – '

'Won't you stay here? I'm not going. My dear child, *do stay*, please.'

'No, no, I know you want to be alone. I want to be alone too. I must go. It is all such a *nightmare* – '

She rose. He wanted to say something loving and consoling, but could not find the words. He said, 'I will see you very soon. Perhaps you will find her, perhaps she will come to you – she would come to you, not to us – very soon everything may be put together, they will run to each other – it will all be – '

Rosalind said, 'No, she will not come, not to any of us ever again, she will never come.'

'Don't say that, Rosalind – we don't know – '

'It's like witchcraft, it's like being transformed into quite a different thing – or like – like in *hell*.'

'Won't you stay with me?'

'No, dear Benet, I want to be alone – I have my things in the hall, and look – Clun has driven the car round.'

Clun had indeed brought the hired car to the door, and then vanished into the greenery as was his wont. Benet helped her to put her things in, those things which had been so precious yesterday. She got into the car, wound down the window and kissed him hastily. 'Goodbye, *dear dear* Benet.'

The car disappeared and he walked slowly back to the house. He thought, they all want to leave me, we shun each other, they think this place is cursed, *that* could not have happened anywhere else, perhaps it *is* witchcraft, somehow it is my fault. *Oh God*. He entered the house and closed the door. He looked at his watch and found to his surprise that it was not yet five o'clock. Earlier he had told Sylvia to go home, though not before she had laid the table for possible remaining guests. There were none. He made his way to the kitchen, then wandered back to the drawing room. A terrible solitude came over him, he felt he was gasping for breath – how could all these terrible things have happened – and be just *beginning* – things that affected everyone, and all his fault. He had been so happy, he had believed he was collecting a family. He must do something, he felt like crying and tearing his clothes. Should he go back to Germany? He couldn't, he had been there too long ago, his sort of life, his long life, had been shattered. He was beginning, something new, something awful, he heard Rosalind's words, it's witchcraft, it's *hell*.

He shuffled into his study, he looked at Uncle Tim's bronze dancing Shiva wildly waving his four arms inside a circle of fire. He looked down at the words he had written the day before yesterday. He sat down.

In attempting to make some sense of Heidegger's involvement with the Pre-Socratics one must keep in mind the metaphysical patterns which illustrate connections and identities and show the (apparently) Many as the One. The One (or the Same) is what it is about. The One has various faces or facets, the approach to it being a grouping (or as one might say bodyguard) of concepts with other names. Christianity emphasises the One, but mediates it through the Three, others through the Two. Too much insistence on the One could, by seeming intolerable, generate a mass of sub-concepts and sub-entities. These of course can exist as saints, minor gods, unrelated virtues, and so on. The force that makes the One is (as often or not rightly) resisted. Heidegger wishes to show us the internal relations between the great Greek concepts, and in doing so to sustain and explain his doctrine of Being, which is supported by a similar inner concept ring.

What on earth does he mean, thought Benet, or what do *I* mean? I thought it would be an escape – instead I am just involving myself in a dark spider's web, the web of *his mind*. And did dear good Célan, they say, visit him in his mountain hut – and Hannah Arendt forgive him – and he dare to take over great Hölderlin, as well as the Greeks? Alas, that awful darkness is there, but for me it is *my* darkness, it is *my* neighbour and *my* heavy chain. I am small and I do not understand. How I wish I had stayed in the light and devoted my life to poetry, not philosophy. I used to write poems when I was young, before I became bemused by *that* philosophy! And now it is all impossible. Only Tim could hold up a light for me in the dark. And the Greeks, the Greeks, even *they* are fading away.

I wonder if I am going mad, thought Benet, as he rose from his desk. What was he to do now? How *could* he blunder about in this raving mess when this day had produced nothing but horror? He went slowly, heavily, back to the kitchen. He tried to eat an apple. He opened a bottle of red wine and drank some. He sat down and put his head on the table, then raised it again. Was he *crazy*? Where was Marian now, floating in the Thames, self-destroyed by poison in some shabby London room, where months, perhaps years, could pass before she was discovered? And Edward – what, with all his busy scheming, had he done for Edward now? He got up and went out into the garden. The garden was motionless, even the birds seemed to be silent. He walked as far as his ginkgo tree. He embraced the tree, rolling his forehead upon its smooth bark. Then he came back to the house and lay down on the sofa in the drawing room and fell asleep. He woke in a haze of misery. The day was going, though it was not dark. Suddenly he decided he must go back to London after all. He hurried about, picking up his coat, and snapping a variety of locks and bolts, and left the

47

house. The Rover was close by under the trees. He got in, and before leaving, laid his head down upon the steering wheel.

There was a great deal of traffic entering London and the sky was darkening. The final jam made Benet curse. What an idiot he was. Was he to spend all night in the car? At last he reached his house, opened the gates, and drove the Rover in as far as the garage. He closed the gates and walked back to the steps which, nearer to the street, led up to the front door. The house was dark. In the faint summer dusk and the dim light which came in from the road he fumbled cursing with his keys. He very quietly undid two locks and slid in through the door. As he closed the door and reached for the light, another light appeared in a room beyond, then a dark figure appeared in a doorway. Benet turned on the light in the hall.

'Hello, Sir, are you all right?'
'Yes, of course!' said Benet.
'Have you any news? Miss Rosalind rang me.'
'No!' said Benet.
'Would you like something to eat or –?'
'No –'
'Well, goodnight – '
'Goodnight, Jackson.'
Jackson was his servant.

TWO

Owen Silbery was sitting alone in his studio. He had had his dreadful recurring dream. He is buried in sand up to his neck, he cannot move his limbs, the tide is coming in, the tide begins to reach him, the spray touches his face, he screams, he tosses his head back, his only possible movement, no one comes, the water begins to attack his mouth, he swallows the water, it has covered his mouth, he cannot scream any more, it begins to cover his nose . . . Owen detested this dream, it made him feel *very sick*, and it particularly annoyed him because he thought that he hadn't even really invented it, it was not *his* dream, hadn't he seen it in a film a long time ago?

It was the next day, the day after the terrible one. The busy telephone had produced no news. Owen had, on the previous evening, driven Mildred to her tiny flat (he had given up asking her to let him buy her a larger one). He had then returned to his house in Kensington, and eaten some oddments out of the fridge, and drunk a lot of whisky and seen the news on television and gone to bed, imagining he would not sleep. However he slept. And now there was this unspeakable horror and a sense all around him of chaos and depredation. And they would be speculating about whether the poor girl had committed suicide. Owen himself had often contemplated suicide and possessed the requirements thereof. And did he not, he reflected, as a painter, imagine, create, and gaze upon what was degraded and vile? Of course such things too became his art and thereby transformed, ha ha! He must remember to drink a toast to Otto Dix. *He* was *real*. Owen was sitting in his quiet studio looking at a half-painted abstract. He hated the picture. *Expressionism, Fauvism, Dada, Cubism, Neue Sachlichkeit, Frightfulnessism. Foutu métier.* He leaned forward and scratched the canvas with his fingernail. He was becoming lazy, and with laziness came idleness, agonising, solitude and loss of being. The only person who had really understood him was Uncle Tim – though even he –

He got up and cleaned the brushes and put them in order and rubbed his hands on a paint rag. He sighed a long familiar sigh. He had silenced his telephones. He moved softly about his studio, pulling up the blinds which had been obscuring some of the windows. The cruel sunlight entered. His studio was spacious, occupying the whole second floor of his house. He had created it long ago when he had had three walls removed and enjoyed for the first time, his own space, his own light. His house was big and tall, bought with his first really big money, a retaliation for his unbearable childhood and the wound about which he never spoke. He kept no servant or cleaner. The plain wooden floor of the studio was kept by Owen extremely clean and tidy. The dining room and sleek kitchen on the ground floor, and the drawing room and 'study' on the first floor, were reasonably in order. There was also a basement which had once (before Owen's reign) housed a maid, and now contained correctly slotted *special* pictures, together with various machines and things. The third floor began to reveal certain 'natural' traits of the present owner, now appearing as the stairs ascended. In one large room there was a huge bed, Owen's bed, never properly made, but randomly covered at times by a huge red counterpane. This bed sometimes reminded Owen of days gone by, when ladies had regularly come down from the north to pose for him, no questions asked. No doubt their husbands were unemployed or had cleared off and they were supporting numerous children. It was no business of his. Opposite, in rows of cupboards, showing only their colourless sides, were other innumerable undisposed of ordinary pictures. Owen sometimes, now less often, pulled out one at random. Now, having left his studio

50

and climbing up the stairs, he entered this room, searching for something. He pulled it out at last, a portrait he had painted once of Lewen Dunarven. He studied it for some time. He put it back again. Not a good likeness. He came out. He felt tired and wanted to lie down upon his bed. However he decided to go up further and look out of the fifth floor window. The fourth floor here, detained him, consisting of a handsome rarely used guest room and opposite, Owen's special treat, his *dark room*, whose walls were covered with *very interesting* photos, including (among the mild ones) a picture of Mishima posing as Saint Sebastian, mentioned recently by Benet. Mishima had died at his own hand. What monumental courage it must take to slash one's stomach open, knowing that an instant later a kind friend would remove one's head. A pity there was no available photo of that.

On the fifth floor, which covered the whole area, Odradek, pet of Kafka, reigned. Everywhere senseless, nameless and timeless entities lay in piles, cardboard boxes, containing unconnected unnameable things lay piled one on another, heavy soiled garments, long ago devoured by moths, innumerable old books, no doubt of great value, kicked to pieces, ancient letters some unopened, broken china, broken glass, ancient newspapers, collections of stones – Owen picked his way to the window and looked out. Below him, stretching away, there were green gardens, filled with bushes and tall trees and backs and fronts of houses, beyond him and above him was the blue enormous sky and just below it, London.

Owen turned away with a sigh, kicked some entities aside, and reached the door. He slowly descended the stairs as far as the reasonably tidy drawing room upon the first floor. There was a large mirror above the fireplace. He looked at himself in the mirror. His copious hair, which had been genuinely very dark, almost black, was now successfully dyed completely black. He had put on weight. Did anyone notice? It didn't matter. His aggressive profile remained the same. Uncle Tim had once likened him to a toad, a particular toad in the garden at Penndean. Owen liked toads. He went to the telephone and released it. Almost instantly it rang. It was Mildred.

'Oh, Owen – have you heard anything?'

51

'No.'

'We've been in touch with the police. You haven't thought of anything?'

'*Thought*? No.'

'You know Benet came back late last night. Has he rung you?'

'No.'

'Were you out?'

'I turned the phone off.'

'Of course, you were working. Are you all right?'

'Yes.'

'May I come and see you? I won't stay long.'

'Mildred, just fuck off please.'

He put the telephone down and switched it off again. He sat down in one of the deep armchairs and covered his face with his hands.

Benet was standing upon the doorstep of a large house near Sloane Square, which was very familiar to him, though he had not visited it for a long time. He was disturbed to notice how anxious he now was, as a mass of memories crowded upon him. He straightened his tie and smoothed down his ruffled red-brown hair. He rang the bell. The bell was familiar. He waited.

The door opened. Anna Dunarven appeared instantly, smiling.

'Oh Benet, I'm so glad to see you! We had no time to talk properly down there, come in, come in, what's the news of Marian?'

'No news, alas, not yet. Anna, forgive me for coming

suddenly like this, I ought to have written, I couldn't find your telephone number and – '

'Yes, yes, I changed it, I should have given it to you, anyway here you are, follow me, you know the way of course, everything is the same, isn't that strange!'

He followed her into the memorable drawing room, he saw the sun shining upon the garden, they stood together by the window.

'Those trees have grown.'

'Yes, that's what I thought at once when I came back. They've kept it all very well, haven't they. This room is all the same, except I've moved things about a bit.'

'I see the old elephant is in his place on the mantelpiece.'

'Yes, would you believe it, they had put him away in a cupboard, I had to search for him! How you all must miss Uncle Tim.'

'We do. We've been missing you too.'

'Oh Benet, you are just the same, your hair stands on end so thick and red and ruffled, like it used to, not a bit of grey, you are so handsome and your eyes – your eyes are *so* blue – '

Anna threw her arms round Benet's neck, he felt her hair warm upon his cheek, he put his arm around her waist. They released each other. They had known each other for a long time, in fact Benet claimed to have introduced Anna, then twenty, to Lewen Dunarven, then thirty. He had met and known them both separately in London, Anna as a friend of Elizabeth Loxon, who was a friend of Mildred, and Lewen as a frequenter of the British Library. He had also sorted things out for Anna after Lewen, a distinguished Irish scholar, had so unexpectedly died. He had known Anna's mother, who had died in France after Anna's departure there 'for ever'. The boy, now nine, or was it ten, years old, had never known his father.

Standing apart, they held hands, surveying each other, then releasing their hands and becoming sombre.

'So what happened to Marian, do you know anything?'

'We know nothing,' said Benet. 'I was wondering if you had any clues or ideas – '

'You don't think I'm harbouring her?'

'Of course not!' said Benet. He had however now reached

the stage of anything being possible. Women take refuge with women. He could at least attempt to picture the degree of despair which must have occasioned Marian's missive. Surely she must be with *someone* – unless some terrible thing had occurred.

Anna, reading his mind, said, 'I might have taken her in, but I haven't!'

'She was very fond of you.'

'And I of her. I have no idea where she might be. I have been so long away.'

'Of course – Oh Anna, it is so dreadful – '

'What did the letter say – just that she had decided not to get married –?'

'Yes. That – and saying sorry.'

'What a shock. Poor Edward. Look, let us sit down.'

They left the window and sat upon the big red velvet settee. Benet looked up at the elephant. He turned to her saying:

'It was so kind of you to come for the – we are all hoping that now you will stay.'

'I might stay, yes, but – '

'Really, stay, and live here, in your own house, not go back to France?'

'Yes, of course I'd live in France too – but I don't know. I might rent the house again later on.'

'You are as beautiful as ever. I love your green dress.'

Anna laughed. 'Do you mind if I smoke? I know you don't.' She reached out for the packet of cigarettes which was lying in the large blue glass bowl upon the long low table in front of them. She lit the cigarette, trembling a little and smiling. She said, 'Would you like a drink, would you like to stay to lunch?'

He thought, she will soon be in tears, I mustn't stay, anyway I can't stay. 'I'm sorry I can't – but could you come and have dinner with me tonight?'

'No. I'm afraid I've got another – '

'Oh Anna, we were all so happy, and now it's pure hell – '

'Are you sure you – all right – but I want to see you again very soon. I may want your advice.'

'Oh heavens – I would do my best! Now I must go and see Edward, poor devil.'

Anna, who used previously to 'put up' her hair in some neat and ingenious mass, now had it undone, tossed back, a smooth rill of straight pale-yellow hair reaching almost to her waist. She raised her hand now to her smooth clear brow, as if enquiring what her hair was up to. Benet gazed at her. Owen, who admired her and had painted her, said she had the calmest woman's face he had ever seen. Her face, devoid of make-up, displayed the faintest glowing shade of pink in her cheeks and lips. Her eyes were pale blue, her lips and eyes expressed often a detached, perhaps wistful, amusement. She could also look pensive, and gentle, and far away. Now, holding her cigarette firmly in her nicotine-stained right hand, she lifted her left hand to the neck of her dress, displaying unconsciously her plain golden wedding ring and diamond and ruby engagement ring which Benet suddenly remembered from the remote past, her wedding, his few and brief visits to her in France, she did not care for visitors; and in that moment he felt a sudden urge to speak of Lewen – and then he thought, she may not want to stay here, where Lewen's dying was so terrible. No wonder she ran away to France.

She said, 'Let us hope for Marian. What can a girl do in such circumstances? She has travelled, hasn't she? She is probably recovering somewhere and feeling relieved. She has realised she just doesn't want to! Everyone will forgive her, even Edward will. They may even come together again later on, why not. Do you think?'

'I don't know, Anna, I just *don't know* – I'm just afraid she'll – I'm just afraid. Look, I must go.' As they rose and moved towards the door he said, 'Where are your pictures? Still packed away somewhere, I suppose, until you decide what to do. I'd like to see that one that Owen made of Lewen.'

'You will come, dear Benet, again and bring Owen with you.'

As they moved into the hall Benet asked, 'How is the boy? Is he here?'

'Bran? Oh yes, he's here, I'll call him.'

'Oh, don't disturb him.'

'Bran, Bran, come and see Benet!'

After a scuffling in the front room, a boy dressed in long

black narrow trousers and a blue shirt appeared. His copious curly hair was dark amber, his eyes a pale brown, his lips red. He gazed at Benet with suspicion.

'Hello, Bran,' said Benet, moving towards him, 'How you have grown up!' He began to reach out his hand, but quickly withdrew it as the child showed no sign of taking it. Benet thought, oh dear, he wants to go back to France!

Anna said, 'He wants to go back to France. But we'll see – it's the school, you know.'

'He looks like his father,' said Benet.

'You think so? Yes – indeed – '

Bran looked at his mother, then quietly receded into the front room and closed the door.

Awkwardly Benet said, 'Perhaps he'll continue Lewen's book – is he interested in history?'

'He's interested in everything, he's extremely clever, but a bit withdrawn.'

Anna opened the front door. 'Well, goodbye, dear Benet – I do hope you'll find – by the way, thank you so much for lending us Jackson, he fixed the thing in no time. Bran took to him at once.'

In Owen's studio Mildred, paying no attention to his stern words, had arrived. Owen, opening the door to her, had returned, leaving her to close the door, moodily to his easel. He was, she saw, 'messing about' as he would put it, with some favourite mysterious subject. This subject it appeared was 'Man stealing a Cat', a subject which he claimed to have collected from some ancient Japanese tale. The man, unable to obtain the favours of a certain lady, has stolen her cat. Owen's version sometimes contained a Japanese flavour, and the proximity of the lady was hinted at though not seen. Interesting aspects of the pictures were the varying expressions upon the faces of the man and the cat. Sometimes the man looked frightened, the cat recalcitrant, sometimes both man and cat looked pleased as if joking, or else the man was wearing an evil grin, and the cat was struggling, or the faces of both were demonic.

After a silence Mildred said, 'He's going to kill the cat. What's that lacy white stuff in the corner?'

'The lady's bedroom.'

'Are we never to see her?'

'She is already dead, strangled.'

Accepting this information Mildred began to pace to and fro in the large room, her skirt swinging.

'Where are your angels?'

'I shall return to angels and to terrified Madonnas. And you are going to India to live in an ashram in the Himalayas and wear a sari and squat upon the ground.'

'I should have gone there long ago,' she said.

'Well, why not go there now, I'll pay your fare. You have been bewitched by Uncle Tim.'

The downstairs bell rang. 'That is Benet,' she said and left the room and ran down the stairs.

Benet was not displeased to find Mildred, where she quite often was, with Owen.

'Oh Mildred – no news? I have none.' He followed her up the stairs.

Owen, still sitting at his easel, put on the slit-eyed cynical look with which he always greeted Benet. 'So you are all running madly about and enjoying every moment?'

Benet walked across the room, picked up two chairs and brought them over, one for Mildred and one for himself. He said, 'It is something to do.'

'At least you can comfort the bereaved.'

'I rang up Rosalind and I am going to see her. Edward's telephone doesn't answer. I have been to see Anna – '

'Why her – did you think she had swallowed the girl? How is she anyway, is she going graciously to stay with us?'

'I hope so. I don't know. I think she wants to stay but Bran doesn't.'

'I don't blame him. I wish I'd settled down in France.'

'Did you see the child?' said Mildred.

'For a moment. He was rather reticent.'

'Just like Lewen,' said Owen.

'We are all in a state of shock,' said Mildred. 'We have to run about, as you put it, so as not to break down – there are so many awful possibilities.'

'We have been through that,' said Owen, 'we must at least now get on with our work. Probably she is sitting somewhere laughing and gloating, she may have gone to Brighton.'

'We must comfort each other anyway,' said Mildred.

Benet said, 'Yes, indeed. I was wondering if you would like to have dinner with me this evening? I just don't feel like being alone.'

'Yes, of course we will be with you,' said Mildred. 'That's all right, isn't it, Owen?'

'I hope Rosalind will come, she wasn't sure when I rang.'

'And of course you asked Anna,' said Owen.

'Yes, but she can't come. It's rather short notice to rustle up guests.'

'I do hope Edward won't just seclude himself in misery,' said Mildred.

'Perhaps he'll shoot himself,' said Owen. 'That would add to our amusement.'

'You must invite Tuan too,' said Mildred. 'And why not Alexander and Elizabeth as well?'

Benet had taken a taxi from his house to Anna's house near Sloane Square. From here he had taken a taxi to Owen's house. Now he was taking another taxi to Rosalind's little flat off Victoria Street. He rarely drove his car in London. As he sat in the taxi he felt a pang of painful miserable guilt. He had felt a brief momentary joy with Anna, he had let himself be amused by Owen. Now he was thinking about Rosalind and about Marian. Of course he had actively been thinking about Marian *all the time*, Marian was what mattered, what filled his mind, what filled their minds. Just now he was also thinking of Rosalind and how he might support and console her. But he knew that beyond these particular matters there was a dark horror which he must not, and indeed could not, thrust away. Marian might be dead, drowned, kidnapped, mad with misery, mad with terror. The end of happiness, her happiness, Edward's, Rosalind's, her mother's, and mine, thought Benet, because in some way it must have been *my fault*! Her life is ruined, perhaps his. And now Rosalind.

He paid the taxi man. He rang the bell of the third floor flat. He pressed open the front door and began to climb. He heard Rosalind's door opening above – and the pain now came back and the fear, the *awfulness* of the situation, its bottomless void, suddenly something out of Shakespeare, the dreadful peril of the Bard himself. He heard her door opening above and thought, I will recall this.

Rosalind held the door open, then when Benet entered, shut it and leaning against it they hugged each other with closed eyes. Then Benet, holding her by the wrist, led her over to the window where a long seat covered with cushions gave a view down the busy little street dusty with sunshine and a narrow glimpse of the great Catholic Cathedral. Here they sat, turned, facing each other, Rosalind with her damp face and red eyes. Benet, suddenly near to tears, said in a gruff awkward voice, 'Oh don't grieve so, dear Rosalind, Marian is safe and well, I am sure.' He cleared his throat and went on, 'She will come back to us, back to you, very soon – she has acted rightly, she has done something perfectly just and proper, something which must have needed a great deal of courage – '

'You mean sending the note, then, at last – '

'A less courageous person would have felt it was already too late, they would have been ashamed, they would think, well, I don't want this, I know I shall hate it, it's all wrong, but I'm so involved now I'll have to put up with it, and I *know* that later

59

on I shall keep on wishing I'd had the nerve to say no, even at the last minute – '

Rosalind, her lips apart, was staring at Benet. 'You think that? But *why* didn't she do it earlier on, find out earlier on, she had plenty of time –? Of course she was confused, and you were all pressing her so – '

'We weren't *pressing* her – ' We were pressing her, he thought, we kept telling her how happy she would be, how happy they both would be, such a perfect couple – he went on, 'It was just when she came to it, to the reality of it, she just didn't really want to marry Edward, she wanted to feel free, and not to have all those responsibilities – '

'You mean the house – '

'Well, yes, but Edward himself, being married to him for ever, after all marriage is – '

'Edward himself – perhaps she found out something – '

'What do you mean, something disagreeable or –?'

'Oh dreadful, how *dreadful* it all is – '

Benet thought, I'm making a mess of this, I'm on the wrong tack. Tim would have known what to do. He said, 'Dear Rosalind, don't weep. We shall see soon what is the better for both of them. I just meant that marriage is a great responsibility and one has to think carefully even up to the last moment – '

'But do you also think that they may soon make it up and then secretly get married somewhere, with no parsons and no bridesmaids, and come back to surprise us all?'

'That is certainly possible too,' said Benet. In fact he had, among many possibilities, envisaged this one also. 'We must just be calm and wait. Marian will come back to us, she will probably send us a signal in a day or two – '

'If she isn't dead – perhaps she is dead – I can see her – dead – '

'Rosalind, stop all this! You must be brave and just wait quietly – I feel sure we shall have good news soon, perhaps even in an hour or two, and you will know at once – '

'There is no good news, for her – or for me – ever – '

'Rosalind, *please* – '

'All right, all right, I'm sorry, dear Benet – I'm so glad you came to see me – I am just talking nonsense to you.'

'Dear, dear child, do not cry – I love you, we all love you, your life is ahead – and really, whatever – all will be well with Marian too – '

'It is very kind of you, but – I think I may lie down for a while – '

'Yes, yes, lie down, I'll go – but please, do come to dinner this evening at my place, will you? Owen and Mildred will be there – '

'And Edward?'

'I don't know, I can't get in touch with him, he may have gone back to Hatting, anyway do come – '

They stood up. He kissed her hot cheek. She was taller than Marian and almost as tall as Benet.

As he was walking towards Victoria Station Benet renewed his guilty misery. Obviously of course, he should have thought of it at once in the gallery. Poor Rosalind was in love with Edward! More hell. He had been intending to go home, but decided now to make one further assault. He took a taxi to Notting Hill, checking the taxi man a little short of Edward's house. He walked slowly on. There was something conspicuous, a ladder leaning against the front of the house. He looked at it, avoided it, and mounted the steps to the front door. He rang the bell, waited, rang again, shouted through the letter box, then stood back. There was no way of getting into the garden. He felt an urge to climb the ladder and look in at the window. What was he imagining? Edward dead upon the floor? He walked hastily away. Now he felt reluctant to go home. He took yet another taxi to Brompton Road and ordered a modest lunch in a small restaurant but found he could scarcely eat. To walk somewhere, he walked to Harrods and looked at some expensive ties, connecting them somehow with Edward whom he senselessly expected to see as he looked around upon the numerous shoppers. He was beginning to experience a loss of identity which now came upon him at times after Tim's death. He left Harrods and walked up across the road into the Park where he strolled along as far as Peter Pan and watched people tossing bread to frenzied swans, ducks, geese, coots, seagulls. Other birds were more cautiously present, herons, even cormorants. This scene and a glance at Peter sent Benet home at last. Here he telephoned Elizabeth Loxon, who said she'd love to come to dinner, but she was engaged that night, he rang Priscilla Conti who had left a message that she had gone back to Italy, he rang Tuan who did not reply, Alexander was not at home, he rang Charles Moxon at his office, who said sorry he and Jennie were going to the opera, he tried Marian's number in vain of course. Exhausted he lay down for a moment upon his bed and instantly fell into a dream that Penndean was in flames.

At dinner of course they had talked about Marian but with silent consent had left this subject for the moment and started up a lively argument about Sonya in *War and Peace*. Owen, though seriously or otherwise was not clear, insisted that Tolstoy, all the way through, had clearly portrayed her as a silly girl, doing what she was told, readily seen through by Nicholas who promptly ditched her, and at the end being rightly described by Natasha as just a moronic cat, humbly attaching herself to the family. This interpretation enraged Mildred, who passionately sided with her as poor brave intelligent selfless Sonya, meanly dropped by block-headed Nicholas, and totally misunderstood by silly mean ungrateful Natasha, who *is* at the end properly labelled by Tolstoy as stupid. After all, Mildred insisted, faithful loving Sonya had rescued faithless Natasha from total disaster by saving her from eloping with ghastly Kuragin. At the end, Mildred explained, Sonya, sitting tired and ignored, dispensing tea as a sort of servant, is a picture of silent selfless virtue! Tuan, who had now turned up, had sided with Mildred. Benet perversely held that Tolstoy, at the end, identifying himself nobly with Pierre, despising both the girls and Nicholas, was of course delighting in Prince Andrew's young son as a blameless icon of the future of Russia. Owen, always ready to tease Jackson, suddenly asked his opinion. Jackson, flitting to and fro from the kitchen, smilingly said he sided with Miss Sonya throughout. Mildred laughed, Benet was irritated. The argument then turned to whether the *Aspern Papers* had been stolen from Pushkin's *Queen of Spades* by Henry James when chatting with Turgenev. After that they returned to the hopeless topic of where was Marian. Then Tuan mentioned that he must go home and quietly slipped away. 'Poor boy can't take the drink,' said Owen.

It was almost midnight, and they had talked again about Marian, when Owen returned to 'Mildred's favourite topic, woman priests, nuns in fancy dress, admit that you are longing to get your hands upon the Chalice! Only remember that the Chalice is the Grail, a magical object, religion is magic! And after all did not the Virgin herself put women firmly down when she took over Athos as her own secret domain where no woman could ever come?'

'The Angel of the Annunciation kneels to the Virgin,' said Mildred.

'Ah, but what is she thinking, poor girl,' said Owen. 'Simone Martini saw into her soul when he depicted her reeling back in fear and horror!'

'Where's Jackson?' said Mildred.

'Our dark angel has flitted away like Ariel. I still can't make out whether he is putting on that accent – '

'Ariel was not an angel,' said Benet.

'Didn't Uncle Tim say that Jackson was Caliban?' said Mildred. 'He was the one who really knew the island, the animals and the plants and was useful and gentle and – '

'He said it of Kim,' said Benet, 'I mean Jackson was like Kim, who used to run along the rooftops delivering messages.'

'Prospero was ashamed,' said Owen. 'Why was he on that island anyway? Surely for some sin, he was suffering secret agonies of remorse – '

'Jackson is suffering,' said Mildred, 'for something, perhaps for something terrible – '

'What did Prospero mean by saying "this thing of darkness I acknowledge mine", what could he mean? Of course Caliban was his son by Sycorax – that stuff about Sycorax having had a child in Algiers was a cover-up – '

'What nonsense,' said Mildred.

'We must expect that Shakespeare felt remorse,' said Benet, 'Macbeth, Othello – '

'Artists know all about it,' said Owen. 'How Titian must have felt it, when he was very old, *The Flaying of Marsyas* – the pain, the pain, the old man must have felt it deeply at the end. I wonder what Jackson is ashamed of – '

'We shall never know,' said Mildred, 'and we cannot judge him. He is more likely to judge us.'

'I bet he has committed some terrible crime and is being punished for it, put in prison – probably he's escaped, no wonder he's so secretive.'

'There is such a thing as redemptive suffering,' said Mildred. 'Weren't there scars upon his back? You saw the scars, Benet – '

'No, I didn't,' said Benet.

'Well, he has been damned like Mildred's Fisher King, perhaps he is the Fisher King in disguise – ' said Owen.

'Perhaps he is a more exalted king in disguise,' said Mildred.

'A beggar like in Tim's India – perhaps he just made it up out of books! Tim certainly took to Jackson, he saw him like an Indian native, something primitive out of the jungle – '

'Jackson does not resemble a beggar,' said Benet, 'or a primitive or – '

'You found him in a cardboard box underneath a bridge, don't deny it, you found him in a basket, he was curled up like a snake and you brought him home, he's a captive, like a ringed

64

bird, poor fellow, he is profound, he must feel like Plato when he was a slave – '

'Must we have Plato in?' said Benet.

'Surely Plato was never a slave,' said Mildred.

'Yes, he was, it's in Plutarch,' said Benet. 'Jackson is really an educated man – '

'I've got it!' cried Owen. 'It's perfectly clear now! Jackson is Benet's illegitimate son!'

'I think you should both go home,' said Benet, rising.

'Well,' said Owen, 'however it may be, in Jackson I recognise my brother!'

They left at last, after standing in the hall and returning to the subject of Marian, and how in the next day or two something *must* become clear. Benet went back to the dining room and looked at the familiar chaos on the table. Usually he tidied some things away before going to bed. Now he had not the heart to. Anyway, Jackson, rising at dawn, would have it all removed and dealt with before he was up. He walked slowly upstairs, gripping the banisters. He was drunk, his heart was sick and heavy. In his bedroom the curtains were not drawn. He walked across in the dark, and looked down into the garden below. Jackson lived there, in the little house of his own which Benet called 'The Lodge'. The light was on in the Lodge. Benet drew the curtains and went quickly to bed in the dark.

On the next day Benet returned to Penn. Before leaving London, still feeling a bit drunk and ashamed, he made the usual telephone calls. No news of Marian, no replies from Edward. Why indeed from Edward, with his misery and his grief and his loss of face? Why had he not stayed in London with Marian on that awful night, what had that *meant*? Why had he not treated her properly? Why had she – ? There could have existed so many wounds and misunderstandings and doubts and uncertainties and secret spites and huge fears between these two. They should have *waited*. Why did they not wait? Because Benet was hustling them along, he was so sure that they were made for each other! Benet now wanted passionately to speak to Edward. Benet loved Marian, and had come to love Edward, he had felt like a father to both of them, he had looked forward so much to visiting them at Hatting Hall, and to seeing their children.

Benet had planned to reach Penn before lunch, but was delayed at the garage and then upon the motorway. As he neared his destination he decided instinctively to go by the loop road, behind the Rectory and over the bridge, rather than the direct way through the village. He had no business in the village. But suddenly it occurred to him that he precisely *had* business in the village, he must *show his face*. He must let them *look at him*, and *pity* him, and get their *sympathising* over with. He drove on, entering smaller and smaller roads and lanes until, at the sign *Lipcot*, turning down a very narrow lane where tall dry prickly leafy hedges clawed the car on either side and feathery ladies lace bowed down over the wheels and there were very few passing places. He met no one. At last he emerged into a larger space above the river and at once, after a few cottages, into the short village street where he parked his car outside the Sea Kings.

The tall Welsh landlord was the first to see him and say 'Was there news of Miss Marian?' and 'What a sad business!' Benet had intended to ask for news of Edward but decided in time that this was a mistake! He set off down the little street where his arrival had obviously been noted. He bought some stamps at the Post Office, picked up the local paper at the newsagent, bought some cheese at the grocer's, and looked so thoughtfully at the window of the little antique shop that the owner, Steve Southerland, came out and led him in, holding his sleeve. At each shop and upon the pavement Benet was met with the bright-eyed curiosity of children, but also from all the genuine sympathy and kindliness and desire to help. Steve Southerland had been so effusively sorry that Benet felt he must buy something and purchased a small cigarette case. He did not smoke. He returned with a suitable dignity to his car which had attracted a small group who waved him off. He drove away up the woody lane toward Penndean. Turning down the gravelled drive he saw Clun emerging from among the trees and waving his arms, but only to ask Benet for news and whether he had had no lunch and whether Sylvia should come. Benet said that he had had his lunch and didn't need Sylvia. He drove on and entered the house. He had had no lunch. He rang Hatting but no answer. He ate some bread and butter and the cheese he had bought in the village, and an apple. He felt terribly lonely. He was startled by a sound which was Sylvia bringing some flowers and asking him if he wanted anything. He stood up for Sylvia, pushing back his chair, and said no. He went to the larder and brought out a bottle of Valpolicella, opened it and poured out a glass. He carried it back to the drawing room and drank two more glasses. He picked up the telephone and rang the Hatting number, but of course had no reply.

Benet's intentions when returning to Penn had been far from clear. He wanted very much to get away from the London scene and be alone. He wanted silence, he even wanted work, the continuation of his book on Heidegger. He thought of driving over to Hatting at once but some terrible exhaustion prevented him. He would go tomorrow. He also wanted of course that *all should be well*, he did not know quite how, with or between Edward and Marian. He wanted passionately to run to them, to draw them together. At the same time he was keeping in mind, though he did not utter this, the possibility that Marian was *dead*. A murder, a suicide, an accident. No, not an accident. Benet still held in his pocket that terrible note which Edward had left with him, which he had perused so many times. Probably he did not want ever to see it again. '*Forgive me, I am very sorry, I cannot marry you.*' What could be more final? Yet might it not be merely a sudden impulse, regretted at once, and she ashamed to say: I didn't mean it? Benet had now recalled many times his conversation with

Edward at Hatting on the day after, when Edward had said, 'You must blame me.' He wondered, what does Edward feel now? Perhaps he rues that little scene when we were so open to each other. By now he resents his emotion, his openness to me, yes, he is cutting himself off from all of us, cursing us even, for having led him into this morass, this *pit*, from which he must feel he can never now escape. His life is destroyed, he will be despised, regarded as done for, a fool, something worse, no wonder the girl left him. But have not *I* done it? He will curse me for all this and he will be right – that talk we had at Hatting when we embraced each other, that was our last meeting, the last moment when we spoke truth and clarity to each other, when we expressed love for each other. I have lost him, and I have lost Marian, and it is all my fault.

These were thoughts which had been continuously at work in Benet's mind, and which were now achieving, as he drank the wine, a hideous degree of clarity. He had come to Penndean for some sort of quietness or solitude, but he was simply miserable and frightened, alone with his demons.

He left the drawing room and went to his study. There on the desk was his book about Heidegger, open at the page where he had left it such a little while ago. Benet perused the page which he had written.

Heidegger's central concept of truth or unconcealment should be understood by tracing it back to the Pre-Socratics, and to Homer, as he explains in an essay, originally a 1943 lecture, 'Wonder first begins with the question, "What does all this mean and how could it happen?" How can we arrive at such a beginning?' Heidegger quotes Heraclitus Fr. 16, 'How can one hide from that which never sets?' What is this hiding and from what? He then quotes Clement of Alexandria who adapts Heraclitus as meaning that one (the sinner) may hide from the light perceived by the senses, but cannot hide from the spiritual light of God. Well, though we may readily understand him in that sense, the Greek was not thinking about anything like a Christian deity. Heraclitus, according to Heidegger, is not thinking of anything 'spiritual' or 'moral', but of something far more fundamental in the dawn of human consciousness. Heidegger here, as elsewhere in his writings, suggests a significant connection between *aletheia* (truth) and *lanthano* (I am concealed, or escape notice, doing or being something) and *lethe* forgetfulness or oblivion. He then engagingly quotes Homer, *The Odyssey* VIII 83 ff. (It is always a relief to get away into Homer.) Odysseus, after his meeting with Nausicaa, now incognito in her father's palace, hears the minstrel singing about the Trojan War, from which Odysseus is now making his laborious way home. Verse 93. 'Then unnoticed by all the others he shed tears.' Literally, he escaped notice shedding tears. Heidegger points out that *elanthané* does not mean the transitive 'he concealed', but means 'he remained concealed' shedding tears. 'Odysseus has pulled his cloak over his head because he is ashamed to let the Phaeacians see his tears.' Heidegger comments 'Odysseus shied away – as one shedding tears before the Phaeacians.' But doesn't this quite clearly mean the same as: he hid himself before the Phaeacians out of a sense of shame? Or must we also think 'shying away', *aidos*, from remaining concealed, granted that we are striving to get closer to its essence as the Greeks experienced it? Then 'to shy away' would mean to withdraw and remain concealed in reluctance or restraint 'keeping to oneself'. Of course this is an example of the persuasive movement of Heidegger's laborious argument when he wishes to read one of his concepts (in this case *aletheia*, 'thought as' unconcealment) into the minds of the early Greeks!

Benet paused, well what *does* it all mean, he thought, and why on earth do I go on with it? Am I not losing my German? Could one forgive Heidegger or be interested in him just because he loved the Greeks? Benet loved the Greeks. But did he understand them, was he a Greek scholar? No, he was just a curious romantic pseudo-historian. He would rather spend his time reading Hölderlin than Heidegger. Really he loved pictures not thoughts. He pictured Odysseus weeping behind his cloak in the hall of the Phaeacians. Benet did not often weep. Perhaps he would weep now, now that *everything* had changed. He thrust the sheets of paper away. He thought, when I am dead what does it matter. He got up and began walking about restlessly. Some tears came, he quickly mopped them away with his handkerchief. He rarely wept – and now it was for Odysseus! These were mad thoughts. The house was quiet, or was it? Those strange sounds were there again: a crackling sound as of something on fire, an almost inaudible little wailing sound as by a small creature in pain, then a sharper brief sound not unlike a knock. Of course it was all nonsense, these were familiar noises, he heard them all the time, the natural murmurs of an ageing house, its little secret wounds, wood rotting, tiles slipping – he went round and locked the doors and bolted and chained them. He went back through the drawing room and out onto the terrace. His ferocious concentration upon Heidegger had for a brief time distracted him. Now he saw the light misted by small clouds, like an evening light, glowing. It must be later than he thought. He came back across the terrace being careful not to step upon the many creeping plants which spread among the paving stones. He went back into the drawing room which now seemed a little dim. He meandered to the mantelpiece and played with the netsuke. He thought, I can do no good. I am blundering about among the miseries of a chaotic scene which I myself have brought about. He went into the kitchen and ate cheese and biscuits and then ginger cake. He ate an apple which he found lying around. He was tearless now, just utterly miserable and helpless. He decided to go to bed and to sleep. However, suddenly he found himself prowling around the house and reflecting upon a quite different matter which now increasingly distressed him. It was Jackson.

THREE

The Past

The legend was that Benet had discovered Jackson curled up in a cardboard box late one night and had adopted him as a weird animal which he imagined he could tame! There were various versions of this nonsense. Benet himself was not at all sure, when later he reeled back his memory, how exactly it had *begun.* Had he really seen strange eyes looking at him in the dark? That area near to the river had been, ever since Benet could remember, some sort of gathering place of various people. Benet randomly, sometimes against the advice of the police, gave money here to people whom he pitied but felt he 'could do nothing for'. The idea 'it is fate', was taken up later by Mildred. Had Benet, much earlier, unconsciously, seen those eyes? *Can* it be that one particular person, sent by the gods, is singled out for another particular person?

Benet had quite recently given up his job and was feeling free and happy. He was more often at Penn, where the house, and now (though not urgently) Uncle Tim, was needing his attentions. He was also being urged by London friends to move from his narrow noisy little abode to some larger and quieter house elsewhere. It was winter, January. After spending the evening with some friends, including Owen, he had become unusually drunk and arriving back by taxi had found some difficulty first in finding his key, and then inserting it in

71

the lock. After some futile struggles with the slippery key he became aware that he was not alone, a man was standing behind him on the pavement. He turned round, annoyed, then alarmed, by the silent unknown figure; then turning his back he returned quickly to his unsuccessful attempt to insert the key. Then a voice behind him said, 'May I help you?' Benet had not heard or dreamt of hearing this voice. The voice was hard to place. All Benet instantly took in was a cool calm voice. A moment later, standing motionless holding the key, he somehow in the dim light of the nearby lamp-post seemed to recognise the man. Without a word he handed over the key. The man neatly inserted it in the lock, opened the door, and, preceding Benet, entered the house and turned on a light. Benet followed him into the hall. At that moment, surprisingly as he thought afterwards, Benet felt no fear. He reached out his hand and the man returned the key. Benet instinctively produced his wallet. Then, and this was a strange moment, the stranger reached out his hand and for an instant rested it upon Benet's hand. Benet, now sobered, took in a great deal. He understood that the fellow was not attempting to steal his wallet, but simply indicating that he did not want any money. Benet said, 'Thank you for helping me.' He moved to the door, which was partly closed, and opened it wide. He wondered if the fellow would say something. But he simply looked at Benet and went out. Benet closed the door and leaned against it.

A great tidal wave of emotion overwhelmed him. He turned and attempted, but failed, to open the door again. In the next instant he decided against this. He was suddenly terribly upset. He should have acted differently, but how? Should he have asked him to stay? Or offered him a drink? Was he waiting for Benet to come back, did he know someone who knew Benet? Anyway he would resent Benet's prompt farewell. It was now impossible for Benet to run after him – how did he even imagine such a thing! He would have to wait until tomorrow. But what for? It was just as well Benet was soon leaving this house and this neighbourhood. He eventually went to bed and slept well.

He woke in the morning with a hangover. He got up. Then he remembered the extraordinary little scene on the previous day. He felt distressed but more clear-headed. Now only a short time remained before he left for a new and larger house, in a safer neighbourhood. Also, during this interlude, he went to Paris to view an exhibition, and stayed for a while. He returned, not having entirely forgotten the matter, but by now feeling free and jaunty. He went out that evening to the opera with Mildred and Elizabeth and a musician friend of Elizabeth's called Andy Redmond. He returned by taxi. It then occurred to him, as it was a warm spring night, to exalt himself further by walking down to the river. As he walked he thought vaguely about 'the poor chap' and wondered if he would be there. A last farewell. A monkey in a box. That was how he had thought of him at the start. One or two others were there but not him. The river was there. He turned back and sauntered slowly up the street. Then he realised that he was not alone, a tall figure was behind him. Benet turned round. He said, 'What is it?'

A soft voice said, 'Perhaps I can help you.'

Benet said, 'Sorry you can't,' and walked on.

A soft voice behind him said, 'I can do many things.'

Benet entered the house and closed the door noisily.

He went slowly up to bed but for a long time he could not sleep. He felt he had been behaving badly. Could he not have been polite? Was he not really *afraid* of the fellow? It was also possible, and this occurred to Benet later in the episode, that the fellow was gay and thought that Benet was! He decided that this was unlikely, and that perhaps the man simply wanted a job. Altogether Benet decided not to think about the little drama in which he himself was playing a rather silly and shabby part. In any case he was now moving to another part of London and could leave the whole weird scene behind him.

In the days that followed Benet was engaged in the chaotic but satisfying task of packing up all his belongings, deciding where the furniture was to go, making sure that nothing was left or lost, and supervising his arrival in a larger and altogether more delightful house with quite a large garden not far from Holland Park. After he had arranged the furniture, inspected the rooms, admired the large garden with its little summer-house, and put all crockery and cutlery in their rightful places in the kitchen, he left, locking everything up carefully, returned to Penndean where he stayed for some time, returning to his books and his work, and entertaining Uncle Tim who was longing to see the new house. Benet was so pleased with his house, he actually delayed his return, gloating and dreaming over it, until Tim kept pretending that by now the house must be gone, at any rate all the furniture must be gone! At last, when Benet had actually allowed himself to reflect upon the possibility that the furniture might *really* be gone, he drove to London with Tim, and with a fast-beating heart, he opened the door. He could breathe, all was well, the house was beautiful, silent, everything was in place where Benet had left it. Uncle Tim followed him. They wandered together all over the interior, and over the garden, admiring the summer-house and discussing the possibility of a fishpond. The sun was shining, it was April. They returned to the house and examined the kitchen and discussed the oven, the fridge, the little scullery with the washing-machine. They laughed and danced about like boys, they had brought a picnic lunch with them. Then the front door bell rang. Tim went out into the hall and opened the door. Benet was struggling, opening a wine bottle. He heard a murmur from the hall. At last the cork emerged from the bottle. Benet came out into the hall to see whom Tim was talking to. Over Tim's shoulder he saw *the man*.

Tim turned round. He said, 'This chap wants to know if he can help you with various things, he says he's talked to you before. Actually we *have* a problem – '

Benet strode forward, Tim moved aside. The man stood in the doorway. The sun was behind him. Although it was a bright day, he was wearing a blue mackintosh with the collar turned up. It was the first time Benet had seen his face by daylight. The sudden glimpse was of a man with dark sleek straight hair and a slightly dark complexion. Benet said hastily, 'No, we've got other arrangements. Please don't come again.' He shut the door.

Uncle Tim said, 'Really, why did you shout at the poor fellow – '

'I didn't shout.'

'You shouldn't have been so rough. I rather liked the look of him, why – '

'I don't want him. I've met him before.'

74

'We could do with some help – '

'Tim, please don't *bother* me, I just don't *need him*, that's all.'

'You said you'd like someone to look after the house when – '

'Oh do shut up, Tim, the man's been bothering me, now let's have some lunch!'

Tim said no more, but Benet could see that he was upset by Benet's curt behaviour. Perhaps in that brief exchange at the door Tim had *seen something*? But what? Some old Indian intuition? They had lunch, the wine cheered them up, and they spoke of other things. But Benet was deeply distressed. He wished that Tim had not seen the fellow.

Tim and Benet spent the night in the house; the house was number twenty-eight, and was called Tara. Tim liked the name which reminded him of Ireland. Benet was at first not sure that he liked it, but in any case the house held firmly onto its name and was so called by all. Tim went back to Penndean, and Benet stayed another night alone to be sure he could. Of course he could, the house was cosy, friendly, benign, altogether the right size and shape. He felt that he could work in the house. He returned to Penn and to his book on Heidegger. When next he came to London he brought writing materials, notebooks, his second fountain pen. He felt a sense of liberation and new life. He felt he was rediscovering London.

Only later as the autumn came and the days grew shorter and colder did he think once again about 'that man'. How had he found Benet's new house? Where was he now? Uncle Tim, who appeared to have imbibed quite a lot of the visitor during the brief visit, occasionally enquired about him. Uncle Tim was getting old. One night in London, Benet had a dream, indeed a nightmare, about a snake curled up in a basket floating in a river. The basket was sinking. Benet thought, of course snakes can swim, he won't drown. Then he thought but perhaps he *will* drown, the basket will pull him down, he won't be able to get out. Swiftly hustled by the stream, the basket was disappearing among the muddy reeds near to a bridge, it was becoming dark, Benet peered down into the water, he thought I *must* get down into the river to make sure that the snake is all right, only I *can't* get down, it's so *dark* down there, and I shall have to *jump*! As he was hesitating he woke up. His first movement was to turn on the light beside the bed. Then he thrust away the bed-clothes and sat up gasping. He thought *light*, yes I must have *light*. His watch said three o'clock. He rose and put the centre light on, and began to walk to and fro breathing deeply. Then he put on his dressing gown and sat down in a chair. Supposing all the lights in the house were suddenly to go out! He got up and went onto the landing, turning the light on. He stood and looked down the stairs, gradually controlling his breath. He listened for some time. The house was silent. He put out the landing light, returned to the bedroom putting out the centre bedroom light, and finally, as he got into bed, the bedside light. He lay stiffly, at last dozing, then sleeping.

When he woke in the morning he remembered first the light, then the dream. He put on the bedside light, then got out of bed, checking the centre light in the bedroom, then the light on the landing. Why was he doing this? He returned to the bedroom and pulled back the curtains, blinking at the bright sunshine. Shaking his head he got dressed and set about his usual day. He had taken over a room, adjoining the drawing room, wherein he now continued his work. His work was, just now, very pleasant, since he was giving himself a rest by continuing a study, abandoned some time ago, of Hölderlin, essential, he now told himself, for an understanding of Heidegger's soul! However even here his concentration failed. He soon got up and walked about. There seemed to be a positive silence in the house, even though he could hear sounds from outside. He wandered out into the garden and went into the summer-house. The summer-house was empty but not tiny. Someone could live in it. It consisted of quite a large room, a small room, a bathroom, a little kitchen bereft of utensils. Benet proceeded down the garden looking vaguely for a place for the pool which Uncle Tim could have fishes in. He had a small lunch, he was not hungry. He considered returning to Penn in the afternoon but decided not to. He read *The Times*. Was he *waiting* for something? He wondered if he would have dinner at a nearby restaurant, but decided not to. However he felt an agonising desire to leave the house. He waited. It was perceptibly evening; he wandered out. He found himself sitting in a tube train, and getting out at a familiar station. Had he just come to look at his old abode? He went along the street, passing his old place, then returning through the station and crossing the road to look at the Thames. He looked about but saw nothing but the evening crowds. He cursed himself. He had dinner at a familiar restaurant where the waiters received him as a friend. He came home by taxi.

As he opened the door he reached his hand sideways to put on the light in the hall. There was a click but no light. Annoyed, he left the door open and strode across the hall to find the switch on the other side at the foot of the stairs. Again there was no light. He stood there in the dark. He moved cautiously toward the dining room. He found himself groping about. He retreated toward the door, which was only partly open, and opened it wider bringing in light from the road. He walked quietly to the stairs and mounted. He felt for a switch. There was light but only from the floor above. Benet stood still. He could now feel and hear his heart. Leaving the light as it was he went cautiously down, crossed the hall and closed the door, fumbling cautiously for locks. Then moving slowly, holding out his arms, as he recalled it later, 'like a ghost', he mounted the stairs towards the light, which he felt might vanish before he reached it. When he reached the second floor he encountered more switches, and successfully turned on other lights. He stood there breathing deeply. He looked back at the dark below. He decided to get himself to bed as soon as possible. He turned on the centre light in his bedroom, he turned off all the landing lights. He went into his bedroom and closed the door. He undressed hurriedly and put on his pyjamas and turned out the centre light. Damn! Where was the bed? He put the centre light on, put on the bedside lamp, returned to put out the centre light. The bedside lamp remained. Good. He struggled into bed and lay down, then sat up abruptly to put out the lamp, knocking it over in the process. Hell! He lay back. He thought he would never sleep, but he did sleep. Was it all an accidental freak?

On the next morning, Benet awoke early to a beautiful blue sky. His head upon the pillow, he smiled. He sat up, noticed the lamp was on the floor, got up and rescued it, still intact. Then suddenly he remembered what had happened last night. He stood quiet for a while. Then he dressed and went downstairs, trying all the lights. They were just as before, intact upstairs, dead downstairs. It occurred to him to try the cellar. The cellar lights were dead too. He stood in the hall. He went into the kitchen, which he had not entered last night. To his surprise the kitchen was intact. He made some coffee. He had intended to go back to Penndean. He wandered out into the hall. He must do something, he must find some expert, he couldn't leave the poor house in this crazy state. He sat down to think, but soon started reading *The Times*.

He heard something, a fumbling at the front door, then a soft knock and knuckles on wood. He went to the door and opened it. The man was there. Benet said, 'Do you know anything about electricity?'

'Yes.'

'Come in.'

That was how it began.

The newcomer, having gone out to fetch the requirements (he evidently knew the neighbourhood) dealt with the mysterious unruly lights while Benet sat fuming in the drawing room.

'All done. Would you like to see?'

'No, thank you. What do I owe you?'

The man drew a piece of paper, already prepared, from his pocket, and handed it over, while Benet opened his wallet and presented the suitable notes.

'Thank you. Perhaps I can assist you on other occasions?'

Benet, now opening the front door, did not reply to the question. He murmured 'Goodbye', his useful visitor passed through, Benet closed the door promptly behind him.

After the visitation Benet wandered, hurried, stumbling about the house talking to himself – he had made a gross senseless blunder, such as *anyone* could see, by letting a complete stranger, possibly a talented burglar, go about all over his house *alone* – he ought to have followed him, instead of which he had shut himself up so as *not* to see what the fellow was doing! He might be anything, a clever solitary, or a member of a gang, or – good heavens – some sort of mad person – Benet had not even checked the work he had done, if he *had* done work – and what was easier than to pretend to be a penniless beggar! It took some time for Benet to calm down. He checked the lights, he inspected the cellar, he *looked* about the house, seeing (but could he be sure?) nothing taken. Then he began to think. Uncle Tim had been alone with the chap – but what had passed between them, had he bewitched Uncle Tim? Should Benet *ask* Uncle Tim? Surely not. Should he go and live in another house? So he was *afraid* of the return of this visitor? Would he have to stay here at Tara indefinitely? At last he carefully locked up the house, the summer-house, the garage and fled back to the country.

Back at Penndean he did not mention the episode to Uncle Tim, but he found himself perpetually meditating upon it. He began to make a memory picture of the man but found it difficult. He was wearing a white shirt – or was it white? Was it open at the neck? Dark hair, certainly no tie. He was, now, 'decently dressed'. He was slightly taller than Benet, rather slim and upright, like a *soldier*, as he had imagined on his first sighting. On the occasion of the key he had refused money, he had, to make this clear, actually reached out his hand, laying it on Benet's hand – his fingers touching the back of Benet's hand. He had *touched* Benet. Well, what did that mean – a gesture of love? Impossible! He had been closer then than now. Well, Benet's emotion – was there emotion – had soon passed! Yet perhaps the emotion had built up later on: the dream, the return to the river. And why had Benet *not* now taken the so recent opportunity of talking to the fellow, who he was, what was his name, was he married, was he an out-of-work actor or something, almost anything could have made some sort of connection! *Had* he been in the army? He stood up as at attention. What about his voice – a northern accent? No. A foreign accent? He seemed to have some air of authority – well, *authority,* had it come as far as imagining *that*! Perhaps he played this game with innumerable people, pursuing them, forcing himself upon them as a handyman, a jack-of-all-trades, so becoming essential – the out-of-work actor story might be

79

the most attractive, easy to palm off upon well-endowed recently married young couples! Yet, ultimately, *was* he a thief, a professional burglar, working for some sinister syndicate?

Down at Penn, time passed, Uncle Tim was ill and got better, Benet read Hölderlin and wrote a little poetry, or 'poetry', himself. He walked about the garden and discussed with Clun and the girls the best site for the Grecian building with columns and swimming pool. However, as everything was looking so beautiful now, he was secretly anxious to postpone this ambitious novelty, whose erection would involve so much violent work with digging and bull-dozers! At least anyone who had studied Benet at that period could have taken him to be reasonably serene. In fact, at this time Benet, still enjoying not being a Civil Servant any more, was considering various trips, to France, to Spain, to Italy, to Greece. In fact his journey, curtailed by the activities of Edward and Marian, went only as far as Italy. And there he had a curious, not exactly 'vision', but 'interlude'.

He was in Venice, where he had quite often been, walking along in the morning sunshine. He had been several times to the Accademia, and was now walking along the Zattere. The light upon the waters, white, gold, pale blue, glinted in his eyes, he was tired and wanted to sit down, on a seat, in a church, but there seemed to be nowhere just now to rest. He had foolishly brought no hat with him. The sun was shining, it was becoming very hot, for this time of year ridiculously hot. Benet began to wonder where he was. Then he was aware of someone walking behind him. He checked his pace to let the other pass. However the other did not pass, altering his or her pace to Benet's. Benet went slower still, and was about to stop. He then became aware of someone, a man, not passing him but walking beside him on his left. The stranger then turned his head towards Benet, seeming to smile at him. Benet glanced annoyed, then anxiously, the brilliant waters still flashing into his eyes. The walker, about as tall as Benet, seemed to be in black, a black figure, perhaps, it occurred to Benet, a monk. But no, it could not be a monk. All this Benet took in in a second. He was troubled by the stranger's silence, and wished he could find somewhere to shake him off, but there seemed, just at present, to be no kind of refuge, and nobody else about. They walked on. At last Benet, still walking, turned round abruptly to survey his curious partner. He instantly felt something pass through him, as of an electric shock. His companion was a man, dressed in dark ordinary clothes. He was turning to Benet, in fact not exactly smiling, but, as he walked, surveying Benet with what seemed a gaze of tender affection. Had Benet met him before? Benet could not in fact see him very clearly because of the exceptional light which was rising up out of the water. He perceived that the stranger had a flash of white at his neck, perhaps a shirt or frill, and that he was carrying a glove.

Still walking and turning his head Benet then saw a young man with dark thick straight hair which fell almost to his shoulders and was cut across his brow by a fringe, while large dark beautiful eyes gently engaged with Benet and lips poised as if to speak. At that moment Benet felt that he was going to faint. He struggled as if against a power to which he must soon succumb. He turned his head away. He saw that he was passing a church on his right hand, and turned abruptly away from his companion, strode quickly, almost falling, into the church.

Once inside he walked several steps and then sat down. The church was empty. He closed his eyes and bowed his head, holding his brow. Some time passed. It was cooler inside the church. Opening his eyes Benet, breathing deeply, settling himself back, gazed about inside the empty church. He

81

wondered if he had actually fainted. He attempted to construct what had happened – did such weird things occur? Of course they did. But this one, was it really anything at all? Was it possible that he had had a visitation or a sort of vision? He was slowly going into a swoon, it was just as well that he had not fallen over. The church was real. He coughed twice, persuading himself of his returning reality. However there was, he began to realise, *even more* to his strange swoon than he had at first realised. Yes, there had been his mirage of another person, walking by his side, a young man with dark fringed hair and beautiful eyes carrying a glove. It was already fading, and he struggled to retain it. But there had been more which he had not, when he had rushed into the church, remembered, there were even many things, besides the walking stranger. Or had he *brought* these things with him? Could he not now sober up and *remember*? Or was it just the *pictures*? Though why *just* the pictures – were they not real people? Yet also somehow present. If he could only make out how it was all present to him, things which he himself had in some sense, and out of the past, *made real*. Though not as real, he thought, as the beautiful young man. Perhaps the young man had been their shepherd. But as they seemed to formulate he shuddered also. He felt like Tobias walking with the Angel. Was this an image of his walking with *him*, the youth, who must not fade? Then as he closed his eyes other things *grew* about him, and he *saw* them, Pharaoh's daughter lifting Moses out of the reeds, Saint Margaret surrounded by terrible serpents, running barefoot holding up her crucifix. And then weeping people carrying a corpse, the terrible heaviness of the dead Christ. Benet stood up, took some steps, then sat again. Were these strange and dreadful images brought somehow to him by that youth, who, leaving him, had passed on? Or was the *whole thing* a complete farrago of sick nonsensical illusions brought upon him by the heat and the flashing movements of the water? Of course the lovely youth was a phantasm, simply the sudden preface of a sickening mental disturbance. Yet why had just *these* things come? Benet got up again. He must get back to his hotel as quickly as possible, fortunately it was not far off.

In fact Benet recovered fairly soon from his curious 'attack', which he attributed to the sun, the water, and walking without a hat. Yet, with his rationality, certain reflections remained, and he spoke of the matter with no one. He was not sure that he remembered all the pieces of the 'picture-show', or whether they had come to him later, and that during his rapid recovery he was binding them up. He thought about Moses and Saint Margaret and snakes, Tobias and the Angel he had perhaps invented later. Other things, weeping people, the Virgin dropping her head in horror at the Annunciation – well, were not these things everywhere? At any rate he hastily left Venice for Paris where he stayed only to see a particular exhibition. Back in England he went straight to Uncle Tim. He found Tim in bed and a doctor in the house. The doctor (a new young fellow called George Park) alarmed Benet, then tried to reassure him. Actually Tim himself recovered remarkably when Benet appeared and Benet blamed himself for having so frivolously stayed away for so long. He stayed then for some time at Penndean, though Tim constantly encouraged him to go to Tara. It was high summer, and the gardens at Penn were so beautiful, and for that too Benet lingered. He could work of course because he had left, before departing, all his Heidegger work at Penn, and anyway Mildred and Elizabeth were keeping an eye on Tara. At last he began to feel a yearning for London and for the British Library and the Parthenon frieze where Mildred once had a vision. Taking some of his work with him he drove to London and to Tara. Dear Tara, how had he left it for so long! Silence. Well, what did he expect? He prowled about the house. He checked the lights which were all sound. Of course Mildred must have been in, he must ring her up. His study was quiet, neat, as he had left it. He set out on the desk the books which he had brought with him. Here now he could work. He slept well that night and on the succeeding night. He thought, *of course* Tim must come here! Why have I kept him away? On the third day, in the afternoon Benet began to feel uneasy. He was remembering something which he could not quite recollect, he was having *dark thoughts*, he was *returning* to dark thoughts. He thought, as a man I have no substance, I wish I had been in the war! He thought darkly about his childhood. He also started to recall that curious *stroke* in Venice, which was now becoming so shadowy. He felt sudden anxiety about Tim. He must bring Tim to Tara, or else go back to Penn. He must go tomorrow. He felt suddenly confused, as if his heart were running too fast.

The front door bell rang. Benet thought first – Tim is here! Then in a second he knew. He went to the door. The man was standing outside. Benet said nothing. The man said, 'So sorry to bother you, I just wondered –'

Benet said, 'Come inside.' This sounded a more peremptory invitation than 'come in.'

The man evidently thought so too, since for a moment he looked surprised, even alarmed.

He stepped into the hall. Benet banged the door. They stared at each other. Benet said, 'What do you want?'

The man hesitated, then said cautiously 'I'd like to be helpful, if you'd need any help, I can do many kinds of things – '

Benet said, 'Go in here,' pointing to the drawing room. The man reflected, then walked into the drawing room in front of Benet, over to the fireplace where he turned round abruptly, gazing at Benet not with hostility, but with caution.

Benet sat down upon the sofa which was facing the fireplace. He pointed to a nearby upright chair. The man sat down, slightly moving the chair so that he could face Benet. Benet felt a curious shock looking into the man's rather intense dark eyes. His dark sleek hair fell over his forehead. He seemed to be young – but probably older than he seemed.

There was a moment of silence. Then Benet said, 'What is your name?'

The man answered promptly. 'Jackson.'

'What is your other name, your first name?'

'I have no other name.'

'Where do you come from?'

After a brief hesitation the man replied, 'The south.'

'Where do you live now?'

'Oh – in many places – '

Benet at this point felt a shudder as if he were about to fall into some weird connection, even a relationship! Why on earth had he asked him in, why had he asked his name? Simply to study his presence? Benet stared at the man. He felt for a moment as if he were suddenly tongue-tied, able only to *stammer* – as if it were *he* who was being interviewed. He stood up. The other stood up too. Benet thought, why should he not 'fix things', why do I have this *deadly suspicion*?

Benet said, 'Please listen to this. I do not want you here, I do not require you here, I have made other arrangements.' He turned and walked back into the hall and opened the door. The man followed and went through the door. He began to speak but Benet closed the door.

Benet went back into the drawing room and sat down. He was very annoyed and upset and puzzled and dissatisfied with himself. He was also frightened.

However, time passed, nothing happened, Benet went to Penn, came back to Tara, and went back to Penn again. He went to the British Library. He visited the British Museum and the National Gallery and the sundry (at present not up to much) exhibitions. He considered going to Berlin, which he had been wanting to do, but put it off. He invited friends to dinner, Mildred, Elizabeth, Robert Bland (a wandering cousin of Elizabeth's), Anna, the Moxons, Andy Redmond (the musician). He returned more frequently to Penn. Uncle Tim was unwell, or he had (as he put it) been unwell. He referred to George Park as 'the puppy'. He was very anxious to visit Tara, and did so once with Benet, bringing on a heatwave and rapidly returning to the country. He was silent, then once more anxious to go to London. Benet consulted 'the puppy' and was told that a brief visit might be viable, only no rushing about. Tim was touchingly delighted, and Benet drove him cautiously to Tara. There for a short while Tim spent his time joyfully exploring the house and garden and commenting on all the new things Benet had put in. The weather was good, and soon of course Tim wished to go farther afield. He told Benet suddenly one morning, that he wanted to go to Kew. '*Kew*!' said Benet, who had completely forgotten the place. Tim went on to say he had never been there since he was a child and he wanted to see if it had changed, was the Pagoda still there? Benet said of course it was, anyway we would be told if it wasn't! Besides he said the weather was too hot, and there was nowhere to park the car. Tim said there *must* be, and everything there was so beautiful, and he wanted to see the greenhouse and the ducks and the geese and the swans – he had enjoyed it all so much long ago – Benet said, *all right*, they would go to Kew! Not today; but tomorrow morning, and he cursed himself for not at once agreeing to what the 'old fellow' desired. Tim was delighted. Benet already wondered if Kew must not mean 'rushing about'. He said now he must go out shopping for lunch and Tim must sit quietly indoors, he wouldn't be long. As he went to the door he felt a wrench in his chest and stopped, pressing his hands to his heart, as he increasingly knew that sooner or later Uncle Tim must die. Oh so much love, so very much love – He opened the door and hurried out. His shopping took some time. When he returned Tim was actually standing at the open door.

'Oh good, you're back! I'm so glad!'

'What's the matter?' said Benet. Tim seemed unusually excited.

'He's back again!'

'Who's back again?' said Benet. But of course he knew.

'That man, I'm afraid he's gone now. Your friend Jackson.'

'Oh, so he told you his name! He's not my friend, but never mind. I hope you sent him away at once. Sorry I'm late.'

'Of course I didn't send him away – I invited him in – he told me all kinds of things he'd done, all sorts – he's a jewel, a real artist – '

'Tim dear, let me repeat he is *not* my friend and there is *nothing* for him to do here – '

'Yes, but there's plenty for him to do at Penn! I've arranged for him to come down!'

It was true. Uncle Tim had been enchanted, *taken over*, by Jackson, and had arranged for him to be driven down to Penn by Benet on the following day!

Benet said at once, 'It's impossible.'

'Why? Damn, I haven't got his address. Anyway we can go – '

'Tomorrow you are going to Kew.'

'Oh, yes – well – we can go another time, next time – I can't get hold of him anyway, and I can't put him off – '

'I don't see why!'

'But, Ben, what's wrong, you've employed him here, he said you were satisfied with his work and of course he wasn't lying – '

'No,' said Benet. 'He was not lying, but – '

'But what? Do you know something bad about him?'

'No,' said Benet, 'I know nothing bad. It's just that – ' How could he explain to Uncle Tim, how could he explain to anyone, even himself! Was he *afraid*? He could see the crestfallen look of distress upon his uncle's face. How could he hurt the dear being whom he loved most of all? 'It's just that we already have Clun and we can borrow from Edward or – '

'But this man is an expert – he needn't stay ages and ages, only a few days perhaps a week if – '

'A *week*? I thought it was a day! Where is he to sleep, in the pub?'

'But, there's piles of room, all the spare bedrooms in the – '

'Oh so he's to be "in the house"! Suppose he rapes Sylvia?'

'Ben, don't make silly jokes! You'll see – '

'Oh never mind, all right, all right, yes, we'll take him with us tomorrow!'

And so it was, and Uncle Tim made a pact with Jackson. Indeed everyone (except Benet) liked and trusted Jackson. He built up part of a brick wall, painted one of the bedrooms, helped Clun to cut down a dead tree, cleaned out the stables, and mended the second-hand mower. He ran errands to the village where, at once, somehow, he made friends with everyone. He was, the landlord of the Sea Kings declared, a 'card'. He was petted by the girls. After four days, tactfully, he returned to London. Tim refused to tell Benet what he paid him. It was at a later date that Benet found himself agreeing that if he were away from Tara for a long time Jackson might

87

look in to see that all was well! Tim even suggested to Benet that Jackson might actually live in the summer-house! Jackson continued, at occasional intervals, to turn up at Penn, especially when Benet was not there. What then was suddenly the most important thing of all was Uncle Tim's health. He had for a while seemed to be remarkably well, not now of course travelling, but receiving visitors. The girls went away with their mother, but other visitors came, permitted by 'George the pup'; the Rector, Oliver Caxton, the landlord of the Sea Kings (his name was Victor Larne), village friends, London friends – but then suddenly he retired to his bed. Now no one came, except the doctor, Sylvia, Benet, and, now staying indefinitely in the house, Jackson. Jackson was now indispensable, an excellent nurse, much respected by the doctor who at last explained instructions to Jackson not Benet. What hurt Benet most in those final days was that sometimes Tim called for Jackson, not Benet. It was not, it seemed, that he was mistaking one for the other. He simply wanted Jackson as well as Benet. He would say to Benet, 'Where's Jackson?' and if Benet said 'Gone to the village,' Tim would be content. What Benet said was of course in all situations perfectly true; at certain times Jackson came as usual to look after Tim, and Benet would withdraw. As time passed Benet watched for signs of Tim preferring Jackson's company but there were none. There was however no doubt that Tim desired Jackson's presence in the house, and once or twice asked anxiously, 'He hasn't gone back to London, has he?' Benet had of course for some time been aware of something, on his part, very like jealousy. Tim had already tentatively mentioned the Tara summer-house, how charming it was, and couldn't Jackson live there? After all they had no idea where Jackson lived in London, and was he not some sort of vagabond, poor thing? Benet gave vague replies. As time went by and Tim was bedridden Benet began to imagine Tim imagining Jackson established in the summer-house! However, as it became more and more clear that Tim was dying, Benet's grief itself obscured what now seemed petty irritations. One thing only added to his torment, he wanted to be alone with Tim when

Tim died – he could not bear to think that Tim might die holding Jackson's hand.

At last it came; it was about three in the morning. Benet, as he was now accustomed to do, was lying upon a mattress on the floor beside the bed. He was lying sleepless listening to Tim's murmurings which sounded so like the sleepy twitterings of a bird. Then there was a little cry, a moan of distress. Benet got up and sat on the side of the big bed. He thought, somehow he knew, that Tim was going. He was lying as usual on his back against a pile of pillows. Only lately he had begun to mumble. Now he struggled, looking at Benet with a beseeching gaze, his lips parted, his eyes wide, frightened. He made a choking sound in his throat, then a sound like 'oh'. Benet leaning forward kissed his brow, then caught hold of one of his frail searching hands and lifted it up and kissed it. He said, 'Dear, dear Tim, I love you so much.' He made efforts to control himself. He said, 'Darling, don't be frightened, I love you more than anything in the world, I love you – rest quietly, dear dear one.' He tried to check his tears. Tim was looking at him with wide open eyes now expressing terror. Benet took his other thin hand upon which a little flesh remained. He said, 'Dear heart, don't be frightened, I love you, rest quietly, dear dear one.' Tim's hair, become very recently so scanty and so perfectly white, was scattered behind him on the pillow like a halo. Benet felt the desperate rhythmic flutter of his hands. Then looking away from Benet with a distressed searching gaze he uttered sounds which Benet could not make out – then suddenly striving helplessly to sit up he cried, 'I see, I see!' These were his last words uttered with his last breath. When Benet leaned over him to attempt to hold him, he was suddenly sure that he was gone. Tim lay there before him with wide open eyes – but the soul was gone, all was gone, Tim was gone. Benet now released his sobs. He turned away from the bed, blind with tears, and opened the door. Jackson was outside on the landing. In an instant of mutual grief they embraced each other, then stood apart wailing with sorrow. In that moment after, Benet found himself already fabricating the notion that in all that precious and terrible time when Benet was with Tim dying, Jackson had cautiously opened the door.

Very many people, many of whom Benet did not recognise, came to Uncle Tim's funeral, many wept. Oliver Caxton performed the service. Uncle Tim's ashes, for he had desired cremation, were scattered in the churchyard. Benet, speaking briefly, wept. People who knew him and people who did not came up to him. George Park in tears clasped his hand. There was to be no subsequent gathering, Benet had expressed his wish to be alone. Mildred, Owen, Anna, all his London friends tactfully disappeared. Edward withdrew. Marian and Rosalind were both with their mother in Canada. He would have to write to them, and indeed to many others who did not yet know. *Oh God*, he sat for a long time with his head in his hands. He got up and walked about, then sat down again. Hating the sunlight, he got up to pull the curtains of the drawing room. As he turned back he thought he saw a figure moving in from the hall. He stood staring. *He had completely forgotten Jackson.* He uttered a low sound of irritation. Jackson came forward a little nearer to him. He was wearing his dark clothes, his face, his head looked dark, he said something in a low voice. Benet said, 'What?' Then he said, 'Of course I will give you your money. I will give it to you now.' He just wanted Jackson to *go*, to *go away forever*.

Jackson moved forward into the dim room, 'Can't I stay?'

Benet now moved back. Jackson, taller, dark, seemed, perhaps Benet had set this up later, like a huge dark slash, a dark thing, something in a dark picture, a monk with a cowl.

Benet said, 'No. Will you go away, please. I will – later – will you just *go – somewhere –* '

The apparition faded away. Benet, after standing motionless for some time, emerged from the drawing room and ran quickly up the stairs into his bedroom, closing the door. He lay down on his bed. So Jackson, who had belonged to Tim, was now to be the property of Benet? Well, did he not *owe* this to Tim?

So it was that Jackson was at last allowed to inhabit the summer-house, later on called the Lodge, acting as guardian, cooking and shopping, looking after the house, and being *always there*.

FOUR

Marian and Rosalind Berran had lost their father when they were young. Their Canadian mother, left with a considerable amount of money, had despatched them to a boarding school in England. Later, after their mother had 'taken on', though not married, a 'new husband' in Canada, the girls, now nearly 'grown up', had spent most of their summer holidays in England, acquiring a flat in London and renting a cottage at Lipcot, just outside the village. Occasionally Ada, alone, joined them there. The connection with Lipcot came through the, now so vaguely remembered, father, an architectural engineer who had somehow met with Uncle Tim in Delhi, and had somehow or other died in an accident when designing a bridge over a river. Tim had only briefly met the engineer, but he had soon made contact with 'the girls' then at school and later with Ada. So there followed visits at Penndean when Tim was there, later when he was not, and later still when he had retired.

Rosalind was certainly considered the more scholarly one of the two, destined she hoped for a career in art. Always busy with exams, she had stayed on in her London flat (now each girl had a flat) and her ambition was to study art history and if possible also be a painter. Meanwhile Ada appeared at regular intervals, providing money and instructing them to get work and acquire rich husbands. Rosalind was happy as a 'swot'. Marian was the wandering one, leaving school at eighteen and going abroad, once in France then in Italy, where she acquired (which Rosalind already had) a knowledge (less thorough than Rosalind's) of the two relevant languages. Rosalind meanwhile staying at home had also learnt German. Marian wanted to see the world, she went away on tours to parts of Europe. She tried to write a novel, but postponed this activity for later. The girls were handsome, friendly, happy, and very fond of each other, though someone (a friend of Owen's) declared that Marian had become jealous of Rosalind because Rosalind was 'really going somewhere' while frivolous Marian was not! Meanwhile, from far back, how far it was not certain, Tim, and also Benet, had decided that when the time came, one or other of those girls was going to marry Edward Lannion.

This was when the bets in the Sea Kings began. Rosalind was pretty but boyish, she was also a sort of a 'scholar', which might count for or against her. Marian was prettier (perhaps it was a matter of taste), while Rosalind was bookish, though perhaps more 'intelligent' if that were counted a 'good thing'. Bets were also laid about whether they were still virgins, when and who was the first boyfriend, or, more wildly, were they actually lesbians and in love with each other! The ultimate union of Marian and Edward was at last, by a small margin, established, though some declared that she was still wild and quite likely to run away with the 'raggle-taggle gypsies oh'. Then when at last the awful news of the vanished bride spread through the village on that morning, many women shed tears, but there was also a considerable amount of lively conjecture, and the 'raggle-taggle' faction were soon crying 'We told you so!'.

'In trying to glimpse Heidegger's path or state of mind after

Sein und Zeit and to trace his thinking about the "things themselves" it is useful here to study his romanticism, the more emotional and intuitive aspects of his mind, in especial his interest in poetry and his particular interest in Hölderlin.' Benet was in his study at Penndean, sitting at his wide-open window. Outside, scattered high up like dots, the swifts were circling in the pale morning sky. At a lower level a large hobby hawk was also circling below them. Benet looked at what he had written and sighed. What did that mean? Was not romanticism deep deep in Heidegger's soul right from the beginning, why mention it now? Had not Heidegger declared his romanticism from the start simply by taking over the Greeks? As for the Greeks, they didn't care, they were gods! And Hölderlin was a god, something quite separate, a great poet, something which transcends the anxious little pawings of philosophers. Not that he, Benet, was a philosopher, not a *real* philosopher, and would never be. Why did he not, from the start, dedicate himself to poetry? Not of course to *be* a poet, but to live with great poetry all his life and understand and love it. English poetry, French poetry, German poetry, Russian poetry, Greek poetry. His Russian was far from good, but Pushkin had aided him and lifted him up. He had tried to write poetry. Should not he try once more? His heart was heavy. He had picked up Heidegger now to distract himself from misery. *There was still no news of Marian.* It was almost as if those who loved her, and should have been grieving and weeping and searching, had now returned to their daily lives. But what could they do, was he not returning to his? Oh this terrible waiting, the phone call from the police, the body found . . . Benet felt, though everyone denied it, that it must have been his fault. Yes, he had tried so ingeniously to bring her and Edward together. How could he know, how much could he see? Oh poor Marian, oh poor Edward, they would never forgive him, Edward would never forgive him, and Marian would not – if she lived. How am I fallen, this base thought was also in Benet's mind. I had to be *King*, even when Uncle Tim was alive I was *King*. Now they will all pity me. Oh God, I am thinking about myself. He stood up, pushing the chair back. A black ball of utmost despair was in his breast. He moved into the drawing room and started walking to and fro.

Benet increasingly felt that all sorts of people were looking towards him and expecting him to act. But how? He had telephoned Ada in Canada on the day of the wedding, though putting the matter rather vaguely. He knew that Rosalind had of course telephoned then and also later. But should he not ring Ada again now, or should he wait for her to ring him? How much could he say, what did he know? He did not fancy long talks with Ada. He was in daily contact with the 'wedding guests' and other close friends, but there was simply no news. *Would* Marian suddenly turn up? Was it his duty to stay at Penn, or to return to Tara? He desired very much indeed to talk to Edward, but it appeared that Edward was 'not there'. He had telephoned of course, and several times driven as far as the door of Hatting, only to be told by his 'staff', speaking with an air of truth, that they had *no idea* where he had gone. Mildred, from London, had told him that she had rung Edward's bell, and in fact watched his house for some time, and there seemed to be no one in. Benet was also upset by a communication which he had received a little later from Anna, saying that she had actually driven down to Lipcot with Bran, she did not say when, but had alas found he was out. Oh God, where was Marian now? Where was Edward? Where was Benet's sanity? He looked at his watch. He decided that he would return to London.

Anna Dunarven was glad to be back in her London house. She had left it, with her son, some time after her husband had died. The horror of his death, so unexpected, so young, had been too

94

much. She fled to France, taking Bran with her. The rich Scottish family who had rented the house during those years and cherished it so well had been 'very nice about it', having their eye in fact upon an even grander house. Anna was well off too, though she made no fuss about it. Lewen, a distinguished scholar, had left her a moderately rich woman. Her flat in Paris, and her house in Provence, though comfy were not large. Now Anna's life was changing. Was it not, she wondered as she gazed down her summer garden, *absolutely in the balance*? She had returned with a positive aim in view. It was time for Bran, now aged twelve, to go to an English boarding school, and he had indeed been accepted by the one where Lewen had been a pupil; he was to go there in the autumn. This sally, getting him into the school, had involved Anna in several brief incognito visits earlier on. Previously Bran had attended an excellent Lycée in Paris, was an ardent and intelligent pupil, good at mathematics, passionate about history and literature, and, beyond English and French, fluent in Italian, good at Latin and now at Greek. Thus far Bran's plan was clear. But what about Anna's plan? Was she to stay on in London looking up her old friends and going to picture exhibitions? She had friends and pictures in Paris. Was she going to retain her Paris flat, her home in Provence? Or if she were to keep only one, which one should it be? Should she buy a cottage in the Cotswolds? She had seen several attractive ones on her recent tour. Or should she, following Lewen's life and work, buy a residence in Ireland – perhaps in Dublin, perhaps on the West Coast, or perhaps both? She couldn't do all these things, and surely London was now essential.

She had indeed returned to London, her London, Lewen's London, as to an expected chaos. She had come of course bringing Bran to his new home, also, as it happened, to see Edward's wedding, where she hoped to meet friends and acquaintances, perhaps even meet new people, other people, all sorts of people. Her father (a solicitor) had run away to America when she was very young, and her mother died when Anna was twenty. Anna's mother had been a promising pianist, but had given up her ambitions when she married a totally unmusical man. After his (welcome to both of them)

95

disappearance, her mother resumed her piano, hoping that Anna, who had kept up her playing at school, might now indeed become a concert pianist. However this was not to be, and Anna married another unmusical, though otherwise angelic, man, Lewen Dunarven, a distinguished scholar in the history of Ireland. Anna had met Lewen through Benet, and Benet and Uncle Tim through Elizabeth Loxon, who wrote short novels under various names, and was a friend of Mildred's.

Anna, looking down the garden, sighed deeply – then, aware of someone in the room, turned round. There were two people, one of them Bran, the other Jackson. Bran ran to her and buried his face in her dress, then stood before her solemn, slightly frowning, narrow-eyed, a familiar look. She ran her fingers through his long curly tumbling amber brown hair and then drew her hand back over his brow. Over his shoulder she looked at Jackson. Bran pulled his head away like a recalcitrant horse, moved away from her and stood staring out of the window. Jackson was there, with Benet's permission, to pin up against the brick wall, at the end of the garden, a rambling vine which had fallen to the ground. This task had now been performed. Anna could not immediately think of another task, but she was sure she would soon be able to. She was very touched and pleased by the speed with which Bran and Jackson had established a *rapport*. Now Jackson was about to leave. He smiled at Anna and advanced to accept the envelope which she reached out to him. His smile was gentle, humorous, mysterious. Anna, who had many strange thoughts, wondered if she might somehow capture Jackson and take him away with her to Ireland. In this drama the idea of his being anything other than a servant did not figure. In answer to Anna's thanks Jackson gave another smile and a bow. Bran left the window and pulled at Jackson's coat. They left the room together and she could hear them talking and laughing in the hall.

Anna turned back to the window, where she could see, at the end of the garden, the piece of the brilliantly green vine up against the glowing red brick wall. Her thoughts reverted again to Marian. Had she run to another man? Could she be dead? Surely not. Anna returned to her own urgent problems.

96

She thought, after all *I am alone* in this, I must not expect to find any help, any help at all.

Edward, so much sought for, was indeed hard to find. Was he dead? Had he lost his mind? Had he discovered Marian and murdered her? After all, had he not always been a bit deranged? Perhaps he had already left England?

Edward had spent the first night, the 'wedding night', at Hatting, and then on the evening of the next day returned to London, where he spent a following day and a night lying low, gaining his information only from the police. Then, rising early, he had left London and spent a day and a night at a hotel with which he was familiar in Salisbury. The day he spent sitting in his hotel room thinking. On the next day he drove down to Dorchester where he paused. The sun was shining from a pale blue sky. He had taken very little food in the hotel. He ate now, ravenously, bread and butter, eggs, coffee at a small 'tea room' which he remembered. He sat there quietly for a while, keeping in touch with the police. Rising and leaving Dorchester he set off, taking a coast road, then descending through a labyrinth of little lanes, towards the sea. He motored on, slowly now, looking downward and looking upward. Now at last, very slowly, he was able to drive the car out onto sandy shingle as near as he could to the sea. He got out, locked the car, and began to walk, looking back at intervals, over dried-up grass, trampling down the dry wild flowers, onto the stony sandy earth to where the earth ended and the stones began. Stumbling a little he went on walking upon the stones in the direction of the sea. He came at last to where the heaped up stones bordered the large now curling now retreating waves. He turned for a moment behind him to check a distant landmark. Then he sat down upon the stones, already made dry by the friendly warmth of the sun. He sat, blinking his eyes, looking out into the glittering chaos of the sea, so many mirrors lifting upward to the sky. His hands picked up the stones, large and small each one so perfect, so smooth, pale grey, dark grey, often streaked, criss-crossed, ringed with white. He sat upon the dry stone heap, looking down upon the lines of the advancing waves, hearing the crash as they destroyed themselves against the stones, dragging them downward in an ever-falling wall. He heard the fierce scooping hiss of the undertow. The sun was shining upon the wide huge empty theatre of the beach where there was no one to be seen.

Edward was in no hurry. Here he was, right above the waves, at the top of the tumbling cliff of stones which were perpetually falling and returning. He dug his boots into the fall of the stones, he felt them faintly shifting down below. The noise of the waves was deafening, like gun-fire, their strength terrifying, the droplets of their spray struck his face like pellets. The breaking waves looked grey and white. Further out the water looked blue, advancing, huge, fast, moving forward in order like galloping horses. Beyond, the line of the horizon was clear and dark as if drawn with a pencil. There were no boats. Ahead there was just the sea and above it the sky, a pale blue above the pencilled line, a few chubby white clouds lounging dreamily below a radiance of gold, but higher up the sky seeming to lose its colour altogether in a trembling stillness of pure light. It is a wonderful day, Edward thought. The stones were warm. A lovely day for swimming, he thought. Only Edward had given up swimming.

Edward and Randall had been on a bicycling holiday, in perfect weather, staying in little accidental inns, free, happy, just themselves. It was early in the season, in the spring. They were very fond of each other. Randall, the younger by two years, revered Edward. Edward lovingly protected his young brother. Their ages were now seventeen and fifteen. The death of their mother, now well in the past, was fadingly mourned by the children, still bitterly by the father. Somehow connected with that sad death was the fact, it was now clear, that the father loved the younger son more than he loved the elder son. All three, aware of this, watched it in silence. Edward certainly felt it as a faint but continuous scar. None of this however damaged his love for Randall, or Randall's love for him. The boys had set out upon their cycling holiday with their father's blessing and his command that they should be *very careful* and *behave themselves*. Earlier, and not for the first time, he had told Edward that he must be *very careful* and look after Randall.

There was a lot of laughing over their departure, at dawn, their rucksacks full of shirts and boots and bathing costumes and knives and forks and plates and fruit and sandwiches, their father and the servants waving them off. The weather was perfect, and they rejoiced as they rode steadily farther and farther away from Lipcot, southward, toward the sea coast. Of course they had gone on many such sallies before, but never quite so far and with quite so much money in their pockets. They were in no hurry. Their rucksacks, soon half-empty, were filled up again in grocers' shops, and they even (contrary to their father's orders) bought a bottle of wine. They were in a hurry to get to the sea, but somehow, it was as they meandered slowly south, still far away. Random nights spent at various small villages carried them to Bath, where they stayed two nights, then on to spiritual and exciting Glastonbury then another spiritual night at Dorchester, where they bought a book by John Cowper Powys, and lingered at Maiden Castle, then on to Weymouth where at last, together with numerous other people, they ran across the sand and leapt into the sea. They spent that night at Weymouth, and Edward suggested that they should stay there for another night. Randall however wanted to press on along the sea road, with its ups and downs and have their second swim in the 'real sea'. Edward, who was now rather tired of cycling, reluctantly agreed. So they set off slowly, upon the main sea road, not without replenishing their rucksacks here and there, and not forgetting the wine which they had not yet opened. The main road was full of ups and downs, sometimes losing even a glimpse of the sea. The sun was now well up in a cloudless sky. The brothers, tired of pedalling or pushing their machines up hills (though it was fun shooting down) decided that they must now find some little road which would lead them to the water, where perhaps there might be another more modest road to follow. After all, as Randall said, it's the *sea* that matters. They found such a little road, sometimes a track, running along, close beside the waves. The sun was blazing down, there was nobody about, slowing they selected a place for lunch, leaving their bikes chained up on the sandier inland. Then, putting down their rucksacks upon the stones, they decided that *of course* they must have a swim before lunch. Here the shore was composed of stones, beautiful stones, light grey, dark grey, smooth like eggs, large and small, their lovely forms covered with lighter criss-cross and speckled backgrounds of paler streaks and circles of pure white. Randall at once ran back and opened his rucksack and began collecting stones. How strange it was that, although the boys had had many holidays by the sea, they had never discovered *this* part of the coast, *this* perfectly magic place with nobody there!

They went down, crunching over the stones, to the edge of the water, where the waves struck the stones and dragged them down. Here they swiftly undressed and plunged in naked. They could master the stones, they could breast the water, they swam far out, where the quiet lilt of the water silently lifted them up and laid them down, then after much dolphin play they were standing and climbing easily up the sloping shore and onto the beach, and on to where they had left their rucksacks. They lay down naked upon warm stones, finding how pleasantly tired the lovely sea had made them. They put on shirts and slowly ate their delicious lunch and opened their bottle and drank a little wine. After that they slept.

Sitting upon the stones they had already noticed, upon a quite high hillock beyond the so-called 'road', a sort of hut, solitary it seemed, not large. Time, they realised, had passed now and they were still quite a long way from their next destination. Soon it might be twilight! Randall suggested that they might spend the night in that hut – it had been such a hot day, it must be a warm night! Edward, the cautious one, said that the hut was not theirs, it was someone else's, anyway it was probably locked up, and anyone might come to inhabit it at any moment, after all they had seen nobody coming or going. Randall said they were miles from anywhere, it would take ages to drag their bikes up to the main road, and he for one was feeling very tired. Anyway it would be an adventure, and they could easily get up to the hut. Edward, to please him, at last agreed, and they set off with their rucksacks, then unleashing their bikes and loading them up and pushing them first along the sandy verge, then, just after reaching the little 'road' that they had come along, discovering a path which seemed to lead straight up to the hut. They abandoned their bikes, chained up and covered over in brambles, in a ditch, and struggled on up the rather steep way with their rucksacks. The hillock was a little higher than it had seemed from below, and it appeared it must be reached through a meadow, after a crawl under some barbed wire. Here they paused for a dispute. Edward said that it was ridiculous, evening was coming on, they should carry on with their bikes, surely they would soon find some pub and relax, as they had done before. However he gave way to Randall's excited begging that at least they must go on now as far as the hut and perhaps – As they reached it, at last, with caution, dragging their rucksacks exhaustedly through the long grass, the sun was falling behind the hills beyond. They stood still for a short while outside it, breathing deeply. They could hear nothing. They cautiously pushed the door, which to their joy was not locked. They stepped inside. The hut consisted of one small empty room, with a pile of wood in a grate with a chimney, which they had not noticed from below. It was all made of wood, the floor, the walls, and the roof, with a delicious woody smell, very clean and neat. Whoever lived there, or more likely visited there, must be a careful, fastidious, perhaps thoughtful, person, they agreed. It was now beginning to be a little dark in the hut. Randall suggested that they could make a fire in the grate, but Edward vetoed this. They would not want to draw attention to themselves – that is supposing they *were* to stay – Randall then discovered beside the fireplace a small box containing candles, and insisted on lighting one at once. He declared that in this little house, which was just for now their own, they would not light a fire, but they must have candlelight to celebrate their feast after which they would sleep. The hut was already very warm from the sunlight. Edward was still anxious, but was overcome by Randall's childish delight. They began to unpack. It was then that Randall suddenly noticed that after all some contents of his rucksack, including the bottle of wine, which he had put in a separate bag, had been left down on the beach! Edward suggested just leaving them but Randall *insisted* that they *must* have their wine to drink by candlelight, it would be so romantic, and anyway the tide might cover that part of the beach during the night. He said he would run and fetch it all in no time, and Edward could stay and light the candles. Edward, who felt very much like resting now, hesitated, then he thought I must go with Randall, he might get lost or fall or hurt himself on the wire. So they set off together in the twilight, back down the hill.

The sun had almost set and the cloudless sky had become a darkening blue. The moon, nearly full, was now faintly gleaming. Randall commented upon the fact that it had been invisible before. A perceptible wind was now blowing. Edward thought, we shall be jolly cold in that hut at midnight! However he did not say that to Randall. They got through the wire all right, passed their bikes invisible in the ditch, then ran down to the track and out onto the beach. They could hear the strange rhythmic grating sound of the great waves upon the stones. It took them a little while to find the bag, now lying almost invisible. Edward picked it up. He felt the wind blowing. Randall had run past him to look at the sea whose harsh grinding sound of the waves breaking was louder now in the quiet darkness. Edward followed him slowly, then as he neared him he saw that Randall was undressing. Edward was at once alarmed. 'Oh Randall, not *another* swim, and it's getting dark, and – '

Randall, now undressed, was standing up, his body pale in the uncertain light, looking down at the crashing waves which were scrabbling at the shifting wall of stones. He cried, 'A moonlight swim, you *must*, come on, the water will be warm – ' He began descending, holding his balance upon the shifting stones, seeming to vanish in the coming waves, then seen instantly a little farther out, bobbing about in the white crested water and waving to Edward.

Edward shouted, 'Hurry up, come in, come back!' He feared the currents, the wind, the grim force of the waves, more savage now, larger, louder, taller, curling over in great white arches, hurling themselves in deafening impact against the slithering wall of stones, and in destroying themselves, each wave in its demise receding, dragging clattering down a grinding mass of sand and stones. Edward stood for another minute watching, he shouted out to Randall, he thought he could see him far out, he thought, I must go with him, I must look after him, oh dear all this is *daft*. He took off his jacket, pants and shoes, he tried to walk, searching for a foothold, then fell down the slope of sand and stones, kept his feet for a second as a wave broke violently over him, then found himself swimming. Here, the surface of the sea was a confused churning mass of white foam, coming and going, sucking back, sucking down, leaping up, then suddenly swinging into a trough, waves fighting with each other. Ordinary swimming was impossible. Edward, almost upright in the water, trying to tread his legs below him, swallowing water, attempting a breast-stroke, managed to keep his head up. He tried to move in the direction of where he had seen Randall. He thought that he glimpsed him in the chaotic darkness and tried to move towards him, but great curtains of racing churning heavy waves struck him violently making progress impossible. He kept trying to cry out, swallowing more water. Then suddenly Randall was beside him, he fumbled in the water, trying to grip Randall's wrist, saying perhaps aloud or to himself, *thank God, thank God*. He thought he heard Randall say 'Can't get out.' He thought, Randall is *terrified* and *so am I*. Holding his brother's wrist he kept on, not exactly swimming, but moving, trying to paw the water with one hand. Low down, between the wave crests, jerking his head up and swallowing water, he had entirely lost his sense of direction. Randall seemed to be jerking away from him or being pulled away. Edward, now putting his trailing legs into violent motion, thought he had caught a glimpse of what must be land, the final breaking of the waves. He also saw, in sudden glimpse, as if a wave had lifted him intentionally up, the moon now very bright. Edward was thinking *I mustn't let him go* – but am I drowning him by holding onto him? He turned his head and glimpsed Randall's gasping horrified face. Then suddenly he felt the movement of the water changing, they were close to the land, to the place where the waves ended their journey and smashed themselves against the perpetually descending cliff of stones. Edward felt the sudden change, he thought, now I must get a foothold, I must *get a foothold*, otherwise we shall fall under the wave. He felt water suddenly lifting him up, he lost his grip on Randall, he was caught inside the curling wave as he tried to stand, above him the dome of the wave, he could not stand, he was dashed down onto his knees, he struggled, feeling for a second the swift strong moving sand of the undertow, now racing back through his fingers, while the running cliff of stones, falling against him, were making him unable to rise, he was choking, drowning. He got up, crouching, attempting to get his legs apart, he thought, *I must stand*, or the next wave will kill me. He braced himself to the wave, and found himself still upright, moving, climbing, stretching out his hands against the tumbling stones. He had lost hold of Randall, indeed he had completely forgotten Randall, now he was crawling, now at last standing upon the shore. He turned back gasping, choking, looking back into the violent chaos of the huge towering waves. Where was Randall now – must he *go back into this hell and die himself*? Surely Randall too must be somewhere near to him, clambering out? Out of the sea, at last, he turned stumbling along, looking out at the waves and screaming. There was no sign of Randall. He returned to the sea, breasting the waves, losing foothold, swimming, choking, then desperately attempting above all with his weary battered limbs, to get back to the land without drowning. His eyes were filled with water. He knelt, he stood, then knocked down to all fours, crept, stood again, desperately at the edge of the sea, staring and calling out. About twenty minutes later or perhaps more he saw Randall, floating face downward, carried in by a wave. He returned to the water, pulling at the limp body of his brother, wailing and crying and screaming, hauling him out onto the stones. He tried to remember what to do, laying him down on his face, pressing his back. It was all senseless and useless. They were alone in the dark on the empty beach. He could find no help.

It was some time after that that a motorist was stopped by a half-clad man, incoherently weeping, pointing down toward the beach. Later, other people came, the police came, Randall's body was carried away.

Edward now, sitting in the sunlight upon the stones beside the calm sea, was crying, wailing. He had never, until now, returned to this place. The little hut was still there, the sea and stones were there, the emptiness and no one. Edward had for many years wondered if he would ever come back. He had never been forgiven, his father had never forgiven him, his father hated him, he hated himself. Everybody remembered, many pitied him, nobody spoke of it of course. What had made him come now, perhaps he knew. He had made another death, that of Marian. Even if she was alive, she was dead. And *between* these two deaths, there was yet a *third thing*, a third crazy thoughtless deed, which must forever be hidden in darkness.

FIVE

Marian, whom everyone was worrying about and searching for, was not dead. She had considered suicide. She had stared down at the shining rails at tube stations and felt in her body the trembling passionate energy which would be needed, timing it carefully, to hurl herself in front of a train. She thought about drowning in some dark place, among abandoned buildings, beside the Thames. But she was a good swimmer and fierce violent instincts would simply prevent her, nor could she imagine thus some slow death. She had no access to poisons. She could of course throw herself in front of a bus, but this might be bungled, leaving her hideously disfigured and damaged. She had always feared high places and could not see herself awkwardly opening windows and climbing onto window sills. All these thoughts were superficial, false, unreal, hideous dreams which segregated her from the ghastly *reality* of what had happened to her, what she had *done*, and now forever after would have to live with.

Now, at present, she was sitting on a bed in a small cheap hotel down a side street near Euston Station. She had cried so much, she was still crying. It was morning. She had, weak with exhaustion, at last slept part of the night. She had dreamed a happy dream, and for a second waking held it. Now the horror was all back again, like a huge steel building collapsing, grinding down upon her. She had *lost*, she had *destroyed*, *wantonly and forever*, everything that was good and happy in

106

her life. She had made an effort to cease her crying, not just the flow of tears, but now the rhythmic wailing, the convulsive repetition of 'ah!' 'ah!'. On the previous day someone had knocked on the door, then opened it, and asked if she was ill. Of course she was ill, but she said no, no, not at all, she was so sorry, she was quite well. Outside the sun was shining. Her watch told her it was morning, after seven o'clock. This was the beginning of yet another day in which she had stayed in the hotel. She must go somewhere, she must do something, but where and what? She thought, I must go back to Canada and never never return to this country again. But why Canada? She could not face her mother, she had ruined her poor mother as she had ruined all the others, all the other people, whom she would never never see again. She still had her handbag with her, her money, her cards. She must *get away*, *somewhere*, and become *another person*. That is the same as dying. Perhaps she should go to a priest. But she had given up priests long ago, as her mother had. Oh her mother, her dear, dear mother – everything had fallen, everything had been destroyed – *and so quickly* – it is like murder, it *is* murder – I am ill, I am very ill, she thought, trying now to check her moaning, I am going mad – am I to run out of here, and run about the streets? My face is swollen and hideous, no one will recognise me. She sat upon the bed, gasping, half dressed, stuffing her wet handkerchief into her mouth.

The condition into which Marian had entered, into which she had *thrust* herself, had origins further back. She loved her sister. But as they grew up her love was, she knew, very slightly touched by envy, later jealousy. Marian was rated more beautiful than Rosalind. It wasn't that. Marian was not sure what it was. Perhaps it was simply a growing up, and a determined parting of the ways. Rosalind had been bright at school, a 'scholar', she was clever, she was going to be an art historian. Marian, though not a fool, and far more naturally sociable, became aware that Rosalind was more sought after, more admired, more witty, more *interesting*. Rosalind knew what she was going to do with her life. Marian had no idea what was going to happen to hers. Both girls had learnt

French, and a little Italian at school. Marian had now forgotten much of hers, whereas Rosalind preserved these, and was adding Russian. They went on pleasant trips to France, Italy, Spain. Marian then decided to go round the world, to brush up her languages, she said laughingly. Anyway she wanted to *travel*, to *get away*, to go to *strange lands* and have *adventures*. This tour came about, funded by her mother, by Benet, more liberally by Uncle Tim; and at last Marian, taking leave of England with lengthy wavings of farewell, turned her face to the wind and felt more deliriously happy than ever in her life. The beautiful white ship, ignoring Europe (which she assumed her wealthy passengers already knew) passed through the Mediterranean, stopping at Egypt, on down the Red Sea, then on to India, down the coast for temples and swimming, on to Ceylon, then at last the long sea voyage to Sydney. The stay at Sydney was proving unusually long because of some engine trouble. This did not worry Marian. She had made pleasant acquaintances on board, but let loose in Sydney she discovered even more delights and interesting friends. She sent postcards home, especially to her mother, Rosalind, Uncle Tim, Benet, and Edward, mentioning the pleasant delay. Just at this time Uncle Tim had died. There had been some argument about whether or when she should be told. At last a telegram finally brought the sad news. Marian sent a reply: *Terribly sorry Uncle Tim. Probably staying on in Australia. Note hotel address.* Marian had already informed her lovely white ship (her name was *Calypso*) that she must now travel on to see New Zealand without Marian. Marian had fallen in love with Australia.

From her hotel in Sydney Marian subsequently sent, not this time a postcard but a letter, to Edward. Marian had for a considerable time been aware that Benet, Tim and others were quietly hoping that she might marry Edward Lannion. Randall's sudden death had damaged the rather stiff but perceptible connection which had existed between Hatting Hall and Penndean. Mourning for that death existed for a long time. Edward left the university; his father died and Edward took charge of Hatting, spending also much time in London, having, at any rate for the moment, given up his historical novel and his poems. At that time too he became better acquainted with Benet and Tim, and also with the girls. On the boat Marian had been thinking about Edward, and had at her hotel composed and recomposed a tactful letter to him. She received a reply from Edward which, though very characteristically cautious, left her in little doubt. This whispered clarification left Marian suddenly not only more happy but more free. Now she was enjoying Australia. Then, before long, she should fly back. She had money in her pocket. Most of all, she could now toy with the idea of being 'the Mistress of Hatting Hall'! There was, in her change of plan, another shadowy consideration. Suppose she were to stay too long away, and find that Edward had found some other bride – or decided to marry *Rosalind*? She wrote a sort of love-letter to Edward, received a vaguely similar reply, and cast away her anxieties.

Marian had by now, though still based in her hotel, ventured a little out of Sydney on various expeditions. She had also acquired some Australian friends, been invited to parties, then to dinner parties. She was, after all, a totally unaccompanied beautiful girl. The bright friendly atmosphere of lovely Sydney suited her, especially so since that shadowy uncertainty had been removed. She would of course go home soon, only not just yet. She wanted to go to the Great Barrier Reef, to the Brisbane Zoo, to Ayers Rock, to see Aborigines, real bush and real free animals, koalas, kangaroos. As happens in Sydney she met all sorts of people. She met a man called Cantor Ravnevik. She met his name before him and thought it a strange lovely name, and she was glad to meet its eccentric owner. They had a drink together, they lunched together, they danced together. He told her about his family and his name. His great grandfather on his father's side had come to Australia from Norway. His mother's family had come more recently from Germany, half German and half Irish, also half Jewish. That, he said, accounted for his name. His other Scandinavian family name, being unpronounceable for Australians, had been smoothed down to its more attractive present form. His parents were dead, he had only one brother, who was older than him, and who ran a sheep farm. He was very fond of his brother, his brother had a lovely wife who was going to have a baby, no, he himself was not yet married. Marian, though still not sure what the man was, began to like him very much. She had felt it proper to mention that she was engaged (or as she put it 'perhaps sort of engaged') to 'someone in England'. She showed him pictures of Lipcot, and Hatting and Penn, and country all around, and Benet and Rosemary and Edward and Mildred and others. Cantor noted these and smiled. He did not ask who the people were. He expressed his wish to take her to the farm. Marian, now feeling 'safe', allowed him to drive her out into the country, and was suitably amazed at the immensity of the farm, the vast distances, the hundreds and hundreds of sheep, 'not at all like England'. His elder brother (Arne Ravnevik) and his sister-in-law (Judith, Jewish, long known to the family, hence Cantor's name) welcomed Marian warmly. When Cantor asked her if she could ride she was delighted to say she certainly could! Then they rode together over beautiful wild country. She found Australian horses naughtier than Canadian ones and they laughed about that. Back in Sydney Marian visited Cantor in his flat and they made love.

Before this Marian had already explained, in answer to a question by Cantor, that she was not a virgin. She had indeed had a few adventures after leaving school, amounting, she said, to nothing. She had of course informed Edward of these facts. Edward accepted them calmly and said no more. Marian had not asked about him, about his previous life, though she was certainly curious about it. She had heard Benet say that 'really nobody knows about Edward'. Marian had asked Edward a few tame questions; she was content to leave more information until later. That would be what Edward would desire. She loved him and was proud to be, as it was emerging now, chosen as his wife. She was also a bit afraid of him, but that of course, would pass. She knew, as everyone knew, of Randall's death. This was a dark shadow, and there might be other ones, in Edward's life. She hoped and believed that love and patience might in time dispel them.

Marian lay down again with Cantor. She lay with her face deep in his blond hair. She had received another letter from

Edward. She had booked her seat in the aeroplane which was to take her home. She told Cantor that she was leaving. He took the news with a little gesture and a slightly rueful smile. She was grateful for his calmness, she had been an episode, he had been so gently beautifully kind to her, but he would easily do without her. He also, perhaps because she was going, told her more about himself, how he did work for his brother, how he ran a literary newspaper, how he wrote a bit, how he attempted to help the Aborigines. Marian, on the point of leaving, was sorry now that she had not questioned him more about the Aborigines. Anyway it was too late and she would never see him again. She gently made a habit in the last days, of talking a little about Edward. The time came for departure. Cantor drove her to the airport.

The time between Marian's return and the completion of their wedding plans was longer than she had expected. When they met again she was shy and Edward was nervous. They lay together in Marian's flat and made some gentle fumbling love with closed eyes. They both, tacitly, reserved this time as a sort of holy preparation. Their great perfect union lay ahead when all would be achieved and revealed. Everyone was delighted with them. Rosalind's feelings (much discussed of course) about Edward were in fact of relief, not (as some believed) of envy. Watching her sister, whom she loved, she could quite early on see her 'made for him and Hatting'. Benet meanwhile, almost too briskly, arranged for the pair to be alone when they might have preferred company. For some unspoken reason there was to be no love-making in Hatting Hall, or of course at Penndean, only in Marian's flat. Hatting was 'out of bounds' until afterwards, until 'after the wedding'. Meanwhile, immediately after the wedding, they were to go (still in secret of course) to France. Weeks had passed and everything was moving in slow motion. Marian's heart beat faster and faster and she was longing for it all to be over and they could be in France.

Something disturbing did occur which Marian felt she must conceal from Edward. She had considered from the first days of her return whether she should tell him what 'had happened to her' in Australia. At first she was ready to tell, only somehow she couldn't quite find the moment, and Edward seemed to have little interest in Australia anyway. Then it was too late and she was beginning to forget it all, absorbed in church services, invitations, dresses, and dealings with her flighty mother. Sometimes she and Edward thought they should just run away instantly to a Register Office! But of course there were always reasons which made this impossible. Meanwhile she watched Edward closely and thought about the 'gloom' which she was now relied upon to send away. As 'the day' grew very near, Edward returned to Hatting and Marian stayed in London, finishing her wedding clothes and packing up a box of 'secrets' destined for various 'worthies'. However, at a time now nearing the date of the wedding Marian received a letter with an Australian postmark. It was of course from Cantor and it was a love letter. Marian cried over this letter, suddenly she felt – what did she feel? She remembered the farm and the horses and – she hastily replied at once that she was getting married, but she gave no details. Cantor replied that she had been so vague about marriage he was not sure whether it was serious! But anyway he was soon coming to England on business and hoped to see her. This was a cooler letter. Marian was already very disturbed, and alarmed at finding herself so. She wished now that she had told Edward about Cantor. Now she could not, it was too late. She spent some time wondering whether she should reply to the letter, but finally decided not to. It was a matter of weeks, now of days, everything was fixed.

Then one afternoon, coming back alone to her flat, she saw an envelope upon the floor with a London postmark. Cantor was in London and this was once again a love letter. He said he was on business, not for long, he was assuming that she was as yet unmarried and would she come and have lunch with him? He would ring her up. The telephone rang. She went into the kitchen and covered her ears. Half an hour later it rang again.

Of course she must answer telephone calls, it might be anybody. She lifted the telephone. It was Cantor's voice. She began hurriedly to babble, no she could not see him today or tomorrow, no not for lunch *or* dinner, she was sorry – as Cantor's charming and familiar voice went calmly on she said, 'Cantor, please stop, please *please*, I cannot see you, I am to be married to Edward.' He said 'When?' Today was Monday, the marriage was on Wednesday. Marian said quickly, 'The end of next week.' She was terrified that Cantor would want to be invited, perhaps 'butt in'. After a short silence he said, 'Well, that's it.' Then he said, 'I'd like to see you all the same. I've got a present for you – well, now it's a wedding present! Can we meet, can we have lunch, tomorrow for instance?' She said quickly, 'Lunch, no, sorry – ' 'Then before lunch then – I *must* give you my present!' 'Oh, *all right*, but not for long and where – ?' She thought, I'll see him and *get it over*! He said, 'I suggest Kensington, Barker's, why not, tomorrow and the ground floor among the shirts, at eleven?' Marian, who had no lunch plans and only a desire not to spend lunchtime with Cantor, said *all right* and put down the phone. She felt extreme irritation and annoyance with herself as well as with Cantor. She had not even asked him for his telephone number – she could have rung up and cancelled it all!

The next morning, the day before the wedding, Marian, talking on the telephone with Edward, suddenly recalling Cantor's tryst, fell suddenly silent. Edward said, 'Are you still there?' Am I still there? Yes, I am still there. Of course she is. A day had passed, another day was to be. Yes, she would come tomorrow with all her 'secrets'. Yes, now, she might be out. 'Oh Edward – Edward – ' He said, 'Don't worry, it will be all right!' She thought, my clothes are nearly ready now, at once, I could go to Penn *now* – only *now* I have to wait for *that man*! But I did want to wait anyway, didn't I? I still have so many little things to do! She set off for Barker's to 'get all that over'.

Coming into the shop and into the shirt department she looked about. Had he not come? Oh be it so! Then she saw him some way off examining a shirt. She felt at once a sort of shock, and put her hand to her breast. Had she *forgotten* him, how *could* she have forgotten him? For an instant she saw him as she had seen him at the very first, before he had seen her, just before someone had introduced him to her, just before he had danced with her, his thick blondish heavy hair 'long enough to tuck in behind his ears', his narrow slightly curved nose, his look as of a picture of some commander, perhaps a Doge of Venice. Venice! She felt slightly faint. The vision passed. He turned, saw her, and waved. She waved. They approached each other smiling, he with his large blue eyes, yet wild, like an animal. They shook hands, smiling, laughing, he kissed her cheek, and they wandered together towards the exit and out into the street, walking and talking to each other. She noticed he was carrying a large leather bag. She asked after the farm, after Judith, had her baby come? Yes, a lovely baby, a boy of course. Why of course! And why had Cantor come to London? Oh on business for his brother, who had all sorts of investments over here, and was even considering a London office. Was he staying long? Not very long, but he had rented a little flat. What was in that big bag? Well, it was, in part, her present! Why in part? If she were patient she would soon see!

Marian had not, in all their quick laughing conversation, noticed where they were going. They had left the High Street and were now in a maze of small streets near Gloucester Road. 'Where are we?' 'Wait and see.' Marian was only now beginning to feel uneasy, and was about to say 'I *must* go' when suddenly they reached their destination. *Stables*. What? *Horses*.

Everything, including boots, which so beautifully fitted, had been unloaded and donned, they had trotted across the road and into the Park. Marian was intoxicated with joy. She had, since her return from Australia, simply given up riding. Now she was back in the saddle, even though in the demure surroundings of Hyde Park. Of course Cantor was a better rider, but Marian was good, they rode knee to knee upon their beautiful frisky horses, Jinny and Samuel. Then Cantor and Samuel went ahead, beginning to gallop, which was strictly forbidden, and Marian had difficulty in restraining Jinny, the horses loved it, the riders loved it, and at one moment when they were close side by side Cantor murmured to her: 'The Last Ride Together.' She had remembered the poem too. After that they took their excited horses back to the stables where Marian kissed them both. After that, as they walked away together, it appeared that it was lunchtime. They had lunch together at a pleasant restaurant in the High Street. It was then that Marian discovered that she had lost her watch. After that she said that she must take a taxi back to her flat, and at first there were no taxis, and when they found one Cantor gave his address not hers. Marian complained but Cantor said he just wanted to show her something and she could easily get back afterwards.

Then somehow they were at Cantor's flat where they were having tea sitting side by side upon the sofa, Cantor with his arm round her. He asked her again when her wedding was, and she replied, 'Wednesday.' 'This Wednesday?' Feeling suddenly very tired she said, '*Yes.*' 'Really? You have been deceiving me!' After that they lay down side by side on the sofa and Cantor kissing her said that she had cruelly deceived him, and anyway she could not possibly be in love with Edward, she did not believe what she was saying, she knew that she was in love with him, Cantor. Marian started to cry. Then they were lying in bed together and she had taken off some clothes. She said that he was deceiving her and that he had *drugged* her, she was frightened, he must let her go, only their arms were round each other, and she had lost her watch. After that they made love and she slept again. Cantor said he was certain that she was going to marry the wrong man, and that it was *not too late*, she must know that it was *not too late*, and he wanted her to write down what *she really felt*. She loved him, Cantor, and no one else, and he wanted her to write this out, and he would show it to 'other people', he *could not bear her giving herself away to someone else*. He made her sit up and write out on a piece of paper, '*forgive me, I am very sorry, I cannot marry you*'. Marian wrote out something and drank some more tea, only now it was whisky, or something else. After that she fell into a deep sleep.

When she woke it was daylight and she was in Cantor's arms and they were making love. She felt for her watch, she had lost her watch, she felt a little sick. Suddenly she sat up, where was she, with whom was she? She started to cry, to sob, and began to look for her clothes, which Cantor handed to her. Cantor sat down on the bed. She struggled, and began clumsily to put her clothes on, still crying. What day was it? Where was she, what time was it? Cantor said, 'I have delivered your message.' 'What message?' 'You wrote the truth. You wrote "*forgive me, I am very sorry, I cannot marry you*".' They have seen it. Only they have not seen me. 'I don't understand. I *don't believe* you. Oh God, what time is it?' 'It is the afternoon, and all is over.' 'What day? oh oh oh – ' 'There is no wedding. You do not want this man. I *know* you do not want him. At this moment he is relieved. As you will very soon be. Rest now, rest my child.'

But Marian continued to sob, even to scream, as she put on her clothes and looked about for her coat and her handbag. Cantor, still sitting on the bed, watched her. He said, 'Marian, will you marry me?' 'No, no, no, I *hate* you, I *hate* you! Oh God, I have been a *fool*, what an awful *fool* I have been, I have destroyed myself – '

'Listen, you did not really want him – '

'No, and I don't want you either, I *detest* you, I shall kill myself. Why, why, why – I don't even know if you tell the truth – you have *drugged* me, you are *hateful*.'

'I tell the truth.'

'Goodbye – ' She ran, holding her coat and her handbag, to the door. She struggled to put on her coat. She tried to open the door, in vain.

'Listen, my child – '

'I must go, *go* – '

'Well, where to? Let us just go somewhere together in my car.'

She fell down the steps, got up, then got into the car, banging the door. Cantor got in the other side, locking both doors, and the car set off. He kept turning to look at her. She looked like a mad creature, transformed, grimacing, her eyes staring with

116

terror and horror. Cantor shuddered, he repeated mechanically, 'I have told them, I have been there in the night.' She uttered a wailing cry, holding her mouth wide open. Then she said, 'I have lost my watch,' and 'Leave me, *leave* me, I *hate* you – ' He said, 'Will you come with me, will you marry me – I am sorry to have hurt you – I must take you away – please *please* – I *love* you. I'm going home – come with me.' He turned to her terrible face, she was crying, fumbling at the door. She said, 'You have destroyed me, you have driven me mad, oh *my wedding day*, let me out, *let me out.*' By now Cantor was crying too. He said, 'Why did you keep on lying?' Then, 'Oh *hell*! I'm going back to Australia.' He turned the car into a side road, then leaned over and opened the door. She slipped out and fled, disappearing among people. Cantor struggled with his seat belt, tried to get out to follow her, then sat back cursing. After a while he turned the car.

Marian ran, then walked, among strange unknown streets, weeping. People stopped, some trying to speak to her, asking what was the matter, could they help. She hurried quickly as if she knew where she was going, turning at random down unfamiliar streets. At last, trying to conceal her agitation and her tears, she entered a little hotel.

Benet could scarcely sleep during those days, he did not know where to station himself, whom he should be watching or watching for. He prayed for some, even slightest, signal from Marian. How could she be so *cruel* as to *vanish* in that way! Surely she knew that no one would hurt her or blame her – yet perhaps the poor child was captive somewhere – or was *dead*. Edward too had disappeared without any word – was it possible that he had found her – found her and killed her – or killed himself? Oh what terrible mad thoughts! Later would they all look back, in sunlight? Was it possible that it might all be *put together* again, the love, the marriage, all made clear and made happy? Perhaps they just wanted a Register Office marriage after all!

Owen was going through a drunken phase because, he said, Mildred was gone into the spirit world. When Marian was mentioned he cursed and said the little fool would never come back. Anna was remote and curt and spoke of 'going away' or 'clearing off'. When Benet rang her she put down the telephone as soon as possible, sometimes at once. Benet had decided that he should at present stay at Penndean, since it was possible that Edward would, might, come back to Hatting. It was also, he felt, most likely if Marian were at some time, ashamedly, to return, he felt sure that she would come to him, and at Penn. But every day just brought more grief and anguish.

In fact, after days, Edward did return, and to Hatting, and straight from there to Penn, where he was told that Benet was. He walked in one evening, after Benet had been making his usual fruitless telephone calls, and came straight to the drawing room. Benet, putting down the telephone, went to Edward and seized his hand. Edward quietly thrust him away. Benet could see at once that Edward had altered. His face was twisted with exasperation and pain. He looked past Benet and out through the open glass doors into the garden, towards the copse of birch trees which the breeze was slightly moving. For a moment he stared out in silence, with the same anguished expression. Then he turned to Benet with a colder sterner expression and said, 'I have not much time.'

Benet, aware of his tallness, said, 'Do sit down.'

Edward ignored this. He said, 'No news of course.'

'No – and you?'

'Of course not! Oh *Christ*, I wish all this was over!'

Benet, already distressed by the intensely cold almost savage vibrations, sat down upon the sofa. He said, 'Edward, dear, do please sit down.' He pointed to a chair.

Edward bared his teeth with an audible '*ach*!' and sat down.

Benet said, 'Oh how much, how *much*, I wish I could make you happy again. I feel I've let you down – yes, I am to blame – '

Edward, his face now twisted again with exasperation, looking away, said, 'Oh – nothing is *your* fault.'

'Well, nothing, I feel sure, is Marian's fault, surely that message was written by the person who kidnapped her – '

'Oh well, we would have heard from the kidnapper by now,' said Edward listlessly, still looking away, out of the window. He went on, 'No, it's not that – it's someone else, she's gone off with someone else, she just had to *get away from me* – it was all arranged – she never really wanted me – *at all.* Just as well, I'm not really – I just wish she'd let me know – a little earlier – but just doing it now – '

'Yes, I know, I *know* – and I'm – so very – sorry – But there were so many things – if she comes back now and wants you and wants you to forgive her – and – and make things right again? Isn't that possible.'

'No, of course not.' He paused. 'You *know* it isn't possible – it's all *hatred*, pure *hatred*.'

'What do you mean, what is – ?'

'Her hatred, my hatred, most of all my hatred.'

'*Please* see Marian when we find her, we don't know her story, she is innocent – you didn't hate her, you don't hate her – '

'I do now, I hate myself – '

'She may be dead, and – '

'I do not believe that she is dead,' said Edward. He paused, then went on, 'Often I think that I am dead – yes, I am or shall be dead. You do not know how much grief I have in me and what terrible things I have suffered, and done.'

'Edward, please, *please*, don't say such *mad* things, there are so very very many things in you and for you – and if you find her you can – '

'Oh, that – I don't know what I think about her or what has happened to her or what she's done – do not talk about her, she is over.'

'And you don't care – ?'

'And I am over too, I mean I am *done for*. I am going to sell Hatting.'

'Edward, no, never, you are *not* to sell Hatting, I *forbid* you – !'

119

Edward, who had been looking round the room with his face once more twisted into a grimace, suddenly looked at Benet and smiled. 'Dear Benet, always playing at my father!' He rose, the smile vanishing. He was thinner, his hair was shorter, jagged as if savagely cut, his face was wrinkled, his eyes narrowed, his lips trembling. For a moment he looked distraught, as if he were going to weep.

'*Don't go*,' said Benet, frightened, rising. 'Dear Edward, I love you, stay with me, don't go away – Have a drink, stay for lunch and – '

'I've given up eating and drinking – I'm just waiting – '

'What for?'

'Just waiting – for the awful thing to go away – '

'But Marian – '

'Not Marian. The dreams – if you only knew how much I am given over to the devil. I bring ill luck and doom. It's all over.' He added, 'I am going to travel abroad. Hatting will be up for sale. Please spread the news, will you.'

SIX

It did not take Jackson very long, using a curving piece of plastic cut from a mineral water bottle, to undo the fragile front door of the house, and then the ancient lock of Marian's flat. He cautiously quietly moved the door, slid inside, and closed it silently. Then he stood still, breathing deeply, in the small hallway, then moved into the sitting room. He had not been there before. Of course, after Marian had disappeared, Benet and Rosalind, with Rosalind's key, had entered the flat, anxious not to find Marian dead upon the floor. They had come to the flat more than once. Edward did not accompany them. They had of course 'made a search'. Jackson looked round. Everything was tidy. That would be the result of their search. The police had also been in, and were said to have watched the place. Apparently, as Jackson heard Benet saying, they had found no clues at all. He himself, he was sure, had entered rapidly and unnoticed. That lot, he thought scornfully, would have no idea of how *really* to search. Of course someone ought to have been staying there all the time. He moved about slowly, noticing Marian's 'things', her clothes hung up in a cupboard, by her, more likely by Rosalind. Her rows of shoes neatly stowed under the bed. She might have left in a hurry, or been kidnapped, or – the china animals upon the mantelpiece, the cushions easily moved, the little desk easily rifled. Jackson pictured Benet and Rosalind finding everything untidy and putting it all back into order, having discovered nothing.

Jackson, following the obvious tracks, looked through the desk, the sofa, the clothes, the bed, under the carpet, inside books, inside china animals, the kitchen, the shelves, the airing cupboard, drawers of all kinds containing clothes or papers or jewellery, all sorts of odd places which might have missed attention. He even found reverently laid to rest by the seekers, Marian's wedding dress. If there had been entities or indication, they might well have been effaced by his clumsy predecessors. He thought, something deliberately hidden, something so obvious as to be invisible. Benet and Rosalind had of course carried off Marian's address book and checked the addresses. And now, alas, Jackson had apparently tried everything including of course the secret drawer in the desk.

He lay down on Marian's bed. Could anything now *come* to him? He was fond of Marian, he grieved for her, he tried to be near her, now, to see her. He was horrified by the 'order' which surrounded him, and by his own utter incompetence. He was a watcher. He had perceived Edward's grief long before it came to view. He had shared Benet's grief. But that was another matter – how had he let himself be cast aside – at last. Because he deserved it? He, the jack-of-all-trades, who now exhibited so few. Owen Silbery had perceived it. Then he had called Jackson 'a ringed bird'. An apt name. Where were the other names now? Yes, he carried a weight, a burden placed upon him by *them*. He had dreamed of something precious, a message carried to an emperor – or to a great scientist. No, not that, but holiness. So now he was suddenly rehearsing for himself woes which he could not understand. Time was passing and no signal came. Not yet. Yes, let him sigh – perhaps he must again move on. Death had removed what he had thought of as a precious jewel. Not for the first time. Oh how he pitied himself. Remorse, remorse.

At that moment in his strange and woeful ramblings, he heard the sudden noise of a bell ringing in the room. He shot up; of course someone downstairs in the street! He fumbled the door and stumbled down the stairs. He opened the door.

A man dressed in some sort of livery or uniform was standing outside. He began at once. 'Oh, here's the letter, I was just going to shove it through, nobody's answered the bell, we've been trying, it's about the lady's watch – '

'Oh I know – ' said Jackson, taking hold of the envelope quickly and tearing it open.

'Is the lady here?'

'She's away for a bit, but back soon – '

'Well, it's not lost, we've got it safe and sound at our place, I've been told to give it only to her, it's a very valuable lady's watch, well, you understand, perhaps she'll come along in person, any time, we've kept in touch with the other gentleman, perhaps you know – '

'Indeed I do,' said Jackson, desperately trying to keep calm and think, 'I got here just after she left, she left a message for me and all about it, you see I've been abroad for some time and *he's* just moved and I can't find his telephone number, actually he's my cousin – '

'Yes, I can see you're a bit like him! What a handsome pair they made, if I may say so, such lovely riders, Sammy and Jinny had a super time. Yes, of course I'll give you his number, I'll put it on the back of the envelope – '

Jackson closed the door with a suitably grateful murmur and raced back upstairs with the booty. He returned to the bedroom and sat down. A telephone number. What was to be done with it? Not surrender it to *them* of course! Try it out – how, when? Now? Who were Sammy and Jinny? In his excitement in glancing at the letter he had not taken in where it came from. Of course he should have kept the man much longer in conversation! The letter was brief.

Dear Madam,
You have left your watch behind and we have it here safely. We have attempted to telephone you with no success. Could you please contact us and come round here as soon as possible.

He saw that the heading was of a livery stable with an address near Hyde Park. So, *Marian* had been there, with a *man*; with *the* man. Should he go round at once to the stables and somehow *find out* who the man was and where he lived?

123

What would anyone tell him? They might be suspicious, Marian's address and her telephone number, and *another* telephone number. My mind is moving very slowly! thought Jackson. How can I find anything out? The only true things were Marian's address and her number. All I can do is – call the other number.

He sat for a while holding onto his heart, which he noticed was now gradually slowing down. Should he not, like a faithful dog, carry the whole discovery to Benet? What use exactly was the telephone number? If Jackson were simply to call the number now and hear a voice, what could he say which would not give him away at once as some sort of enemy? If the man just slammed down the telephone, that would suggest something. Anyway, Jackson checked himself, all this is on the assumption that 'the man' is some sort of dangerous or at least unpleasant character! He might be someone whom Marian had just picked up, or knew from long ago, some sort of innocent party, or – was it not wiser to tell Benet who would ask the police who would check on the number? Jackson's burning curiosity overcame his common sense. He lifted up the receiver and dialled the number.

Silence. Then a woman's voice. Marian's? No, certainly not Marian's. 'Hello.'

Jackson, who had not carefully thought out what he was to say, said, 'Is he there? I've got a message for him, or for her.'

'Oh he's gone,' the rather pleasant woman's voice replied. 'He left us rather suddenly.'

'Oh, and about her?'

'I don't know, they went away together, he came back alone and stayed a bit, then he took up all his things and left –'

'Please excuse me, but could you tell me to whom I am speaking –'

'I'm so sorry, I'm Mrs Bell, I am from the flat downstairs, I've got the key of the upstairs flat and –'

'Could you tell me where he is now, do you know?'

'Oh yes, he left me an address and telephone number, but – well, he asked me not to tell it to people – may I ask who you are?'

'I am his brother.'

'Yes, yes, of course, he mentioned you, so I may tell you – '

Tuan, although a pet of Uncle Tim (who gave him his nickname) and also a favourite of Benet, remained, as everyone agreed, something of a mystery, not a sinister one of course. He was also called 'the Theology Student'. He gained a First at Edinburgh University, and later taught for a while at a college in London. Now he worked in a bookshop and appeared to be perpetually studying. He was said to have been a student of a student of Scholem. This might or might not be true. He was Jewish on his father's side. His Jewish father had, when a small child, escaped with his family from the holocaust and settled in Edinburgh. When his father married a Scottish Presbyterian girl, there was some stir in the Jewish community. The grandfather was particularly annoyed, but became more forgiving when the little boy appeared. Tuan could recall sitting on his knee, also walking in his funeral. Earlier still, Tuan could remember his father calling him Jacob and his mother calling him Thomas, and Thomas sometimes gaining the upper hand! Tuan's father spoke Hebrew and Yiddish to the infant boy, an only child, sent him to a Judaic Liberal school, took him to a Synagogue, made him wear black clothes and skull caps, and insisted on a *Bar-Mitzvah*. So, at school, he was formally called Jacob but somehow or other sometimes Thomas, or rather Tommy. His parents, as far as Tuan could remember, never seriously quarrelled, his mother never attempted to advocate the austere Scottish religion which she constantly practised, and they continued successfully to love each other passionately. It was Uncle Tim who later changed Tommy to Tuan, taken from Joseph Conrad's novel.

As a student at Edinburgh University Tuan had developed the general 'interest in religion'. As an academic in London he was encouraged by his open-minded college to teach and lecture on 'history of religion'. Tuan wandered about London sampling various forms of worship. He came to certain conclusions. Later, his observant colleagues accused him of 'taking it all too seriously', also 'enjoying it all too much'. They accused him of 'frivolity' which was far from being true. He was simply discovering mysticism. This discovery did not, he felt, detach him in any way from what he could now see as virtue and goodness, which he had perceived in his parents. He wrote home to them, often amusingly, about the other 'dons', about his digs, about the picture galleries, about a jacket he had bought in a sale; but he was unable, he felt as yet, to explain what he was discovering about religion. In letters he frequently begged his parents to consider coming to live in London. At first this seemed a possibility; then there was a shadow, something about his father's health. Tuan came at once, finding his father cheerful, 'getting better', 'not to worry'. However he could see his mother had been crying. He stayed for several days during which his father was getting 'much better'. He talked to the doctor. He went back to London. He rang up every day and heard his father's cheerful voice. He returned to Edinburgh and found his father 'well, though tired'. He spoke to his mother and to the doctor. He decided to stay for several days and rang up the college. His father said that he should 'go back to his work', but Tuan was now afraid. His father 'rested in bed'. Then Tuan saw his father asleep, unconscious. Then soon after, dead. He organised the funeral. He wept, his mother wept, there were many mourners. After this Tuan stayed with his mother for many days. They sat and cried together. She refused to have any visitors. He wanted her to come and live with him in London. She did not want to, she wanted to stay on in the house where she had lived for so long. Tuan said all right, he would leave London and come and live with her. She said no, he must 'do his work', he could come and see her, and she might come and see him. She did not want any other people, not yet anyway. She could look after herself, after all she had been looking after Tuan! She said, 'The doctor will help me, you know he comes every day, and if you like Annabelle can come too.' Annabelle was her old cook, now retired. She begged Tuan to go back to his 'ordinary work'. At last Tuan said he would go back to London, but only for half a day, to fix some things, provided the doctor came, and Annabelle stayed with her all day. She must ring up Annabelle *now*. He heard her ring Annabelle. He made sure of the doctor. He went to London, to his university, announcing his hasty retirement. He caught an afternoon train, he took a taxi to the house. He passed the gibbering doctor on the stairs and ran into her room. She seemed to be asleep. But she was dead. There were pills beside her. She had written, 'I shall meet him again.' Her only reference to life after death. Later he found out that Annabelle had died two years ago.

After this time, which was before he met Uncle Tim, Tuan curtailed his duties at the college where he continued to teach once a week. He also now went regularly to Edinburgh partly concerning his father's affairs. He spent many of his days wandering in the poorer parts of London. He thought very much about his father and his father's intense goodness, also about his mother and her terrible act, and of the words she had left behind her. The act was noble, the words a mystery. Religion and its forms. In his wanderings, at that time, he entered many places of worship, some even very strange. Was he, he sometimes wondered, being merely what his colleagues dubbed him as 'frivolous'? He was searching, but so were countless other people, and his searching often seemed pointless nor could he find anyone with whom to discuss it. He also visited numerous varieties of religious bookshops, in the Charing Cross Road and then in even more secretive and exotic areas, and bought and read a great many books, and continued to enter a great variety of places of worship. In due course he began to conclude that true religion *must* be a form of mysticism.

He had become more profoundly interested in Judaism and decided that to understand *anything* he himself must write a book. He hastened to begin the book, but then paused. He had taken for his subject the great Spanish Jewish mystic Maimonides; soon however he found himself, in the next century, discovering Eckhart and with him the various lights of the English mystics – and why not run quickly on to Spinoza – religious values, mystical values? He stopped writing his book and decided that he must, and for a long time, *read* and *think*. These problems he confided to no one. He found himself continually returning to the relation, the difference between Religion and Mysticism. Could there be Religion without Mysticism, Mysticism without Religion? Between these two where does Good lie – where does Love? Where is the Ultimate, and what is it? Where is Knowledge? Tuan was in love with Mysticism. Could this be bad? Where do sin and evil lie – indeed where can they not lie? It was about this time that Tuan met Uncle Tim. Amid these amazing seekings and ever opening vistas there was yet another darkness in Tuan's life which had been revealed to him and which he had not revealed to anyone else.

Tuan was at work as usual in the 'small room', which he did not call his 'study', in his ground floor flat in Chelsea. It was evening. The flat consisted of three bedrooms, the small room, a little dining room, a large drawing room, the hall, the kitchen, the bathroom and a very small garden. Almost all the walls were covered with books. Tuan rarely had visitors. He had some college friends, but many of these had gone away. He had in fact found in London no really close friends until he had met Uncle Tim. Tuan had seen and known Uncle Tim instantly. Their meeting in the train was mutual. It was, for

Tuan, a revelation, a meeting with a kindred soul. Not that Tim could help him much in his studies, except that they could converse about Indian mystics. It was a matter of, not exactly a master, but a wise fellow soul or brother. The affection they had for each other was mutual, but while it was often boisterously conveyed by Tim, it was secretly stored away by Tuan – so that the others did not really notice it. Tuan was of course also fond of Benet, to whom he turned more after Tim's death. That loss had been terrible; Tuan held it quietly to his heart. He was also of course fond of some of Tim's, and Benet's, friends, such as Owen, Edward, Mildred and of course 'the girls'. Tim and Owen used sometimes to tease him about 'the girls', meaning Marian and Rosalind, and also about 'girls' in general. Owen especially used to enjoy informing him that he must know by now that 'girls' were just 'not the thing!'. Tuan used to smile silently at this. In fact he had had no intercourse with either sex nor did he wish for any. He was tall and thin, his nose, faintly hooked, was thin, and so was his rather long neck. His smooth skin was of a uniform dark goldenish colour, his dark thick hair hung down very straight. He had large very dark brown eyes, questing and timid like those of an animal. His long thin hands, also brown, were mobile, often he would cross them at his neck, then send them flittering away from him like restless captive birds. It had been suggested by some that his nickname, taken by Uncle Tim from the novel, suggested not only wary timidity but fear of some fate which was bound sooner or later to catch up with him. However there was no clear evidence for this conjecture. The dreadful disappearance of Marian, the destroyed marriage, the lack of news, had distressed him very much as it had the others.

Thinking of this, he had laid down his pen. He picked it up again, but began to realise that he was tired and losing his concentration. He got up and went into the drawing room and began to walk about. Now he became conscious of sounds in the street. He thought of going down to the river, which was quite close, but decided not to. The bell of his flat rang suddenly, a long ring. He felt annoyance, wondering what it was, almost certainly it was something tiresome. He wondered if he should ignore it. The bell rang again, longer this time. Frowning he went to the front door and opened it. A woman was standing outside. It was Marian.

Tuan, pulling the door wider, stepped out and caught her as she seemed about to fall into his arms. He pulled her over the threshold and quickly closed the door. She collapsed onto the floor. He knelt, then sat down beside her, gasping. He lifted up her head. Her eyes were staring, her mouth open. For a moment he thought she had fainted or was in some sort of fit. Then she seemed to look at him. He tried to pull her up, supporting her head, but she resisted, then seemed to help him, thrusting her elbows back to lift herself. She fell back again, then he felt her hand somehow finding his hand. He said breathlessly, 'Marian, oh Marian, dear Marian – ' They were still for a moment, he now lying almost beside her on the floor. When he made another attempt to lift her, she aided him, and they reached a sitting position. He said again, 'Marian – ' She nodded as if he had only now recognised her. He got up awkwardly, then with a little of her help, hauled her up to her feet. He put his arms around her, feeling her warmth. They moved, as if dancing. He helped her out of the hall and into the drawing room, where she sank down into an armchair. He stood before her. 'Marian, dear dear Marian, don't worry, don't be afraid, I'll look after you – oh let me get you something – ' He did not know what – food, drink, milk, alcohol – or else – He murmured softly, saying 'oh dear, oh dear – '

Marian leaning back in the chair was now breathing deeply, holding one hand up to her throat. Her other hand, lying over the side of the chair, was holding the entangled loop of the handle of some sort of large bag. She was wearing a loose coat. He could now see her face, which he could scarcely recognise, he thought at first because of some ailment, then because of continuous tears. Her hair was tangled, unkempt and darkened as if wet, clinging to her head like seaweed. He said, 'Dear, dear Marian, don't be, so – ' He couldn't find the word. 'Don't grieve, you are safe – '

His murmurings seemed to be of help to her. She sat up in the chair and began clumsily to put herself in order, untangling the bag, smoothing her hair, patting her face, adjusting the neck of her dress, visible through her coat. Then she began to take off her coat, revealing a dark red cotton dress with a white collar. He helped her, awkwardly. Standing before her he said, 'Would you like some tea or coffee, some hot drink, or perhaps wine or something? – Something to eat?' This clumsy programme seemed to soothe her a little. She seemed to be wondering what she wanted. She spoke in a low husky voice, 'Yes, could you bring me a little whisky with a lot of water.'

Tuan ran to the kitchen – even as he ran all sorts of enormous problems were gathering in his head. He concentrated on the whisky, in a glass, what kind of glass, with the water separate or with, hot or cold – He was too anxious to get back to her, so afraid of her suddenly getting up and running away, he hastily made the decision, two glasses, one whisky one water, upon a tray – but he must also feed her – perhaps she was starving – he ran back.

In the brief interim Marian had opened her big bag, getting out a small mirror from a smaller bag, and found a comb which she was dragging through her hair. She asked him to pour some of the water, yes that much, into the whisky. Tuan, though not a serious drinker, felt he must have some whisky too, but could not move from his position of standing in front of her.

She said, 'I am so sorry, Tuan – '

He was so glad she used his name. 'Dear dear Marian, don't worry. I'll help you – '

'I don't want to impose on you.'

'You are not imposing, I just wish I could – '

'I won't stay long.'

'*Please, please* stay – do you want to – is there anyone you'd like to telephone?'

'No, *no*, don't ring anybody, *please*, you mustn't tell *anybody*.'

Tuan hesitated. 'Not even Rosalind?'

'No, *no*, not *her*! *Nobody* – '

'You must have something to eat, you must stay here, I have

a spare bedroom, I want you to stay here, you must be so terribly tired, and you must eat something now, *please –* '

'All right – just give me something – anything – I – '

He rushed to the kitchen and came back with some hastily buttered bread and some cheese and a slice of cake. She drank some whisky but took only one mouthful of the bread. It seemed she could hardly swallow it.

'Marian, listen, I've thought of something. They are all terribly upset, they think you might be dead – '

'I might be, I nearly was, I ought to be, I will be – '

'But oughtn't we just to let them know that you are not – just tell them – I wish you could talk to someone on the telephone, you needn't say where you are – '

'I have destroyed two men. I am going away – far away – '

'Look, I am going to ring Rosalind, I *must*, I can't do this by myself, she loves you, she will tell no one, she will do anything for you – and I *must* ring Jackson too.'

He went to the telephone. He paused. Silence. He lifted the telephone and rang Rosalind's number. She answered.

'Hello.'

'Rosalind, it's Tuan.'

'Oh Tuan – no news I suppose?'

'Listen, I want you to do something – you are alone?'

'Yes – '

'Will you come round to my place *now, at once,* and *tell nobody*?'

'Of course I will, I'll get a taxi.'

Quickly he rang Jackson's number, but with no success. He ran back to Marian. He had expected her to scream. But she was sitting with her eyelids drooping, her head fallen to her breast, her lips parted, covered with froth. He pulled his chair close to her and took hold of one limp hand. Still staring down, she slowly drew it away, her tears now falling as she leaned back, closing her eyes, seeming to fall asleep. He thought it wise not to speak again. She uttered an almost inaudible lamentation.

After twenty minutes the door bell rang. Tuan got up hastily and went to the door. He let Rosalind in and closed the door. She stood beside him, leaning back against the door. He put his fingers to his lips, then said softly, 'Marian.' Rosalind nodded. She murmured, 'I thought so.' He pointed towards the drawing room door. Rosalind went towards it, went through it, and it closed behind her. Tuan went out of the front door, shut it softly, and walked down to the river. He saw a telephone box and could not resist trying again to contact Jackson, this time with success.

'I thought I might find you here.'

The speaker was Jackson, the hearer was Tuan.

Tuan had reckoned on staying away from the house, though keeping it carefully under observation, for about half an hour. He had just turned back and was leaving the river when he encountered Jackson.

A curious partly silent friendship between these two had existed from the start, from their first meeting with Tim and Benet. In company their eyes fleetingly met, one the junior guest, the other the servant. They talked too sometimes, but as accidental encounter, not as any mutual invitation. Tuan was shy, and instinctively took Jackson for some sort of wise father figure, but of course this was a silent invention of his own. He didn't like it when others teased Jackson, or when Benet chided him.

They stood together in the street looking at each other. It was late evening, the sun was below the buildings on the other side of the Thames. Jackson stretched out a hand which Tuan seized with two hands. They began to walk back together.

'I stopped outside the door,' said Jackson, 'I could hear the girls talking inside.'

'Thank heavens you've come. No one else knows – I hope.'

They reached the door and Tuan opened it with his key.

The sound which had been audible now ceased as the two men came in. The drawing room door was open and Marian was now sitting on the sofa with Rosalind kneeling before her. Both girls were crying. Now they leapt up. Rosalind came forward to greet Jackson. She put out a hand, then embraced him. Marian simply disappeared, taking refuge in one of the bedrooms.

*

Jackson, who had had difficulty in finding a taxi and had then decided to dispense with one, had walked through the eerie brief darkness of the city, meeting with other such strange solitary walkers, he knew such creatures, he was one himself, they gazed at each other as they passed. And he found himself remembering his past and thinking about his future – was his future, some entirely new and different future totally unknown to him, about to begin? *Had* he a future?

Jackson now recalled the more immanent events of the evening. Marian had locked herself into her bedroom, and had refused to open the door except to Jackson. They sat on the bed together and Marian kissed Jackson's hands. Jackson, who had in his time performed the duties of a priest, felt his own familiar pain. She promised – she would not kill herself. She shed more tears. After that she said she was so terribly tired that she must now go to sleep, and of course she trusted Jackson 'not to tell'. She was indeed so exhausted that she then lay down and fell asleep before him. Jackson had then quietly retired. Meanwhile Tuan and Rosalind had been trying to compose an anonymous communication to be sent to Benet to say that Marian was alive and well! However this was discouraged by Jackson as being too dangerous, and they in any case bowed to his wisdom. After this Jackson set off walking and thinking.

When he reached Tara the dawn had by now become the day, it was indeed nearly nine o'clock. He observed the garage and then went into the house. It was clear that Benet was still away. What a wonderful relief that at last Marian had been found, and was now in such excellent hands, for the present at any rate! He felt very tired, and was about to set off for the Lodge when he suddenly remembered, how could he have forgotten her, *Mrs Bell*! She who had so kindly given him that address and telephone number, since he was after all that person's brother! He must see to that too even if it were now just a matter of curiosity.

Jackson had given the driver the address by memory. He had written it down carefully as Mrs Bell had pronounced it, but had now somehow left the instructions behind. However, recalling what he had so carefully recollected, he was sure he was right. The region was north London, 'near to Lord's' as the driver had remarked. St John's Wood, Lisson Grove. The taxi stopped near a church. Having paid the taxi he walked along the road upon the other side. The address was a large Victorian house, verging upon the pavement, which had been turned into flats. The flat in question, he remembered, was number three, perhaps a first-floor flat. He looked up at the windows. He thought, what's the point of all this, now that Marian's back. She won't run. They'll soon persuade her to come back to some sort of ordinary life. Why should I want to dig up some stuff which she evidently regards with fear and horror? He crossed the road and walked up two steps to the door. He surveyed the small number of bells and pressed number three. Silence. With a sense of relief he pressed it again, preparing to depart down the steps. Then a male voice said, 'Yes?'

Jackson, taken aback, said 'Oh – hello – '

Silence. Then the voice said again, 'Who are you, who is there?'

Jackson replied, 'Your brother.' He thought what an idiot I am, now he'll put the phone down!

But he did not put the phone down. He said after a brief silence, 'Come up,' and then put it down.

Jackson entered, closing the door behind him. He paused in the hall, then heard a door opening on the floor above. He mounted the stairs, saw the open door and went through it, closing it behind him. He saw another open door before him and entered a room.

Sitting behind a table covered with papers was a young man with thick long dark hair and large wide open staring brown eyes. The young man was looking at Jackson with intense annoyance, but also with curiosity, his full lips pouted. His long legs were stretched out under the table. Jackson thought at once, Spanish, like a sailor, looks Greek too. And tough.

'What is the joke?' said the young man in a cool smooth voice.

Jackson thought, Australian? He replied, 'I do apologise – I just want to talk to you.' Do I? he then wondered. What have I got to say? I'm feeling terribly tired!

'Why did you say you were my brother? How did you know I had a brother?'

'Someone said I looked like you.'

'Who said that? Who do you know who knows me?'

Now I come to think of it, thought Jackson, no one really said I looked like him, oh yes, the chap from the stables said so, after I'd suggested it. He said, 'Someone who had seen you said I looked like you.'

'*Who was it* who said that?'

'I don't know, he was just a chap at the door, and when I said I was your brother – ' I'm going to faint soon with exhaustion, Jackson thought, I ought to have waited, but then –

'So you go round telling people whom you don't know that you're my brother? But how the hell have you heard of me?'

'You're famous,' said Jackson.

'I'm not as it happens, and as it happens you don't resemble me. You are a liar. What are you up to? Are you queer?'

'No.'

'You're drunk, or else you're out of an asylum. What's your name?'

'Jackson.'

'Jackson. What Jackson?'

'Just Jackson.'

'I suggest you *get out*, Jackson. You're lying. This is just a game you play with people's bells. You say I'm famous. Do you know my name?'

'Well – ' said Jackson, 'it is true that I do not know your name – '

'So you are a filthy liar. Will you get out pronto, Mr Jackson, or shall I kick you down the stairs? I know your sort, you're looking for money, you try to frighten people by saying you know something about them. Well, you won't frighten me, you're just a mean pernicious creep, now get out – '

The man rose suddenly and came round the table and before Jackson could move he had seized hold of Jackson's arm, twisted it behind his back, and was frogmarching him towards the door. Jackson had not expected this. Yet why not? He was

136

a damn fool, he had got it all wrong, he should have waited and *thought* and put things in order, he should have had something *sensible* to say and said it at once. As it was – he kicked his adversary in the shins and as he felt the grip on his arm relaxing turned using his free hand to seize a handful of his adversary's shirt and with his other now free hand to deliver a push upon his shoulder making him stagger back. It was all over in a moment. They stood looking at each other – the other man made a savage spitting sound like a cat. He bared his teeth, then adjusted his shirt. Jackson adjusted his. He thought, this is just luck, since I'm so tired – I simply don't know what to do, I don't know now what to do or what to say.

He said, 'I'm sorry. I didn't mean this. Don't let's fight. I want to talk to you.'

The other said, 'Get out, Jackson. I could *kill* you, you know.'

Jackson thought, I must keep him talking, I've got to give him some sort of *signal*, I ought to have done that at the beginning!

He said again, 'I'm so sorry, forgive me. It's strange that I don't even know your name. All I know is that you went riding with her – ' His body was hurting somewhere, he looked round for a chair.

The man moved back behind his desk. He sat down, putting his hand up to his throat. 'Are you her husband?'

Jackson found a chair against the wall and sat on it. He thought, we are now in a different game. How am I to play it?

'No, I'm not, I'm just a servant, a messenger. She isn't married to anybody – '

'What's the man like she was going to marry? Has she run back to him?'

'No, she hasn't. Look I'm sorry, I'm just making confusion around here – '

'You know, I helped her write a note saying she didn't want to marry him. I took it down the motorway at night by car while she was asleep.'

So that was what happened, thought Jackson. Anyway I must go. He stood up.

'Don't go,' said the man. 'Just sit down.'

Jackson sat down with half his eye on the door.

'Listen,' said the man, 'I don't know what sort of fellow you are. I've just been in hell. You said you were a messenger – '

'Did I? Well, yes – '

'Would you take a message to her from me? My name is Cantor.'

Jackson had seen all this coming in the last few seconds. He felt sorry for the man, but rather dazed by the situation he had got himself into. He said, 'What sort of message?'

'That I love her and want her to forgive me and marry me.'

Jackson said, he had now already thought this out, 'Give me the message. I shall do what I can.' Cantor had opened a drawer in the table and was hastily writing. He put the paper into an unsealed envelope and passed it to Jackson. They stared at each other. Jackson rose again, put the envelope in his pocket and turned towards the door. Suddenly Cantor rose and moved around the table. Jackson stopped. Cantor strode towards him. Then reaching out he thrust something else into Jackson's hand. Jackson glanced down and saw that it was a hundred pound note. He stared at it. He smiled, dropping it upon the floor, then sidled out of the door, closing it after him. As he hurried down the stairs he heard no sound behind him.

Tuan had not imagined that after spending part of the night talking to Jackson, he would be quite unable to go to sleep. In fact after Jackson had left, Tuan walked about the flat softly, in bedroom slippers, excited, upset, sometimes pausing, gasping, ready to cry. He had carefully checked all the windows, already closely secured against burglars, and locked and bolted the front door and placed the key in a pocket of his jacket. How perfectly extraordinary, unimaginable, unforeseen, to have suddenly both the Berran girls under his roof, and under his *protection*! He had to stop and breathe deeply. Of course he had known them through Uncle Tim and then through Benet, but he had never been, or expected to be, really close to them. He had even at times felt closer to their mother, who had occasionally turned up, and had made a special game of teasing Tuan! He did not mind her teasing, which made him feel older. Now what was he to do? He wished he could have kept Jackson. One thing was certain, he had done right in summoning Rosalind. Rosalind had commonsense and could carry responsibility. He would in some way be able to 'hand Marian over' to her sister. She had already begun to calm Marian down, and had even brought sleeping pills for Marian to take. But why should Marian come to me, he wondered – perhaps indeed she would not want to go to Benet – but would she not have been better running to Mildred, or Elizabeth, or some girlfriend or friends unknown, somewhere else in London, who would shield her? Why me? He felt perturbed, but also a little proud. Yet what was he being proud of? He thought, she has come to me because I am a sort of nobody, a strange half-and-half being, without any strong or terrible emotions – like a fawn who finds a sleeping princess in a forest. It was all chaos, accident – would she stay with him, perhaps for a long time? But how could he and Rosalind go on deceiving the others, who would continue to be so intensely anxious? Softly treading, at last Tuan began to turn off the lights in the drawing room. He took off his jacket. A soft light shone in the corridor, and the doors of the two rooms where the girls were sleeping were slightly ajar, separated from his own larger bedroom. He peered round the door, slightly moving it, into the first room, where Marian was. He could not see her, only a bundle of bed-clothes pulled over her head. She was asleep. He moved to the next door, which was a little more open. Rosalind was lying half undressed upon her bed, she had evidently been too tired to get herself into bed. One long leg was showing, one distraught arm stretched out across the pillow, her head thrown back, her soft golden hair spread upon the pillow. He heard her soft breathing. He moved quickly

back. He thought, I'll just rest on my bed for a while, I'll be
sentinel. He was wakened in the morning light by Rosalind's
terrible cry.

They ran about the flat helplessly, calling out, as if they could
find her somewhere, under a blanket or a shawl. How on earth
had she got out? They went to the front door intending,
equally helplessly, to run about in the road. The front door was
locked. Tuan picked up his jacket looking for his key which he
had put as usual into his pocket. It was not there! Marian must
have found it during the night and left, carrying her belongings
with her, locking the door from the outside and keeping the
key. They were locked in! Of course they were not really
locked in since Tuan had another key, except that he could not
find it! After some search he located it and they went out into
the street, into the sunshine, people hurrying about – what
could be done? They hurried back inside. Then Tuan rang
Jackson's number, in the Lodge. No answer. He continued to
ring at intervals. No answer. If Marian had gone to any of the
others they would hear the news soon enough. Tuan had
nothing to do but wait and curse himself.

Benet, having ascertained from Clun that Edward Lannion
was now in residence at Hatting Hall, decided he would go
there and confront Edward. He was not quite sure what such a
confrontation would achieve, or even contain, but he felt he
must now see Edward face to face and discuss the whole
situation. It was now as if he were *blaming* Edward for the
situation – but of course he was not. He just wanted *something*
from him, perhaps just comfort of some sort – though of course

it was for him to comfort Edward. His heart yearned toward Edward, who must be suffering some unspeakable tragic horror. Benet's present unhappiness was also connected with Jackson. Some of his friends, especially Anna, had begun to 'borrow' Jackson, whose various talents were indeed remarkable – and Benet had agreed. But now, of late, it was all *too much*, Jackson was, it seemed, becoming too casual and perfunctory about when he might absent himself. All this thoroughly annoyed Benet; but it also hurt him in some deeper sadder way.

He was now extremely, even frenziedly, anxious to see Edward again. Perhaps Edward was mad, perhaps he was considering suicide? At first Benet had intended to drive round, but then decided to walk. Now the memory came to him with greater force – was it possible that Rosalind was madly in love with Edward? Of course it was possible. And Edward? Another wilder but suddenly, also vividly conceivable, possibility was that Marian had now actually *taken refuge* with Edward, and was *hiding* in Hatting Hall, where perhaps Rosalind was visiting her? Was she there now, ashamed, not yet ready to emerge and announce that she was ready to marry him? Would Edward have forgiven her? Yes, it was *possible* that Marian had now returned to Edward and was living with him in secret.

Benet set off down the drive and then down the path to the road. The sun was shining, it was a sunny morning, puffy white clouds coming and going. He crossed the road, climbed over the stile, hurried down the path and reached the bridge. Here he paused and took off his jacket. The bridge swayed and creaked. He thought, I must speak to Edward about this bridge. At least the village children don't dance on it anymore. He looked down at the swirling waters of the Lip which were tugging at the stems of the tall reeds. Onward onward onward forever. Dazed, then getting his eyes into focus, he could see the trembling alders beside the water, and up the bank the masses of wild summer plants in flower, some coming, some going, willow-herb, foxglove, marjoram, meadow-sweet, ragged robin, every year, every century, every millennium, and further up the bank, coltsfoot, stitchwort, campion, scarlet pimpernel, forget-me-not, every year, every year, so beautiful, so beautiful. He stood spellbound, almost tearful; and so much evil, so much evil. He left the hollow tilting planks on the bridge and pressed his way upward upon the almost invisible pathway through the thick dry grasses of the still unshorn meadow. He reached the chained-up gate and climbed over it into the next wild but roughly scythed field not far from the top of the hill. He blinked into the sunshine. Some movement was made among the shaded trees, some large brown thing, oh yes, the *horse*, now slowly moving towards him. Benet stood still, letting the horse approach him – he stroked the huge head and face which was so gently being thrust towards him, he drew his hand down over the damp nose and caressed the sleek side, he felt the warmth of the terrible loneliness of the great beast, as he lowered his brow against it. He detached himself quietly and hurried forward toward the trees where, as the crest began to flatten, he could see a hedgerow and another gate. He went on, now breathlessly, still not achieving the top and the great view down. Now suddenly, resting, he could see below him, Hatting now well in sight, its great tall windows gleaming, its turrets and battlemented roof warm and red in the sunshine. He strode down now over shorter grass and then, now upon the level, to the final gate and the tarmac road. He crossed the road onto the mown path which led to the open gates and began to hurry, now running upon gravel, past the huge mulberry trees and up the steps to the doorway. He tried the door, which did not open, then rang the jangling bell.

Millie opened the door, smiling when she saw Benet. Edward, emerging behind her, took charge, saying 'Oh, it's you!' then, 'I've been in the billiard room.' He then turned his back on Benet and crossed the hall returning to the billiard room. The room was huge, receiving a slant of sunlight. Edward went to one end of the table, leaning forward upon it on his elbows, then straightening up. He picked up a billiard cue, then put it down balancing it awkwardly. It fell to the floor with a clatter. He said, 'I was playing against myself. Well, I suppose one always does that. I mean, trying to – Let's sit down. Not in the sun.' He sat down on a velvet-cushioned chair against the wall.

Benet approached and sat upon a similar chair, pulling it away from the wall so as to survey Edward. Edward was gazing at the floor, frowning intently, as if tracing something, his mouth open, his eyes wide as if startled, with one hand drawing back a lock of his dark golden brown hair, tugging it, then letting it go, then seizing it again. He seemed to have forgotten Benet.

Benet said, 'I hope you don't mind my coming.'

'Oh? Not at all – not – at all. But there's nothing there. I shall be going away soon.'

'Where to?' said Benet cautiously, almost murmuring. 'So you *are* selling the place?'

Edward did not answer this question. Then he said, 'I've just muffed every shot – right from the start – I ought to have – now it's all impossible – I've just got to go away – '

Benet then said, 'I suppose *you* don't know where Marian is? I just wonder if – perhaps she'll come back to you?' He immediately regretted this remark.

Edward did not seem surprised. He said 'Oh no – *that's* over – and I'm – relieved, you know – now it's – nobody – '

'If you mean nobody loves you you are quite wrong! Rosalind loves you – you know she does – we all love you, Owen, Mildred, Anna – '

Edward murmured, still staring at the floor, 'Oh no – no – *no* – ' He shuddered. 'How kind of her. But there's – nothing – nothing – *nothing* – '

'I came over the hill just now,' said Benet. 'I met the horse.' He had begun to feel that Edward was falling asleep.

This slightly animated Edward. 'Yes. He's the only horse left. His name is Spencer. He's old, old. It's amazing that he's still alive.'

Benet said, 'He is lonely, he wants love.'

'Yes, yes. I'm going soon, you know – everything will go.'

'Oh *Edward*,' said Benet, '*don't, don't* – you don't mean that you are going to sell Hatting? Of course you don't – all this will pass – you must *stay* with us, you are *ours*, we won't let you go!'

Edward stood up and resumed his pose beside the billiard table. Benet rose too. He thought, I too have muffed it! He

143

moved forward, looking at the balls. He said, 'Do you remember how we used to play "Freda", running round and round this table, you and me and Uncle Tim and the children – ' He checked himself hastily.

Edward picked up one of the balls and threw it violently against another ball which in turn propelled two more balls. He stood watching with a frown. 'Yes – we ran and ran – and ran – I'll run you back to Penn. I imagine you don't want to walk back.'

'That wooden bridge is getting rickety,' said Benet. He added, 'Yes, thank you. I'm going back to London today, maybe tomorrow.'

It was nearly midday and Tuan and Rosalind had not yet been able to contact Jackson and give him the dreadful news that Marian had gone. They kept trying to imagine that suddenly she would run back. They told each other that at least she knew where there was a safe haven. Rosalind, supposed to be going back to her flat, wanted very much to stay with Tuan, although he regularly told her to go.

'Rosalind, do go back to your flat! Marian might be trying to get in there – I mean – '

'She won't go back to my flat, it's too public. And anyway – '

'Oh God, if only I hadn't fallen asleep – '

'It's time to try Jackson again.'

Tuan tried Jackson's number but there was no answer.

'She might have gone anywhere. Do you think we ought to raise a general alarm?'

'Not yet.'

'She must be terrified. She wouldn't go to Owen or Mildred, certainly not to Anna. She'd be ashamed.'

'She's ashamed *here*. It's my fault – '

'Or my fault. Oh Tuan – what can we do? Jackson should have stayed, we should have *kept* him here. All the same he is a strange man – '

'He is Jackson,' said Tuan. 'You think he's mysterious and needs some profound explanation?'

'Yes. Perhaps he's on the run from somebody or something.'

'Yet we are trusting him now.'

'You had a long talk with him last night. Do you often have long talks with him?'

'No, never alone, just a few words at Penn and Tara – I have felt then – a sort of electricity – as of a strange animal, a *good tame* animal.'

'I know, I love him too, I love you.'

'You had better go,' said Tuan, 'you *must* go. We must *wait*. I here, and you there.'

They were sitting side by side upon the sofa.

Rosalind said, 'I want to know more of you – if you don't mind – '

'There is nothing to tell.' He began to move away.

Rosalind took hold of his right hand and held it. She said, 'You are a mystery, but don't be! I love you, please love me – '

Tuan gently removed his hand. 'Dear Rosalind, please go – what matters is Marian.'

'Oh Tuan – you are engaged, you have someone else – oh my heart breaks, I love you so much – '

'I have no one – '

'But you want a man?'

'No, no, just – you don't know me – '

'You have darkness in you – let me send it away – '

'You want some one, but it's certainly not me – I have nothing to give you, you must think about Marian, not about me. Don't you *understand*? Now will you *please* go back to your flat, dear Rosalind?'

'But I want to stay with you, I want to know you, I *do* know you, I want to please you – oh my dear, just let me love you – '

Tuan shook his head. He went again to the telephone. No answer. He found Rosalind's coat and gave it to her. She rose. She went to the door, he opened it and she stumbled out.

When Jackson had reached Tara after his visit to Cantor he again looked first at the garage. Benet's car was still not there. He then entered the house. It was entirely silent. There were two or three letters in the hall, one he saw from Anna. He felt that he was losing his grip on time, perhaps on everything. He was extremely tired but must keep his wits about him. He paused. Ought he not now to go out shopping, in case Benet were to arrive? Or should he try a dodge which he despised, telephone Penn, wait for Benet's voice, then put down the telephone? He was feeling hungry, but there was plenty of food in his own kitchen. He thought, what day is it? Is it morning or evening? Of course he would telephone Tuan. He was absolutely exhausted, ready to drop, he ought to have taken a taxi. He let himself out of the back door into the garden, locked the door, and trudged towards the Lodge. The sun was shining. He recalled that he had forgotten to lock up the Lodge before leaving, thank heavens Benet hadn't seen that! He opened the door. Something was different. There was a strange smell. Something was wrong. He looked through the open door of the bedroom. There was chaos on the bed, someone was lying there. It was Marian.

'Do stop crying,' he said. He had asked her why she had run away from Tuan. He felt relief but also terrible confusion and distress. He must get her away before Benet came, he must get her away *at once*! 'Won't you let me take you back to Tuan? You are safe there. You are *safe*.' But of course she was not safe. He did not want her to run away again, but he could not keep her here and certainly not 'hand her over to Benet' against her will!

'He didn't want me,' she said of Tuan, 'I knew he wouldn't want me, he would soon have told them, Benet and – them all.'

Half lying upon the bed, half undressed, her face distorted, she seemed like a wounded animal in her moaning repetitions. She was attempting to pull up the sheets, clutching them with one hand, leaning back on the pillow.

'Nobody wants me. I have destroyed my being, I am nothing, *nothing*. Can't you *see*? I can't stay here with you.

You are very kind but you want to get rid of me, you have to. I came here only to get away – now I'll be moving on – '

'No you won't, I won't let you! I'll find you somewhere safe, I won't let you wander away – perhaps you'll let me talk to someone –!'

'No, no, *no*!'

'But, Marian, you must realise that you have done *nothing wrong* – '

'How can you say that, I have done *everything* wrong, I am like a – like a spiteful rat – everyone will – oh I don't know – want to *kill* me, I must be *killed* – '

'Marian, stop this nonsense! You decided that you did not want to marry – if you had married *then* against your own will and reason *that* would have been wrong, for both of you, Edward does not hate you or blame you – '

'Edward *hates* me. *Everybody hates me.* There has been a terrible dreadful wound, a huge bleeding scar, I must go. It was wrong of me to come here. I'll only harm you if I stay. I am mad. Benet may come. I'll just – tidy myself – and then I'll – go – I'll *disappear* – '

Sitting on the side of the bed, holding her breasts, she was sobbing, and trying to choke her sobs. Jackson thought, *of course* I will *not* let her disappear. But where can I take her to where she will *really* be safe? She may actually *recover*, perhaps quite soon, or – now I must keep my head. *Shall or shall I not show her that piece of paper?*

He said, 'Tidy yourself, yes, disappear, no! Oh *do stop*! You must *get dressed*. Have you eaten anything here, no? Then we'll both eat, I'm hungry too. Benet is away at Penn, he's staying there for several more days, he won't disturb us.' This was a wild guess.

He left her alone for a while, closing the bedroom door, locking the front door, and tactfully closing the kitchen door, leaving access to the bathroom. He suddenly felt something 'coming over' him, like a dark cloud, of course tiredness, but something more. He started shaking his head like a horse. A loss of identity. He looked at the telephone. He seized it and rang Tuan's number. As soon as Tuan made a sound he *whispered*, 'She's OK. Keep quiet,' and put down the receiver.

147

Then he silenced the telephone. Then he thought, *is that wise?* Then shaking himself again he set about rapidly putting together something like a breakfast, bread, butter, marmalade, milk, coffee, but of course it wasn't breakfast, it would be, wouldn't it, more like tea. He put out chocolate biscuits and a currant cake. He listened, then said, 'Hello.' She emerged from the bedroom wearing the dark red cotton dress with white collar which she had been wearing at Tuan's flat. What had she been wearing when he saw her, so few minutes ago? He could only partly remember, he could recall a black petticoat, a brassière showing, dark stockings, the red dress upon the floor. He felt a terrible anguish. What on earth could he do for her now? He smiled, bowed like a waiter indicating a chair. She sat down, staring up at him. She had powdered her face and combed her hair.

'Breakfast is served! You like coffee?'

'Yes.'

'Would you like some bacon? It wouldn't take a moment.' He had forgotten that.

'No, no! Just coffee. I've got to be going anyway. I mustn't stay here.'

'I shall be going with you. *Please* eat something. Look, I'll put some butter and marmalade on that bread.'

He stood, dealing with the bread and marmalade. At least she did not object. She sipped coffee.

There was a strange smell in the kitchen, the smell that had been in the bedroom. He breathed it in thoughtfully, a mixture of sweat and perfume.

She said to him, sipping the coffee, 'How old are you?'

This startled Jackson. He wondered which of his ages he should most tactfully offer. He said, 'Forty-three.'

People rarely asked him. He thought of a number. He also recalled, as he always did on these occasions, his first meeting with Uncle Tim, when they looked at each other, when Tim asked him, and then in silence looked again.

She drank half of the coffee, but declined the rest of the breakfast. He looked at her and thought how beautiful she was. He was about to say, how beautiful you are.

She said, 'Thank you for harbouring me. I *will* go, I will have to – I must go away, *right* away, I must *disappear*, I don't mean suicide. I have just wrecked my life. I shall have to make a plan. I shall go abroad *forever*. You cannot realise how desperate I am.'

'It may help you to say all this, but none of it is real. People have experienced far more terrible things and recovered from them.'

'Have *you* experienced such things?'

'You are not a criminal, you have not done any dreadful deed, just be quiet for a while, go back to Tuan and Rosalind, or stay with Rosalind, no one will blame you, don't you realise that! I will take you back now, you must *rest* – '

'I *don't want* to stay with Rosalind, I came to Tuan not Rosalind – all *that* is over anyway!'

Jackson thought, yes, she was ashamed before Rosalind. 'Never mind Rosalind. You could just stay with Tuan, he would care – '

'No, no, he likes Rosalind, I *can't rest*, I won't destroy myself, I shall just hide, I shall take another name, I shall go far away to a place where no one will find me – '

'This is all nonsense. I won't let you disappear! Can't you just understand about Benet, I could talk to him, I wouldn't say where you were – '

'I *have said* that I *will not* see Benet –!'

'I'm sorry, all right then Mildred, or – '

'I shall leave this country, oh – *you don't understand what terrible pain is like!*'

Jackson thought, I'm getting nowhere with this. Let me try another tack. He said, 'Listen, Marian, at least answer me some questions truthfully, I mean calmly. You have been speaking of how you have hurt Edward and made him hate you. But Edward does not hate you and you have not really hurt him. I believe that there is *someone else* too whom you think you have thrown away, who you *imagine* hates you – is there not such a person?'

Marian flushed. She said, 'How do you know these things? There is someone else whom I have damaged and who hates me far more than Edward does – that person is a demon and would kill me. You see, I am doubly destroyed.'

Jackson took the piece of paper out of his pocket and handed it to her.

On the same day of Benet's visit, Edward Lannion had returned to London. He was profoundly upset, made even more so by Benet's clumsy idiotic insinuations, suggesting that perhaps Edward would take Marian back, was already perhaps hiding her somewhere or then, put off that track, that he, having hurt Marian, might like to take up Rosalind instead! Benet's attentive sympathetic eyes, his familiar kindly face, now faintly reminiscent of Uncle Tim, his evident desire to *touch* Edward, to comfort him and stroke him, made Edward ready to wail with abhorrence. Of course Benet had been so kind to him. But now – and also the tiresome reference to the bridge, and to Spencer, as if tactfully drawing attention to some misdemeanour – all this was too much. For a while Edward stayed in the billiard room, moving round the table, catching the balls by hand and making them move each other. Why had he gone into the billiard room anyway? It was so reminiscent of the past. The sheer dark heaviness of the table suggested the past, the far past, a place where he had been innocent and free, very very long ago. He remembered his father, his father's gentle solemnity, before the catastrophe. He pictured his dear mother dying, so young, his father weeping, he and his brother crying. His brother drowning. He thought about Marian. Then he drove in his sleek red car very fast to London, put the car in the garage, then walked about, stopping and staring blindly at things, avoiding certain places, then driven by hunger to a little Italian restaurant which he had not seen before where he ate little, realising it must by now be at least the afternoon. From the terrible moment of Marian's communication, and indeed before that, yes well before that, Edward had struggled secretly and silently with his great dark demon. He had drowned Randall, failed Marian, perhaps killed Marian, and there was *another hideous fault*, an *old* fault which he could not remedy and which might well finally drive him to suicide. He could see no possible road, even one far far ahead, which could lead him to happiness. *Happiness*! Not to joy, not even to continued sanity. There was only one thing which he might do, one *real* thing, but it was now more and more clear that he would not do it. He paid the bill and walked out into the warmth, among the colourful crowds who jostled him in friendly ways. He passed noisy jolly pubs, their doorways wide open, spilling onto pavements, somewhere, perhaps in some park, birds were singing, the rich sky hung cloudless, there would be no dark, was not that the evening star? He blundered on, feeling that he would fall. He was lost. At last he took a taxi, returning to his house, to solitude and nightmare.

When Jackson had handed Marian the piece of paper he had not known what response to expect to Cantor's message. *Marian I love you please please come back to me, please marry me.* They had been sitting at the kitchen table opposite to each other. She was determined to go away forever, she had dreadfully hurt Edward, he hated her, she hated him, no, she would not see Tuan, she would not see Rosalind, or Mildred or Benet! It was after this that Jackson had tried to conjure up 'the other', at least hoping for some kind of clement change. This did not occur.

Marian read the message, she read it twice as if calmly, then tore it in two and threw it on the floor whence Jackson retrieved it. She said nothing, looking at Jackson with a tense savage coldness, he saw her teeth chattering, he saw them bared.

He said awkwardly, 'You know his writing.'

'Of course!'

'But don't you believe what he has written?'

'No, it's nothing, *nothing* – '

'You think – well, what – a sort of trap?'

'He hates me, I hate him, all that is *over*. You don't know what he's done, you don't know what I've done, you don't understand how far far away I am now – '

'Marian,' said Jackson, 'don't be angry with me. Listen, I have been to see Cantor, I have talked to him – '

'*You went to see him*? How did you find this, he gave it to you –?'

'Of course he did, where else did I get the message from –?'

'You have met him, you have seen him, you have talked about me, do you think that pleases me – I *detest* it – do you think I'll run to him just after that? Everyone is *cruel* to me, everything is *mad, mad, mad* –!'

'Oh Marian, don't cry *please* – '

'Don't you see that I *hate* myself – '

'No, no, you mustn't, you don't, you must *believe*, you must go where love is, this is a *truthful* message, do have hope, he loves you, I know he does – '

'I have destroyed everything around me, everyone despises me, even if they try to be kind they despise me, you despise me, I hate it all – '

'All right, suppose I drive you to Mildred, or to Elizabeth – '

'I don't want to see them, *I hate* them – oh Jackson, help me, help me – '

'I'll stay with you, I'll be with you.' But what on earth can I do, he thought, *I am so tired*. He wondered if he were actually falling asleep. He moved his chair round the table and put his arm round her shoulder, holding on to her white collar and gripping the fabric of her summer dress. For a moment she yielded, leaning her head down, then stiffly moving away. Tears were coming down her cheeks, she touched them with the back of her hand.

'I stayed in a hotel then,' she said, 'I'll find somewhere. I can get money from my bank. I'm going to leave the country as quickly as possible. Thank you, thank you, I must go now, *now* – '

'Wait,' he said, 'I'll go with you, I know a little quiet place, a lodging house, no one comes, I'll take you there, you could be quiet – let's go now – '

He led her, holding her hand, carrying her suitcase, looking anxiously at the house, out of the garden and through the side door by the garage and out into the street. He hurried along, pulling her after him, until he found a taxi.

'You're sure no one will find me?'

'Yes yes. I'll come tomorrow – '

'Oh Jackson – in so little time – I have destroyed my life – '

'All will be well with you, my dear dear girl – '

In the taxi he sat sideways looking at her, touching her, touching her face, kissing her hand.

'It's a little secret place, I know it, it's flats, all separate, I'll come along tomorrow!'

They got out of the taxi, Jackson paid the fare. Holding her wrist he led her towards the house. He pressed the bell for flat number three.

'Yes?'

'It's me – I've got a friend – can I come up?'

'Yes!'

'Good – just leave the doors open.' He said to Marian, 'It's just up the stairs, don't worry.'

Cantor left the upstairs doors open. Jackson entered first, leading Marian. Then he released her, dropped her suitcase, and stepped back.

Cantor was standing in front of his desk. When he saw Marian he opened his arms. When she saw him she gave a loud cry and would have fallen to the floor had he not caught her in his embrace. She did not struggle.

Jackson stayed a moment or two, then closed the door on the landing and hurried down the stairs. Another job accomplished. Or was it? Would she come running back? Or would she simply run away and get lost again? He felt exhausted. He had had no sleep since – since when? He realised that it was now evening. It was very hot. He couldn't find a taxi for some time, and had to walk most of the way back to Tara.

Jackson, at a little distance from the house, approached cautiously. Had Benet returned? No car visible, perhaps in the garage, no. He went up the steps and in at the front door. He walked about. No, Benet had not returned. He became

153

conscious of the terrible exhaustion, how dreadfully tired he was – in the old days he had been able to carry on day and night! He was also very hungry. He went into the kitchen. He went into the larder. He sat down at the table. He ate some bread and butter, he sipped a little white wine from an almost empty bottle in the fridge. He very rarely drank alcohol. Was he celebrating his success with Marian? Ah, but was it a success? He must wait until tomorrow. He thought of ringing Tuan, but that too had better be left till tomorrow. He looked at the unseemly chaos upon the table. He appeared to be dozing. He got up. He would feel better soon. He went into the drawing room and sat down upon the sofa.

Benet left Penndean early in the morning. Yesterday had been hot, today was to be hotter. He had rung Edward on the previous evening 'to cheer him up' but Montague had told him that Edward had gone to London. He rang Edward's London address in the evening and when leaving in the morning but without any answer. He felt depressed and irritated. He had also rung Tuan in the evening, hoping to find someone at home, but Tuan sounded rather confused and hasty, perhaps about to go out. He rang Rosalind who seemed to be rather tearful and incoherent. He rang Anna, but she was out and Bran answered the telephone rather curtly with a French accent, put on, Benet thought. Of course there was no news of Marian.

He reached Tara early, although he had been briefly detained by a queue just entering London. The sun was already becoming extremely hot. He put the car into the garage, then mounted the steps at the door of the house. He opened the door. A waft of loneliness and sadness came to him. He thought of Marian lying dead in some dim rented room, he thought of Anna's wild tears, what did they mean, Rosalind's tears, Edward's awful coldness, his dreadful hatred. 'I hate her now, I hate everybody.' He moved slowly across the hall, peering into the various rooms. He noticed a deplorable disorder in the kitchen and paused. He was increasingly conscious of a rift between himself and Jackson. Who did Jackson think he belonged to anyway? He seemed to be always away, helping everybody but Benet! Perhaps Benet had better 'hand him over'! Benet had purposely refrained from ringing him up, so as to find him out in some sort of ignominy! Benet felt a little ashamed of this, on his part, a lack of trust. But really things were, were they not, going a bit too far! He wandered slowly out of the kitchen, back into the hall.

The sun was shining, it was very hot, he took his jacket off and undid his shirt. Where was Jackson anyway? Perhaps he was doing something in the garden. He went down, and out of the back door. No sign of Jackson. How beautifully warm and sunny it was. It was early. Perhaps Jackson had gone out shopping. Benet made for the Lodge. The sun was striking the back of his neck, and he put up his hand to protect it. He knocked, then opened the door. Silence. He called out, then entered the kitchen. He was shocked to see upon the table another scene of disorder. Also there was a strange smell. He crossed the kitchen and threw open the door of the bedroom. What he saw appalled him. The little room was in total chaos. The bed dragged about, the mattress visibly dislodged, the sheets hanging down, the blankets tangled in a knot upon the floor. He stood still, breathing deeply, gasping. There was a strange nauseating smell. It looked as if there had been some sort of struggle – animals, or people – fighting – making love – *horrified*, he closed the door, trying to think. In the kitchen the table seemed to have been for two. What had Jackson been up to in the Lodge? He might have had some, any, woman there. Or a *man*! Benet quickly moved out into the sunshine. He felt like weeping or shouting. Whatever it was, Jackson had been wantonly deceiving him. How could he have been so idiotic, so wanton, so *stupid*, as to leave these traces behind! Where was he now, was it possible that he had a *man friend*? Benet returned to the house. He stood for a while in the hall, trying to *work out* the senseless madness of the whole situation.

The telephone rang. He rushed to it. It was Anna.

'Oh Benet dear, hello, is there any more news?'

'No, I'm afraid not – of course I'll let you know if there are any developments.'

'You rang Bran, didn't you, I hope he wasn't naughty or – '

'No he was very kind – I've been hurrying about rather.'

'By the way, I wonder if I could have Jackson for tomorrow morning?'

'Yes, I expect so, he's not here at the moment, I'll tell him – in fact, *yes, yes*, you can have him!'

'Benet, thanks so much, you are an angel, and so is he!'

Benet put the telephone down. Where was Jackson, just when he was desperately needed! 'Oh *God*, I feel so tired,' he said aloud. He thought he would go into the drawing room and lie down. He could scarcely walk for tiredness. He pulled himself along, pushing open the drawing room door, then closing it behind him. He moved toward the mantelpiece dragging his steps. He put his hand on the back of the sofa and moved forward.

Then *something dreadful*. There was some *awful thing* upon the sofa. It was a man. *It was Jackson.*

Benet came round and looked down. Was he dead? No, he was breathing, he looked *terrible*. He was half clothed, he was fast asleep, and he was apparently drunk.

Benet bent down and sniffed. Yes, *drunk*, and *deeply* asleep. He stood there meditating, looking down upon the heavily slumbering man. How utterly wretched he looked, his jacket crumpled up upon the floor, his shirt undone to the waist, his chest showing, he had not shaved, he looked dirty. He was certainly dead asleep. Benet looked down upon his closed eyes, his long eye-lashes, his dark tangled hair, and sighed.

Benet went back into the hall and sat down upon a chair. He put his hands upon his face. He sat there for a while breathing slowly.

At last he reached out and took some paper out of the small table which stood beside the chair, and wrote. What he had written he laid upon the table. He sat still for a while his hands upon his lap, his lips open, his eyes glazed. He fumbled for a large handkerchief in his pocket. He got up quietly and put together some belongings. He left through the front door, closing it gently, and went down the steps. He went to the garage and drove his car out, and returned to Penn. Fortunately there was not much traffic.

Jackson woke up. He had a headache. He lay still for a while. Where was he? He recalled having taken Marian to Cantor. What became of that? He would have to ring up. Better, just go over. He tried to lift his head. Difficult. Yes, Marian had been with him. He began to sit up. The bright sunlight from the tall windows dazzled his eyes. He fell back again. He thought, the mountains, Tim and the mountains. Messages – that was what Tim saw – just at the last moment – when he said – I see, I see.

Jackson sat up and looked about. Where was he, in what place, where? Of course he had been with Marian – he closed his eyes. He opened them again. He was in the drawing room at Tara. He listened. Silence. He tried to get up but fell back. He became conscious of a headache. Why on earth was he in the drawing room, *sleeping in the drawing room*, with all his clothes on? Well, mostly on. The thought rushed into his head – he must have been drunk! After all he had had no sleep for two days and plenty of extremely tiring things to do! He had been in the kitchen and eaten bread and butter, then that little wine, all the same – just as well no one had seen him sprawled out on the sofa! He stood up carefully, then picked up his coat from the floor. The bright sun was dazzling him, he must get out into the hall. He dropped his coat again and began to tidy up the sofa. He was horrified that he had been drunk, which he hardly ever was. Surely no one had been there, impossible. He went out into the hall, went up the stairs, came down again. He thought, I must tidy up the kitchen. I left it in a mess, what a terrible stupid fool I am! Then he thought, shouldn't I telephone Cantor and find out if it's all OK, she hasn't run away again or something. As he approached the telephone he suddenly saw a sheet of paper with writing upon it lying upon the table. He picked it up. It was from Benet.

157

Dear Jackson,

I returned to find you drunk, sleeping in the drawing room. I am sorry to have to say this, but I need as a butler, helper, man-of-all-trades etc., someone who is constant and reliable, not a drunk, and not likely to be always somewhere else. You must know how much anguish we are all suffering. I also believe you have been disgracefully entertaining a woman in the Lodge which I find *most objectionable*. Moreover: I agreed that you might occasionally, with my permission, do odd jobs for my friends. It now seems that you are constantly to be found in other people's houses, not in mine. Bluntly, I believe that you have found my establishment rather dull, and found more entertainment elsewhere. There may be some satisfaction, for both of us, that you will have no difficulty in obtaining other employment. I enclose in a nearby envelope your pay for this quarter and for several weeks thereafter. I am now returning to Penn for several days during which you will have time to pack up all your goods and go.

Yours sincerely
Benet Barnell

Beneath this, in a hasty scrawl, was written:

I am sorry. I trusted you.

Jackson folded up the sheet of paper and put it in his pocket. He left the pay envelope where it was. Then he stood motionless, looking down, for some time. Then he sighed deeply. What a senseless blunder. A modest amount of wine combined with two days and nights' constant activity with very little food and without sleep. Of course he was not used to wine. As if that mattered. He uttered a long sobbing sigh. 'I trusted you.' Anyway it was true that he had been for some time away from the house. Any point in trying –? No. He moved away from the table. Then he returned: he could at least telephone Cantor. If only *that* has not also ended in tears!

He rang. 'Hello, is that Cantor!'

'It absolutely is Cantor, and Marian is here, and you are the hero! Won't you come round and see us? You have made us *so happy* – you really really have – you have *rescued* us – you must be a *magician* – wait a moment, Marian – '

'Jackson darling, it's Marian, it's really me, I feel I've been made into some wonderful absolutely new person, I've simply lost my old self, and so *quickly*, and *you did it*! It's like a lot of confused rubbish being suddenly jumped about and made into a perfect being, I mean I thought I had destroyed myself – '

'And me, Cantor, – back to Marian.'

'I know I've been awfully bad – '

'No, she hasn't – Cantor again – '

'Yes, yes, but really and truly we might have simply lost each other, I was absolutely broken, hating myself and thinking about suicide – '

'So was I – then *you* appeared like a *god*, dear Jackson – '

'I'm very very pleased,' said Jackson. 'Everyone will be so glad. Will you send the news around, or shall I, or – do you want to keep it quiet for a while –?'

'Well, really we're off to Australia almost at once, aren't we, darling.'

'Yes, dear Jackson, Cantor has finished his business – '

'*You* are my business, angel.'

'Anyway we'll be off, and we'd be glad if you would tell *them* we've gone, but *of course* we shall come back! They won't murder us, will they?'

'Certainly not,' said Jackson. 'They'll be delighted, they may even come to see you!'

'I expect we've made a bit of a nuisance of ourselves, but they haven't made much fuss of it, have they?'

'No, they haven't, they've been very sensible, they just wanted to know where you were. I mean you, Marian – '

'Of course they don't yet know about *me* – or do they? I expect they've had other things to do!'

'Jackson, dear heart, I know they must have been bothered at first, but you can tell them that we're sorry to leave so soon – '

'When are you leaving?'

'We're leaving by plane tomorrow – but we'll be here again.

I shall write a letter to Benet explaining it all – he's not too bothered is he?'

'Oh no, no – '

'Jackson, do come over here *now* – '

'No, I can't.' What time is it, he wondered. 'But oh I am *so glad* – '

'Where are you now, by the way?'

'I'm at Tara. Benet is at Penn.'

'Wait a minute – yes darling, yes – Marian thinks she'd better just telephone from the airport, and write later.'

'Whatever you do,' said Jackson, 'please don't bring me in!'

'But you're the – never mind, all right – Marian will ring – don't worry – of course we'll write to Benet later on, he's the one, isn't he, he'll forgive us, won't he, we'll *both* write – '

'Yes,' said Jackson. 'Please *both* write.'

'Oh – yes, yes – It will be simple, and we'll write to you too – where should we send it to, Tara or Penn?'

Jackson closed his eyes. Oh – *dear*! He opened his eyes and said, 'Could you direct the letters for me *via* Tuan, it will be easier, Benet will be away soon and I – Marian will know, she will give you the address – '

'Who's Tuan? It's a lovely name – '

'Look, my dears, I must stop, I'll think of you both tomorrow up in the air – '

'But you *will* come, my dear brother, won't you, and we'll be back – '

'Yes, yes, be well, be happy, you have made me very very glad – don't forget, when you write to Benet, *don't* mention me!'

Jackson tidied up the kitchen, then he spent some time cleaning up the scene in the Lodge. This was not easy. The bedroom was a tangled wreck. It occurred now with force to Jackson that *this* had been the picture which had confronted Benet not so long ago. No wonder . . . He thought, of course it was all a *mistake*, what he imagined was *not true*! Should I not simply *stay here* and tell him what happened? Well, what did happen? Somehow he could not bear it, to have to explain or apologise or crawl to Benet. Some of what Benet said about his going out to other people's houses was true, though surely he had almost always *told* Benet, and *asked* – Benet was often not interested or away. He had never wasted Benet's time or in any way cheated him. Well, all this could not be sorted out now. He worked on the scene for some time, he folded things and washed things. A terrible anguish crushed his breast. Everything had come down. He brought out his two large suitcases and filled them up, then, since there was so much left over, emptied them again and filled them carefully, tagging on a few plastic bags. He ran back to the house, looking about him in case he had left anything of his own behind anywhere. He felt he was going mad – so many other matters – he was ready to weep – he pulled himself together. In the Lodge he checked his luggage again. He picked up his coats, then put them down. Where was he going? Ought he to go back into the house? Of course, he would have to lock up everything and leave the keys, he had forgotten that! Also – should he leave any sort of statement, explanation, apology in the hall for Benet to see? No, there was nothing to say.

He put on his overcoat, slinging his mackintosh over his arm. He lifted up the suitcases, the mackintosh running down over his wrist. He dropped the suitcases. He had pocketed the house keys, but the Lodge keys were hung up in the kitchen. He put the suitcases outside, together with his mackintosh and bags, closed the Lodge door and locked it, picked up the suitcases then began to walk slowly towards the house. He went round to the steps which ran up to the front door. He left the suitcases, bags, and mackintosh beside the gate. He took off his overcoat and dropped it. He went up the steps and let himself in. He went through the hall and down to the lower level and the 'garden door'. He locked the door and returned to the hall. He laid all the keys down on the table on top of the envelope which contained the pay which Benet had kindly left him! He looked round the hall. He did not look into the drawing room or the kitchen. He went out of the front door closing it carefully behind him. As he went down the steps he heard the telephone ringing inside. Down at the gate he put on his coat, then put on his mackintosh, then, clinging on to the rest of his luggage, made his way out to the road, closing the gate with his foot. He began to walk slowly along the road. Soon he saw a taxi and gave the taxi man the address of a hotel.

SEVEN

Tuan, who would normally on that day have gone out, was staying at home in case of telephone calls. It was still quite early morning. He was also so unhappy and so distressed he felt he must hide himself away. He decided to resume his studies of Maimonides but could not concentrate. He walked round and round the room, drawing his hand over the books. His father had been a devout Jew, but not a Jewish scholar. Could he, Tuan, become such a thing as a Jewish scholar? Jewish scholarship, Jewish mysticism? Religious values, mystical values? What is mysticism, can it relate to philosophy? How does all this relate to 'God', is there a God – a *living* God, does that not mean some sort of *limited person*? The great difference between the Jewish God and the Christian God.

Distracted, he thought of ringing up Benet. But if he rang him he would have to make some account. Of what? Well, of *anything* – at present he felt *guilty* of *anything*! Something about Marian – but what could he say? Oh if only *that* grief could be removed. He had been rude and hasty to Rosalind, of course he had to tell her to go, but had he not done so in an unkind way? He now very much regretted the sort of sinister things he had said to her – moreover, somehow, he had said too much. He wondered if he should go to see her, but that was *impossible*, and now she would avoid him. He had rung Jackson's Lodge number at intervals, but that was silent. What was happening now to Marian, where was she? Oh poor Marian. He could not ask questions now, he was an outcast.

The door bell rang. He ran to it.

'Oh, Rosalind, have you any news?'

'No. I waited a while for telephone calls, then I went over to Tara but I couldn't get in, I mean there seemed to be no one there!'

'Thank you for coming here. Don't go away yet – '

'Tuan, darling, are you mad!'

'What do you mean? I am sorry, I have offended you.'

'Let's sit down.'

They went and sat down on the sofa. She took hold of his hand.

'Tuan, I love you, I want to marry you.'

'Dear, dear Rosalind, you don't know me, this is just an impulse, a hasty movement, after all the distress we have been through. You are being very kind to me and I wish you well with all my heart, but we must think about your sister – '

'But you love me, I *know* you do, we want each other, there has been a barrier and it is broken, I am the only person who understands you – of course I think about Marian, but – '

'My dear child – '

'I am almost as old as you. How old are you?'

'Thirty.'

'Well, I am nearly twenty-three, so we are just right! I know, you have had dreadful troubles, perhaps because of your parents, I know you grieved so much when they died, I am sorry, I know I must not speak of that – and yet in time I must, I must speak of *everything*. I have been watching you ever so long, ever since Uncle Tim found you on that train from Edinburgh – '

'Please – '

'He told us about that, and how he loved you at once. I have loved you at once.'

'Will you please *stop* – '

'He gave you your name – what was your other name?'

'Thomas, but – '

'You have a Jewish name too, will you tell it to me?'

'Where did you – never mind – it is Jacob.'

164

'I love that name too – but I shall keep it secret between us. Uncle Tim also told us what your name meant, Tuan, how it was a tragic and a noble name – '

'You are a child, a charming child. But please do not go on with this talk, it will lead us nowhere, it would just lead into the dark.'

'You have sorrows – oh please forgive me – I want to hold you and save you – '

'Yes, you are a child, a thoroughly romantic child. I am very very far away from you. Forgive me. I have to be alone.'

'To be forgiven and to be alone forever? Like Jackson!'

'Why do you think like that about Jackson?'

'I don't know – I think he is going away – I don't want him to go away – anyway he is very lonely – '

'He is a strange man, and he is a good man.'

'So are you, let us return to you. I want you to tell me something about your life.'

'Rosalind, I *cannot* – there is no life – I mean there is – nothing to tell – '

'Oh come – there is something you know of, something you have seen, the suffering of someone else – you have been so secretive, so shy and reticent – '

Tuan stood up, he walked several paces to and fro. 'Enough, *enough*, dear Rosalind, please go now. You came here because of Marian. There are things I cannot explain. I should not have spoken. Please leave me, oh *please leave me.*'

Rosalind said, 'You must understand my love, you must *believe* in it, you must not let *that* destroy my love, our love, for I *know* that you love me. And I have loved you for a long time, I am not a child, I cannot leave you, I want to be entirely with you, I want your suffering to be my suffering. Please at least tell me *something, please* – '

Tuan walked up and down the room in silence, then sat down again, drawing up a chair opposite to her. 'All right, I will tell you something. Just one thing. I will tell you and it will distress you, and you will tell no one else.'

'I will tell no one else.'

'It is about the past – oh the past, how soon it can vanish and be forgotten. Even the hugest and most hideous things may fade – yet such things also must never be forgotten – '

Rosalind said, 'The Holocaust?'

'Yes. Perhaps there is nothing more to say – '

'*Please* – '

'It concerns my father and my grandfather. It is a story that my father told me. It was when the war was already on. Many people, our people, for a long time did not realise what terrible danger they were in. Many stayed till the last moment. Many stayed too long. My grandfather was a lucky one to escape – to escape by an ordinary train, to pass a frontier, to board a boat and to come to Britain. My father described to me the fear, the terror, of those last moments in that train – my grandfather, my grandmother, my father and his sister – Time was passing and the train was still. My father was then fourteen, his sister was twelve. His sister had been crying because, when hurrying away from the house, they had left the dog behind. My grandfather explained that they couldn't take the dog, and anyway they couldn't go back now, when the train was leaving at any moment. Our house, abandoned, was quite close to the railway station. Then suddenly his sister pushed her way through and jumped onto the platform and began to run. My father tried to run after her and stop her, but my grandfather violently took hold of him and wouldn't let him go. My father kept crying, I'll stop her, I will, I'll bring her back, but my grandfather just gripped him, holding him violently, while the train was still. The time, the terrible time was passing, and my grandmother kept crying, surely by now she will be back. Then suddenly the train began to move. My grandmother was hysterical. My grandfather and my father looked out of the window. 'She is here, she is here!' But already the train was moving too fast. The last my father saw of her was his sister standing on the platform with the dog in her arms.'

Rosalind was crying. 'And of course –?'

'And of course they never saw her – they never found a trace of her again – my father told me – he never told my mother – my father said to me, he said more than once, that he could have stopped her and brought her back, if his father had let him. And then he blamed himself. "When she jumped down

166

and started to run away along the platform, I could have got free and run after her. I could have seized her and pulled her back to the train. Only my father would not let me, he held me so violently!" '

Rosalind had covered her face with her handkerchief.

'So, Rosalind, you see – and that – that was – and is – with me. And *more* – and *more* and *more* I think of her, I think of *them* – millions, tens of millions – how can there be such evil, it must be held up before the whole world forever. My little story is *nothing*. Now do stop crying.'

'I am sorry, it's *so much* – but can I not love you and be with you all the same – will it not be better for you, I mean – '

'*No, no* – '

'Perhaps you want to marry a Jewish girl – '

'Not that. I just can't – I must carry it, for my father and my grandfather and *all* – that burden, forever, that pain – the *whole thing* – I'm sorry – that's why I cannot marry – anyone – I am so sorry. Well, I know you can't understand – '

'Perhaps I could – ' said Rosalind. 'Perhaps something, I think I might – but let us just wait a while – I am so – taken away. Just let me recover. I can come to you – in a little while – *please* – '

'I am very sorry, I didn't want you – to have any illusions. I know you will say *nothing* of this to anyone.'

'Have you told anyone else?'

'Well, yes. I have told Jackson – now I have told you – foolishly – it must stop here, it must stay with me. Please, dear Rosalind, *go away* – your being here torments me. *Please.*'

He went to the door and opened it. Rosalind picked up her jacket and her handbag and went out through the door.

Owen opened the door. He stared at Jackson and at the suitcases.

'What's up? Come in! Are you going on a cruise?'

'No – I hope you don't mind looking after this stuff while I'm away.'

'Certainly, bring them in, gosh they're heavy, are there bombs in? Just shove them there. What's that taxi doing?'

'I don't want to bother you, I'll be away for a while – I must go now – '

'Oh no, you won't! I'll get rid of the taxi, just sit down in that chair.'

Jackson sat down. He closed his eyes. Owen paid the taxi and returned and shut the door.

'Now get up and we'll go and sit in the drawing room and you'll tell me *everything*. Lean on my arm.'

Jackson had, he was sure, not intended to stay with Owen longer than was necessary to leave the luggage. But the thought of 'sitting down' overcame him and he weakened, feeling that at any moment he might fall down and go to sleep. He followed Owen into the drawing room. They stood opposite to each other. Jackson reached out one hand to hold the edge of the marble fireplace.

'You look dead beat,' said Owen. He reached out, seizing Jackson by the shoulders, detaching him from the marble and shaking him, then guiding him gently to an armchair. Jackson sat down.

'I'm sorry, I just wanted to park that stuff, I'm most grateful, I really want to go on – '

'Where to? I won't let you go. Has Benet kicked you out?'

'Yes. He left a letter – '

'*What* – has he *really* kicked you out? I can't believe it! What have you done – or rather what has *he* done? All this is madness! Thank heavens you've come to me. But really, you can't have done anything wrong, it's perfectly impossible, you don't do wrong things!'

'It's all my fault,' said Jackson. 'He was fed up with my going round to do jobs in other people's houses.'

'Well. What were you doing in other people's houses?

Maybe he had a point! You've never done much here! No, no, I'm just teasing, how *dare* I tease you when you're so terribly tired? I'm *very* surprised at Benet losing his temper. He'll want you back tomorrow.'

'I don't think so. I messed things up. I really must go out, go on – '

'Where to? Who to? I'll go with you. I've often wondered where you were going! Let us go together!'

'I don't want to – '

'You are about to say you don't want to be a nuisance and so on, but you must realise, you must be *certain*, that I am *very glad to see you* and I *am going to hold on to you*. Now sit quiet here. I shall bring some things to eat and to drink and we shall sit at this little table. You seem ready for a dead faint.'

Leaning back in the armchair Jackson experienced a strange though faintly memorable sensation coming as if from long ago as of being embraced by a huge warm watery substance which rose gently above his head, not death, not drowning, but coming as it were to his rescue. He let his head fall gently onto the back of the chair. He closed his eyes for a moment. He heard Owen's voice far away. He went to sleep.

He woke up. Owen was looking down at him. He sat up. After a few seconds he remembered. He said, 'I am so sorry. I think I slept.'

'Yes, you did. I didn't wake you. It's just as well I pulled you in here. Time has passed. Now you shall eat and drink. Then I shall send you to bed.'

'What time is it?'

'Nine o'clock.'

'*Nine o'clock?*'

'Yes, in the evening. I forgot to tell you about Mildred. She's gone to India where they wear saris and squat on the ground. God or Krishna has sent you to me. Now let us eat and drink and be merry.'

Owen had laid out a little table with whisky and red wine and orange juice and ham sandwiches and olives and plums and cherry cake. Jackson stared at these. The whole business of Tara and Benet's return came back to him. He felt sick with shame and grief. He hung his head. He also wondered whether Marian and Cantor were all right, and whether they were now far away. He drank a little orange juice, and some water which he asked Owen to bring. He ate a ham sandwich and an olive. He felt an extraordinary burden, like an animal clinging to his back and shoulders. He said to Owen, 'I'm terribly sorry – '

'I know, you want to go to bed. I can see – tomorrow you'll tell me – I hope. Come, I'll help you up, I'll get you up the stairs, hold onto me, that's right, come on, just another flight up, we're nearly there, I always keep this place ready, just in case, only no one comes, only you – that's an omen, there's the bathroom, can I get you – all right, all right – I'll pull the curtains, it's a huge bed you know – no I won't, not yet anyway – I can't tell you how glad I am that you have taken refuge with me. May I kiss you – will you kiss me – thank you, darling, I love you, goodnight, dear Jackson.'

Jackson woke up. He was lying in a bed, in a strange bed, in a huge bed in a strange room. Sunlight was coming in through slits in heavy curtains. His head was being lifted by a mass of big soft pillows. He breathed quietly, he tried to lift himself by his elbows, but fell back. Was he in hospital? No. He remembered yesterday, that terrible long day. Yet he had slept so much of it – why was he always sleeping? He remembered where he was, and Owen helping him up the stairs. Dear Owen. Then he remembered yesterday morning, when he was asleep on the sofa at Tara. Oh *God, Tara – Benet*. And the *end* of all that! He began to get out of bed. Where were his suitcases and things? He saw them in a corner of the room. Owen must have brought them up when he was asleep. What a wretched miserable furtive creature he was yesterday – and today. What could he do, where would he go, to what to whom could he now appeal? He loved Owen, but he could not stay with Owen.

He got out of bed and pulled back the curtains. The sun blazed in. He did not look out of the window. He opened one of the cases, then closed it again. He had been wearing his clothes in bed, except for his jacket and his shoes. Sitting on a chair he slowly put these on. What next? Nothing next? Everything seemed to be *finished up*. He got up to go to the adjacent bathroom. He opened the other case and found his sponge bag, his shaving material, his razor. He walked very slowly, like an old man. Well . . . He cut himself shaving and left some blood on the towel. He came slowly back into the bedroom. He told himself to *buck up* with little effect. He sat on the bed. He could not stay, he must leave as soon as possible. He must make *other plans*, altogether *other plans*.

Now suddenly he could hear Owen running up the stairs. He stood up and tried quickly to make himself look tidy, look sane.

Owen burst into the room. 'Oh, Jackson, you're awake. You haven't heard the wonderful news!'

'What news?'

'Marian! She's alive and well, she really *is* alive and well, what a goosechase she has led us, Benet has told me over the telephone, he's telling everybody, he's so happy – '

'How splendid!' said Jackson. He sat back on the bed. 'But where has she been all this time?'

'The little minx, she has been in hiding with her lover, he's an Australian – '

'How amazing! She might have let us know sooner.'

'Yes indeed! But what a relief, and what damned fools we've been!'

'So now we shall see her, with this chap – '

'Well, no, not yet I gather, they're leaving for Australia today! The wicked teasers! Benet got the letter just this morning – and then the dear villains actually telephoned him from the airport!'

'They telephoned him!'

'Yes, both of them, I expect they'll be airborne by now. No

wonder they're running away! They've caused such a bother –
but somehow now we shall have to forgive them, won't we!'

'Yes,' said Jackson.

It was the previous evening, before the Marian news.

Of course Rosalind had come back, how could she not. She
came knocking late upon the door. This Tuan had expected
and feared. Since she had left him he had been in anguish. He
had stayed at home all day. He had not telephoned Benet, he
had not telephoned anybody. He was quite unable to concentrate on his work. He employed himself by tidying up the
house, cleaning the kitchen (though it was already clean),
sorting the books (some of them were out of order), washing
his shirts, and mending a tear in an old coat. Sometimes he
walked up and down, he moaned and put his fingers in his
mouth and bit them. What was he to do, what was he to *do*?
He ought not to have told that hideous story to Rosalind –
indeed having told it must suggest that he should never see her
again. Even to tell it to anybody was a sin, why this one little
story, when the *whole thing* was so *eternally hideously
immense*. He, his presence, his being with her, was darkening
everything for both of them. His having told it to *anybody*
made it a thousand times more vivid, more violent. His father
must have known that *he* should not tell that tale to his son,
and he must have regretted it afterwards. Perhaps telling it had
seemed to be some great necessary duty, some gruesome *detail*
picked out of the *black mountain*. But what good had it done?
– it had damaged Tuan, and now Tuan had damaged Rosalind.
He thought, she will *resent* it, not at once, but later. Should he
now leave London, leave *them*, return to Edinburgh for good?
It was not a bad idea. There were things he might attend to

there. He considered ringing up Rosalind – better than sending her a letter – to tell her that he was very soon going away.

He opened the door for her and she slipped through. He closed the door quietly and followed her into the sitting room. He said, 'Have you any more news of Marian?'

Rosalind looked surprised, then distressed. 'Oh no news. If there were Benet would ring up. Has he rung you?'

'No. Why have you come here?'

'I'm sorry – I want to see you again – let me stay, please.'

'We have said enough.'

'What do you mean? Can we not sit down? Please let me talk to you.' She sat down upon the sofa.

Tuan stood, staring at her, his hands behind his back.

She said, 'I am frightened of you. Do not look like that – '

'I am going away. I mean going away for good. I am going to Scotland.'

'If you go to Scotland I shall go with you, I shall go wherever you go, I love you.'

'You hardly know me. Your love is a dream. And I am a demon. Oh Rosalind – '

'You say my name.'

'For the last time.'

'Do not be cruel to me, do not hurt me, *please* – '

'Why are you wearing that dress?'

'I thought – I just thought you might – well – like me – in this dress – '

'You think about *that*?'

'Tuan, let me stay with you tonight.'

'I saw you when you were sleeping.'

'Then let me stay with you now, let me go with you wherever you go, I shall not be a burden, I shall work for you, I shall make money for us – you are not gay, are you, well, I know you are not – '

'You are a *fool*. Oh *God*, I am not myself. Please go away. I ought not to have done it, I have damaged us both.'

'Tuan, *stop* – just be quiet – let us both be quiet together, I love you, I have always loved you, you remember that evening at Penn – before that, what happened – I wanted so much to

173

talk to you, to touch you – I was in love with you then – you say you saw me when I was sleeping – oh my dear love, let me stay with you. Please, in the name of Uncle Tim, who found you on the train, he said you were like a Greek boy, and he said you were so sweet and gentle like a dear lovely good animal, and then he gave you your name out of a book – '

'A name of doom and death. That shadow will be upon me always, and now I have spoken it, it is heavier and darker. I am sorry, I am *very sorry*. Now please *go away*, Rosalind.'

'I want to sleep with you tonight.'

'How can you say that when Marian may be dead? Will you now *go away, please.*'

Rosalind was gone. Tuan sat motionless until late in the night. Then he lay down for a long time in the darkness with open eyes. On the next morning he was awakened by Benet joyously announcing that Marian was absolutely safe and well, had talked to him on the telephone, and was going to Australia with her *fiancé*! Tuan considered ringing Rosalind, but of course Benet must have done so. He turned off his telephone.

After Owen and Jackson had had breakfast, Owen became calmer.

'I've never had a day like this in my life. No, I'm a liar, of course I've had all sorts of quaint days. But this is a thoroughly odd one. What could be odder than *you* turning up – we belong to entirely different worlds, a different ether, a different planet – we do all sorts of different things – but now we shall be able to explore each other – don't be afraid – we shall be *amazingly creative* – we're awfully alike just now, you know – he's chucked *you* out, and *she's* chucked me out! We are now to recover – to the devil with them – we shall enter a new life – maybe we'll talk of other people too, not *them* of course – and exchange all sorts of secrets. I bet you won't though. You've always been an absolute clam. I shall try to prise you open. Or like an oyster – yes, an oyster, and there's a pearl inside, I know that. You shake your head. But how can you be sure? The oyster isn't sure. It's something that grows in you without your knowing. Mildred said something about you, damn her I forget what, something nice of course. You shall teach me wisdom, I shall teach you painting, that's all I can teach – perhaps you will become a great painter, far better than me. I think you've got a *quest*, isn't that so, Benet was a dead end, now you are free, look now, I'm serious, I can set you free, well, that's boasting, you'll set me free, anyhow you'll become your *real self*, you're rather weird you know, and you've got so many trades, probably secret ones too – and you're silent – let's go somewhere together, but not yet outside the house, I won't let you outside the house, not yet anyway, like a dog or a cat who might run away and get lost, I'll show you my cat upstairs, cats, that is, in pictures of course – how old are you by the way? – you are an avatar with a broken wing, you may be two hundred years old for all I know – never mind, we'll get very drunk – but now we'll be free, we'll *do over* the house like magic housemaids.'

Jackson listened carefully to every word, feeling a deep affection for Owen, his huge head and pale face and thick pouting lips, his often watery blue eyes, his big nose and dangling black, probably dyed, hair. Jackson, tired, was content for that time to be Owen's captive, his magic housemaid. Owen's 'doing over' consisted first of all in climbing to the very top of the house, past the spare bedroom to the attic, where there was another bed standing upright, just visible, amid a mass of heterogeneous *things* which thickly covered the invisible floor: old moth-eaten clothes, broken articles of furniture, dusty filthy broken-backed books, stones of various sizes, ancient trunks and suitcases, broken glass, old photograph albums falling to pieces, useless lampshades, smashed up china of every description, boxes crammed with innumerable small objects, ancient newspapers in faded yellow piles, broken toys. Into all these Owen waded, kicking them aside with his large feet clad in shabby canvas shoes. He said to Jackson who was cautiously following, 'I call these my entities, children of Odradek ha ha, little gods, arcane sources of my inspiration, slaves of disorder. Sometimes I pick one up at random and bring him down, a privileged one, don't you know, like this, he can bring good luck.' He picked up a small bronze tortoise with one foot missing and put it into his pocket. 'Now look at this.' He kicked his way to the window. '*See*, beautiful London under a clear blue sky, the Post Office Tower, what a vista, handy for suicide, the Natural History Museum tower, jolly good tower that, the Albert Memorial, the Albert Hall, a dozen Kensingtonian spires, Kensington Palace – let's go down, mind the broken glass, hold onto me going down, there's your bedroom, I see you've made your bed, a good omen, now let's look at the Horrors, I'll put the light on, all right, you're not amused, I live by their dark passions, those deformed entities, never mind, let's go down and look at my four-poster bed, and then some real pictures, here in the studio, these are the versions of the Japanese cat, I can see you are tired. I'll dig you out some old friends and then I'll stop, here is Mildred when young. Edward with his father, here with his brother Randall, you know that ghastly story, no wonder poor Edward, yes, all done by me, I'm not all that young, that's Anna with Bran as a baby, how sad that Lewen never lived to see his son . . . '

Benet, suddenly hearing Marian's voice on the telephone, had nearly fainted with surprise and joy. He was to take in a good deal in a short time. Marian was very well and very very happy, she was with her Australian *fiancé* at the airport – yes, Australian, *fiancé*, airport, they were to be married at once, over there, she was sorry she hadn't rung sooner, she hoped she hadn't caused trouble or anxiety. Here the Australian *fiancé* intervened, only Benet could not understand what he said. Laughter. Marian's voice again – yes, I am with the man I love and I will love him for ever and ever! Then, dear Benet, do hope you will visit – must go, kisses, kisses.

Benet sat down, holding on to his heart, some tears, then crazy choking laughter. After that seizing the telephone. He enjoyed sending the news about, but only for a short time. The others were ready enough to continue its dissemination. He was relieved to find no answer from Edward. He asked Anna if she would ring him, but she was just going out. He returned to Rosalind who said she would make sure that Edward knew. He returned to his previous grief. Jackson.

Benet had fairly soon repented of the ferocious letter he had left for Jackson. He felt ashamed at his anger and his haste, also distressed by what the others might think. He realised also that he had put Jackson out into a market where he would be readily snapped up! But was it not just that he was making a fool of himself. He had lost not only a valuable handyman, but a potential adviser and *friend*. He had blundered, he had muffed it all, and he could not see how he could ever mend the damage. Already perhaps Jackson had become the servant, or as he now saw it 'servant', of perhaps Anna Dunarven, or Owen, or Edward, or Rosalind, or the Moxons, or Oliver Caxton, or crazy Alexander, or Elizabeth Loxon, who had expressed so much interest in him, or Priscilla Conti, only she was still in Italy – but *Italy*, that would be just the place for him to go to! Or perhaps by now he had vanished forever into the depths of London, a London now in which Benet would never ever find him. What on earth would Uncle Tim have said – how right Uncle Tim had been.

Where was Jackson now? Benet recalled how and where he had first met Jackson. He recalled the stages of their, so strange, acquaintance. Jackson near the bridge, following him to his house, the voice behind him saying, 'May I help you?' At that moment their eyes had met. Benet remembered those eyes. Then how Jackson had actually *touched his hand*, indicating that he did not want any money, or was that what it meant? Had it indicated some much larger possibility, some *signal* offered to Benet in vain? Then again later once more in the dark: 'Give me a try, I can do anything.' Why had it seemed then artificial, as if spoken by an actor? Then when Benet, having moved to Tara, had almost forgotten the ghostly figure, the same insistent person had appeared again, seen by him this time over Uncle Tim's shoulder! Uncle Tim's dismay and reprobation when Benet shouted at him. And at last when he had let Jackson in. Why had he done that? It was Uncle Tim who had done it, castigating Benet, so (for him) sternly, for not 'taking Jackson on'. Yet why should he have, at last, taken Jackson on? Well, was not Jackson as valuable, as talented as he had claimed to be? Even more so. Was it really something like *fate*?

Yes, it was Uncle Tim's doing. Tim had loved the fellow. Nothing could be done about that. Then, at that moment, Benet recalled with a shaft of pain Uncle Tim's death-bed, and how close he had been with Jackson just for that brief moment. Oh, if only Tim were here. Perhaps, thought Benet, he had *really* belonged to Tim, he had followed Benet because of Tim, he had *put up* with Benet because of Tim! Still, I met him first, Benet thought, and then reflected how evidently possessive that thought seemed to be after all. Still, it was over now, and his relation with Jackson had never been less than awkward. He should be relieved. If only he had not written that vicious letter. He could easily have done it politely, even with regrets. I don't think after all, he thought, he would now sell himself to one of *them* – that would be spiteful. Still, it was rather awful of him to run away for so long – but perhaps he had really been finding Marian? Anyway he must have been concealing things and telling lies – perhaps he knew where she was all the time! Most awful of all: Marian and that fellow had carried Jackson away to Australia!

They are all leaving me now, he thought, they are falling away. I can't even get any company! Edward is depressed and angry and saying he will sell Hatting. Owen won't talk to me.

Anna says she'll go back to France as soon as Bran goes to school, and she'll sell her London house. Mildred has run away to India. When I ring Rosalind she is almost rude and puts the phone down. I wonder what – of course, he thought, we have only just been released by Marian, and now there is quite a new scene! Why not *Edward and Rosalind* – is this not now *quite obvious*? At least I can do some sort of work on *this*! Benet had been sitting in his study trying to work on Heidegger, but reflecting upon Jackson and 'the others'. Now he began to see how incompetent he had been; he had kept on seeing Marian marrying Edward. Now Marian herself had opened a way for Rosalind! There was already evidence upon both sides! When he had come over to see Edward on the awful afternoon of the broken wedding he had found Rosalind with him in the Gallery. She might have been there for a long time giving him tender consolation! Such secret ventures and visits were of course very well, only Edward himself had nobly kept them, perhaps sadly, at a suitable distance; but now that Marian had declared herself *hors de combat* it was open arms for Rosalind! No wonder she did not want to waste telephone time with Benet!

Of course Rosalind was profoundly relieved when she received from Benet the news of Marian's eloping to Australia with an Australian! She had of course been worrying very much about her sister. But she was even more concerned about her other problem, that of Tuan. Rosalind waited for three days. Waiting was agony. She painfully checked, held back, all the violent desires and movements which tore at her heart. She felt, as she had never felt before, her *heart strings*. She sat often during these days, in the chair beside the window, breathing deeply, and trying to read. She had never in her life felt this sort of pain. She thought, this is like the pain of dying must be when you know that you are mortal. She cried a lot at first – later she simply sat with her lips apart, gazing down at where her hand rested, upon her knee, upon her breast. The window was closed and the room was hot. After the first day she did not look out of the window, she looked at things in the room, only intermittently at her book. (It was *A la Recherche du temps perdu*.) Sometimes she tried to think about painting. She had *ceased* painting. She must paint again soon – in the future – only there was no future, except one which was a dark chasm. To her surprise she slept fairly well, as if her ordinary healthy body had not as yet received the message or realised the possibility of mortal pain. She thought, people talk of dying with love, but they don't really believe it – at least not many do, I suppose some people – yet not very many – have felt this sort of anguish – when it is really a matter of life and death – though perhaps I won't die – yet I can't imagine going on living. What she checked too during this time was the steady powerful violent instinct to run at once to Tuan. Some higher wiser intuition told her to wait. At the end of three days she could endure it no longer.

On the fourth day she woke up early and lay in bed curled up like a snail, her face covered with her hands. She got up and dressed slowly. She had, on the previous evening, selected a particular dress, a very simple brown cotton dress, loose, with long sleeves and no design. She would also take with her a loose black cotton jacket. She assumed that the weather would be warm and the sun would be shining. It was Saturday; this too had entered into her calculations. She sat on her ruffled bed and stared at her watch. She got up and looked at herself in the mirror and adjusted the neck of her dress. She smoothed down her glowing pale fair hair which she had lately cut a bit shorter – she regretted that now. She looked at her eyes – she had done so much crying – she tried not to cry – she must not cry now. The response of this resolution was a rising flood of tears which she could only just control. She turned away and consulted her watch again. She had already decided to walk to her destination. It was just before eight o'clock. She was ready to start.

Tuan opened the door. He said rather vaguely, 'Oh – hello.' After a short hesitation he moved back from the door, leaving it to her to enter and close. She had been carrying the black cotton jacket which she had had with her before, she now remembered to put it down on the same chair. He stared at her. 'Why do you come?'

'Oh, Tuan, you know – '

'It's all the same – '

'Could I stay just for a bit, could I have a cup of tea?'

'Oh, all right – but – '

'It's hot out there.'

Tuan receded into the sitting room and she followed. She evaded the sofa and sat down on an upright chair. Tuan had now gone into the kitchen.

'Tuan, don't worry about the tea, I didn't mean tea, I meant just lemonade – '

After a brief silence Tuan returned and gave her a glass of lemonade, which she sipped then placed on the floor. She said, 'How are you getting on with your work?'

'Not very well.' He pulled forward a chair on the other side of the room, but did not sit down.

'It's – what is it?'

'It's about – great thinkers – in the past – you know I do other work as well – '

'Yes, at the shop. I'm afraid I don't know anything about your thinkers.'

'Neither do I, I mean I know very little, I'm a dismal scholar.'

'Surely you aren't "dismal".'

'I just mean I'm an ignorant scholar. Listen, Rosalind – '

Tuan had now risen and was walking to and fro.

'Rosalind, I'm sorry. Your presence here disturbs me. Please could you go away? Forgive me for the awful performance I put on. I cannot expect you to share or even understand – '

'But I do understand, I try to understand.'

'You are made for happiness and freedom, in your own world. I am someone out of another world. I have displayed my sorrow and my burden which I ought not to have done. I have thought about this. You pity me. I feel the great extent, the great ocean of your pity – but you have been overcome by my story and you take this terrible shaking and this shadow to be love, the openness of love – as it cannot be – your destiny is in another area, in *another world* – and *now* you are duly liberated into its great space.'

'Why *now* – do you mean – oh *heavens* – '

'You belong to England, to the beauty and nobility of its history. Here you are at home, you are a princess. You are young, you are free, you have now before you the completeness of your possibility – you can be happy in your own world, with your own kind. And now that Marian is gone – '

'How does Marian come in? Are you hinting that I am now free to marry Edward –!'

'I can now see your world, which is not mine. Yes, Edward or another. I am sorry to say such things. Oh Rosalind, how *can* you!'

Tuan, who had been striding to and fro, sat down upon the sofa covering his eyes. Rosalind came to sit beside him.

'What do you mean? Surely you know, you see, that I love you, *only you* – '

'I told you the last time – '

'How *can* you speak of Edward like that! Can't you recognise real *love*? I love you desperately and deeply and to the end of time, I love *you* and I *know* that you love *me* – you *do* love me, don't you, please say that you love me – please take my hand.'

Tuan took her hand, then released it. He said, 'Don't cry. Well, do cry if you must.'

'Have you got a handkerchief, I've lost mine.'

'Yes, here take this big one. Rosalind, you are still a *child*. We are two very different people, we come out of two very different worlds. Marriage is a mystery, a very profound and difficult matter, it can be a terrible mistake, a *lifelong* mistake.'

'Not if we love each other as *we* love each other. Love overcomes all – I *know* you love me, Tuan, I see it, I *know* it, we shall be together, we *must* be together, I want to be with you *always* – '

He thrust her away and got up and resumed his pacing up and down. She watched him breathlessly, holding his handkerchief in her hand.

He said, 'I have told you various reasons why we cannot marry, even if you love me – and love can be unreal and ephemeral. I should say too that I have never been with a woman, or a man.'

'And I have never been with a man, or a woman.'

'I have had my own terrible – inward – problems and difficulties – '

'So you keep saying, but *I* am here and our love can hold us and cure us. We can both earn money, and even if we were *very* poor it wouldn't alter – '

'No, no, no – I told you last time – '

'Oh my dear, I am so tired, do let us stop fighting, I want to lie down, let us at any rate lie down together, in there, let us at least *rest* together, please please my love, come with me. Let us go there together, come – ' She rose and reached out her hand.

He stared at her, then took her hand. He let her lead him to the bed. They sat down on either side of the bed gazing at each other.

Rosalind felt faint. An extraordinary wave of being which she had never experienced before overwhelmed her, even as she sat, a disintegration of her body, so painful, so weird, like a sudden electric shock. She leaned away from him, pulling off her dress. Tuan sat still, watching her, and his eyes were quiet and calm, as if he had been thinking, gazing at her dreamily for a very long time. He was breathing deeply, his lips apart. He began to unbutton his shirt, then paused.

'Come to me, hold me, Tuan darling, surely we have won – '

'Perhaps *you* have won, my child. However it remains to be seen – '

'Well, thank God all *that's* over at last,' said Owen as he sat in the kitchen watching Jackson making a *ratatouille* for lunch. 'But fancy her rushing off with that Australian fellow. I wonder if he followed her, or perhaps he was here all the time.'

'I wonder,' said Jackson.

'She might have let us know a bit sooner! Well, she might have made up her mind a bit sooner that she wanted the Aussie and not our poor Edward.'

'Indeed,' said Jackson.

'She's dragged us all through hell, especially Edward, of course, but also Benet. Still, I'm sorry for Benet, I mean about her not marrying Edward. That night – of course you were in London – when that ghastly message came through the door. I wonder just how it all worked out – was her Australian friend already there, was it he who wrote the message for her, no, it was her writing wasn't it, or perhaps simply that she realised that Edward was not for her, she didn't really like him, and Benet had engineered the whole thing.'

'Possibly,' said Jackson.

'Edward has been very elusive hasn't he. Benet said he was terribly depressed when he went to see him at Hatting. Edward is the kind of chap who would go into a depression and stay there.'

'Maybe,' said Jackson.

'You *will* stay with me, dear? You heard how I dealt with Benet when he rang up and asked if I had any news of you! I nearly choked! All right, I won't bother you, not yet anyway. I'm just so glad that you're with me. I do think about suicide. Well, that's a boring topic. You know Mildred's gone to India. I can hardly bear it. Perhaps one of her gods brought you along instead. Of course you're still suffering from shock, I wonder just what Benet – well, I won't enquire, whatever it is he's a bloody fool, perhaps I'll go round and horse-whip him, no I won't, I bet you wouldn't let me, you are so forgiving – Damn, what's that, go and see will you, darling, it can't be Benet so soon – no, I'd better go, it might be anybody.'

There had been a ring at the front door bell. Owen opened it. It was Mildred.

'Oh *God*! You're back again, you bitch, I thought you were

gone *forever*! Are you coming to say another last sickening farewell? What do you want? If you're going please *go now* as far as I'm concerned. If you want to shed your tears of farewell once again, oh bloody hell – just when – oh, all right come in – come up to the drawing room, will you, I'm in the midst of something in the kitchen – don't start crying already, everybody's after me, come on, and please *stay* in the drawing room till I fix something, otherwise I'll scream.'

Owen pulled Mildred up the stairs to the drawing room and closed the door upon her. Then he ran down to the kitchen and closed the door there. Jackson raised his eyebrows.

'Listen, don't make a *sound*, it's Mildred, confound her, I don't want her to see you, just *keep quiet* will you, I'll get rid of her as soon as possible, I promise, just you stay here, dear boy – just close the bloody door and *keep it closed*.'

Jackson nodded.

Owen then hurried back to the drawing room. 'So you're back again, or are you, you can't stay here you know, all right, you've come to tell your story, it's damned inconvenient, yes, sit down, and I'll sit down too – '

Mildred's story, briefly, was as follows. She had put her flat up for sale, but she had not decided where she was going to live in India. She had been to the British Museum to consult her gods but had received no definite answer. She was inclined toward Calcutta, the abode of Mother Teresa, a place of absolute squalor and misery, where, however humbly, one might add one's tiny offering, on the other hand – during this time of painful indecision, as a sort of penance, she had gone to the East End of London, to prepare herself for more terrible scenes in India. Here, entering a church at random, she had met an Anglican priest who was working there, and been moved by his humble holy selfless way of life, a light to all kinds of people who came to him in their brokenness. Of course Mildred had seen many other such, but simply this particular glimpse of his simple life, the possibility of so pure a heart, brought suddenly to Mildred, as she was waiting for an illumination, a new ray of light. It had become clear to her that it was after all *not necessary* for her to go to India, she was not so called, what was needful was there before her. What was now so necessary, coming to her in a beam of light, was the preservation of Christianity in the form which the time, the new century, demanded, like the other great religions who knew how to mediate the past into the future, to preserve in this pure form the reality of the spiritual, keeping and cherishing what was profoundly and believably true, onward into the new eras of the world. This deep mystical understanding, which had once belonged to Christianity, had been therein eroded by the great sciences and the hubris of the new Christian world which had kept their Christ and God as stiff literal persons who cannot now be credited. But what is *real*, the mystical truth of Christianity, as the great mystics saw it, Eckhart, Saint John of the Cross, Teresa of Avila, Julian of Norwich, as it was now seen by the few great saints of today, *that* is what must be preached now, where it is needed, in the West. So, Mildred concluded, it is here, in England, in London, that I am destined to preach religion in my own very humble way, and not in India. I even went to the British Museum and stood before the great image of Shiva, and saw him nod his head!

'Well, blow me down!' said Owen. 'And what about that priest of yours, when are you going to marry him?'

Mildred laughed, and said she hoped now to be ordained as priest herself. 'I may yet hold the Chalice!'

'You'll want the Grail next,' said Owen. 'See how your eyes gleam!'

Mildred said, 'The Grail *is* the Chalice! I'm sorry to have bothered you, but I had to tell you I was still here – don't be angry with me, dear Owen. Now I must go.'

'All right, all right. I'm glad you'll be doing your act here, not there, after all. But to the devil with that priest.'

He led her down towards the front door where, seeing tears, he kissed her. She put her arms round his neck. The front door bell rang.

'Oh fuck,' said Owen, and thrusting Mildred away opened the door. It was Benet.

'But what exactly did you say in that awful letter?'

Owen, raising his voice and preventing Mildred and Benet from beginning a serious conversation on the doorstep, had managed to push Mildred out, pull Benet in, and pull Benet up to the drawing room where he informed Benet he was sorry, he just had to rush down to the kitchen to put something on. Having closed the door upon Benet he hastened to the kitchen where he whispered to Jackson, 'Benet!' closed the door upon Jackson and ran back to Benet, closing the drawing room door.

Owen had rarely seen Benet so upset. However he had no intention of 'relieving his mind' and every intention of punishing him. Benet, rambling, had been saying he so much regretted sending Jackson such an 'awful letter'.

'Well – I said I was fed up because he was always disappearing – '

'Yes, always going to the rescue of someone else. You haven't seen him since? But what *did* you say in the letter?'

'I said he'd been drunk, and he *was* drunk, at Tara, I've never seen him so overtaken – he was asleep on the drawing room sofa dead drunk.'

'What did he say?'

'Nothing, I just left him asleep, then I wrote the letter and left it in the hall and went back to Penn.'

'Good heavens, was that all?'

'I said I needed someone more reliable, and that he had had a woman in the Lodge – '

'Oh – *had* he?'

'I thought so – I never made that out. I said evidently he found it dull with me and this was the last straw, I was going back to Penn and wanted no traces of him when I got back to Tara.'

'And were there any?'

'Absolutely none.'

'Were you pleased then?'

'I kept telling myself I'd done something very sensible, and he had been very sensible to go away – but then – '

'You had second thoughts?'

'I began to be sorry and shocked and wondered how I could have been so hasty, I ought to have waited and *talked* to him, perhaps he had been taken ill, and after all I knew so little about him – '

'Oh there was very little that any of us knew about him – I doubt if we shall see him again.'

'And I started thinking about Uncle Tim – '

'Of course Tim loved Jackson, he gave him the love that Jackson wanted, and after Tim died – I thought at the time that Jackson wouldn't stay long with you.'

'I had a dream, Uncle Tim was looking at me, then looking down at the floor, and there was a long black shadow on the floor – and that was – Jackson – '

'Well, I expect we shall never know, I thought he'd vanish – he may have died of grief, killed himself, thrown himself under a train or something.'

'Oh how I wish I hadn't written that idiotic letter, just that *letter*, why did I write it, I was just spiteful, vindictive, I must have been *mad* – '

'Well, there it is – some people are so sensitive. I expect he's gone, starved himself in some miserable hole in loneliness and sorrow – he was so silent – perhaps he just felt he had run his course – '

'Oh, Owen, I shall never recover, he will never come back to me – I shall never see him again – it's all my fault!'

EIGHT

Edward put something into his pocket, then set off early from his London house. He began to walk slowly along taking deep breaths. He had carefully chosen his tie, but now after a while he took it off and put it away. His demeanour, his walk, his eyes were evidently strange, since at times people stared at him and even turned to gaze after him. He walked as if marching. He did not appear to be in a hurry, rather to be in some state of quiet relentless determination. His arms were swinging, his lips were parted, his eyes appeared to be sightless. Some who saw him likened him to a man bent upon suicide, or else who had committed a murder or was about to commit one. He walked as if at any moment he might fall stiffly flat upon his face.

As he neared what was evidently his destination Edward began to reduce his already slow pace. He also began to look about him, moving his head slowly to and fro. At one point he actually stopped beside a lamp post and slowly raised his arm and, still staring ahead, took hold. Here his face altered, his eyes began to put on a puzzled expression, as of one who has come a long way and is now lost. A kindly woman even paused and spoke to him. Edward's head turned slowly and peered at her. She walked hurriedly on. This set Edward in motion. As he continued to walk slowly his face began to wear an anguished look as if searching for something or as one repenting of some dreadful act. A clergyman actually turned and followed him before deciding that he was simply drunk. At last he paused and stood at the corner of a road, then squared his shoulders. He even uttered a little sound like a bird or some small animal. Here, turning down the road, he quickened his pace again and began to shake his head violently as if waking himself up. He stopped outside a house, and with slow deliberation rang the bell.

Anna Dunarven opened the door. When she saw who it was she gasped and it was as if she might faint. Then she opened the door wide. Edward came in, then stood still in the hall while Anna closed the door and passed him, moving towards the drawing room. Edward followed her. The room was full of sunlight. She turned to face him and said, '*What do you want?*'

Edward replied, 'You know what I want.'

Anna sat down on a settee near to the fireplace. She covered her face. Edward picked up a chair, placed it opposite to her, and added in a matter-of-fact voice, 'I want to marry you of course –'

They looked at each other. Edward stretched out his hand. Anna took it in both of hers. Tears came from her eyes. He did not move his position. After a few moments Anna released his hand and stared at him. He moved onto the settee and they closed their eyes and put their arms about each other. Anna murmured, 'Thank God!' then, moving apart, they stared at each other.

'I'm sorry,' said Edward. 'I am *very* sorry. But I didn't know what to do. Of course I'd been thinking about it forever since –'

'So had I. Sometimes it was torture. But I didn't know what you knew.'

'And I didn't know what you wanted.'

'Really? I came back to see you marry another woman! That was the final torture, the last giving up of all things.'

'Anna, *don't*, I have been in hell.'

'Have you not deserved it? You would have married Marian! You had a narrow release.'

'Oh God – yes – I saw you in the churchyard.'

'I saw you in the churchyard – you were hiding behind a gravestone.'

'Yes. I wanted to see both of you.'

'Ah – indeed – *both!*'

'Then I thought I might meet you somewhere, with Benet or – '

'I kept clear – I knew if I met you in public I would –'

'I thought you were avoiding me.'

'Only in that sense. Now my dear boy –'

'Anything can still happen. You must save me.'

'I must save all three of us, now and forever! You haven't opened your mouth?'

'No, of course not!'

'And I have said nothing.'

'And he?'

'He – well, you will see, don't be afraid. He is a very wise boy, he will not talk.'

'You mean he knows – I suppose it had to be.'

'It must be. He found out anyway!'

'And the future?'

'That will look after itself. We are strong and so is he. But really all will be well.'

'So. May I marry you *at once?*'

'All right, I can't remember how long it takes in England –!'

'We shall have to go somewhere else.'

'Maybe, but only for a time. Edward, don't be frightened, what matters is that you have actually *come*. Oh, I can hardly believe it!' Closing their eyes they held each other, then thrust each other apart and looked.

'You are so young, Anna.'

'Yes, yes, yes, be it so! But why didn't you come sooner?'

'I was waiting for a signal – no I wasn't, I'd just *given up hope*. I felt since everything was so damned crazy –'

'I was waiting for a signal. I even went down to Lipcot and looked at Hatting, just the outside, just for an instant.'

'Was I there?'

'I don't know. I just wanted to say farewell – I was so absolutely miserable.'

'I'm sorry. We'd better sell Hatting.'

'No, we won't, why should we, certainly not!'

'Now we are arguing just like – all right we won't!'

'Oh my darling, you have come so far, you have come home to me at last. You have been so brave, my dear knight!'

'And he? I felt everything was against me. Something terrible may still be against me.'

'You mean Bran.'

'I may be blown to pieces. Where is he?'

'In the garden. Shall I call him in?'

'So soon – yes, I shall die in the interim.'

As Anna left the room and ran down the steps Edward sat with closed eyes, leaning down and holding his head in a savage grip. When he heard again the quick footsteps outside, he stood up hastily, putting his hand to his heart.

Bran hurled himself at Edward. For a second Edward thought he was being attacked. Then as they both, entangled, fell back onto the sofa, Edward knew that something, the most important thing of all, was well.

'Oh Edward, Edward –'

'Oh Bran, dear Bran, you're not cross with me?'

'I love you, I love you, I've thought so long that you might come one day, I waited for you so long, then I thought you would *never* come –'

'Well I've come now, whatever anybody says, I've come and we'll be together, won't we! Oh I'm so glad, my child, my dear dear child!'

Then the three of them were all talking at once, hugging each other and crying and laughing and wailing with joy. What had seemed so utterly impossible had now come to pass. When they were a little calmer, and Anna had suggested eating something and Bran had declared he was so happy he would never eat anything ever again, Edward took something out of his pocket and passed it to Bran.

Bran took it solemnly, looked at it, then gave a little cry of 'oh!'

Edward said, 'It's yours.'

Bran nodded his head and was about to put it away when Anna reached out for it and took it. 'What is it?'

'It's a stone,' said Edward.

'Yes, but what does it mean?'

Bran retrieved it and put it in his pocket.

Edward said, 'It is the stone which shattered my window on *that day*, the day that was supposed to be the day before my wedding.'

'You – Bran, *you* did that, you broke that window?'

'Yes,' said Bran calmly. 'Somebody had to start something.'

'How naughty – but oh how –'

'How magnificently bold,' said Edward.

'But did *that* do anything to you, make you suddenly change your mind? It might have done.'

'It upset me very much and –'

'Upset you very much forsooth! You *knew*, but you did nothing! It was really Marian who saved you! May I see the stone?'

Bran produced it and gave it to his mother who studied it and gave it to Edward. The stone was beautiful, dark, rounded, streaked with white and green stripes. As Edward took the stone in his hand his face twisted for a second. He returned it to Bran who put it away again with a proprietary air.

'Where did it come from?' said Edward. 'I couldn't make it out.'

'From a lovely beach in Brittany,' said Bran. 'Oh do let us go there, *Maman*, don't you think –'

'Oh, we'll go everywhere,' said Edward. 'Until your school term begins, you know – but always now we'll all go together to lovely places –'

'Oh school, yes – actually I'm looking forward to that,' he said with dignity.

Bran had run away. They could hear him mumbling and sobbing and singing like a bird upstairs. They, downstairs, were also sobbing, sitting on the sofa and embracing each other and having fits of hysterical laughter.

Edward said, 'We must sober up, we must work it all out, lay it all out, see the picture of what has happened.'

'Yes, yes, but now we have time –'

'You didn't feel guilty? You know you were the creator of it all!'

'At first it was pure anguish, I just didn't know what would happen, or what I had done, what sort of thing I had done –'

'Indeed, dear girl, of course, I could not approach you after *that*, I didn't know at all how much you might have remembered – or *intended* – it might have been like a rape – or just what you wanted. I thought sometimes that what you wanted was –'

'What?'

'That I should *not have remembered anything*, anything that mattered, that really happened, on that night, and that it would all simply have vanished into black forgetfulness. Perhaps it all hung upon your telling me a certain lie.'

'Yes. I told you that I was pregnant – I didn't want anyone to know that it was impossible for Lewen to have a child. We had kept it absolutely quiet because we didn't know what to do. We discussed it, we thought of adopting, but I wasn't sure, it was such a gamble.'

'You were looking for a thoroughbred!'

'Yes, Edward! Of course I had to stick it out, to wait and see if anything was going to happen and what that happening would be like, there might have been nothing at all. I was in such a state, I was fighting against time. And then Lewen went into a coma –'

'You remember Doctor Sandon, he was your doctor, he was ours also. I overheard him talking to my father –'

'You mean that you found out – ?'

'No, not really, I scarcely took it in at the time. I only thought about it on *that* evening, when you invited me in for drinks and –'

'So you – Edward, you were an angel!'

'Let us say a gentleman. Actually, I guessed from the start that I was somehow being made use of. But I was so much in love with you, I would have done anything – though I didn't really know what had happened till the next day – then I started to think! And, well, I had to think for a long time!'

'And you have been thinking ever since? Oh Edward –'

'Before you went to France you went to Ireland.'

'How did you know that?'

'I went to Trinity College, Dublin, and said I was a scholar of

Irish history and asked to see the genealogy of the Lewen Dunarvens up to date, and there was Lewen and the date of Bran's birth.'

'Oh my dear! How thorough! Yes, and Bran was born in Ireland. That was safer. When did you go?'

'Soon after Bran was born. Then you stayed in France. But – well – I've wondered why exactly you did it – it wasn't for me. You told me a lie.'

'Yes, I told you I was pregnant. I loved Lewen so much, he was such a great man, we wanted a child so much, but then he was beginning to be ill, then very ill, and the doctor told *me*, but not *him*, that he would never be able to beget a child, and I so much wanted there to *be* a child, and then when he went to the hospital –'

'No one knew that I came and spent that night with you.'

'No one. I wasn't sure whether or not you had taken it in at all –'

'Oh, I took it in!'

'You were so extremely drunk.'

'You made me extremely drunk!'

'Then I told Lewen I was pregnant with his child – and he was so happy – and then of course I told the others.'

'Oh *God* – I loved Lewen so much – And Bran?'

'I think Bran has some sort of second sight.'

'He is like me. He looks like a Cornishman. I saw that in the churchyard. How much of all this has he worked out I wonder? Anyway enough to break my window.'

'Yes, and it was the photographs –'

'The *photographs*?'

'Yes, I kept so many to punish myself. I thought I had kept them from him. I realised he had found out something when he stopped asking questions. And then here – the stuff I brought with me – I couldn't stop him from rummaging in the loft, and then when he met Jackson, they went up there together –'

'*Jackson*?'

'Yes, I –'

'Jackson mended the window which Bran broke. We talked about things. I think Jackson has second sight as well. He's a very strange chap, far stranger than people think. And he keeps his mouth shut.'

'Bran loves him, so do I.'

'Yes, and as Bran said, somebody has to start something.'

Tuan was alone. It was evening. He had sent Rosalind back to her flat. It was not that they had had some immediate quarrel. Rosalind would come back the next day. It was just that Tuan was suddenly gripped by fierce, terrible anguish. He felt a pain as if he were being cut in two. He thought I am under a curse, I *cannot* marry! He had lost track of the day, of the time. Between the moment when he had taken off his shirt and some other moment somewhere in the afternoon he had been in paradise, no, that scarcely described it, a kind of *total change* as if some quite *alien rays* were transforming his body and because his body and his mind were one. Perhaps like someone undergoing, still conscious, a very serious operation by a wonderful surgeon whom he trusted utterly, and all the time his eyes were open. Some intense golden light was falling upon him, penetrating, transforming, dissolving inside his body. Of course, Rosalind had been *there*. Her pain, her joy. He recalled them getting up at last and eating a little and drinking a little and laughing strange crazy laughter and shedding lovely tears. He remembered saying softly 'oh, oh, oh,' and going on saying it. It had all *happened*, and it was *true*. It was later in the afternoon, or was it already evening, that the pain had come on. Tuan had never been in a hospital, but he thought he knew what it was now, he recognised that particular anguish, which he had kept from Rosalind. They had managed to put on their clothes, and they were crying, only their tears were like soft arrows falling into a pool. Tuan, standing upright, soon to be doubled up with anguish, told her, 'You must go, you must go *now*, but you will come back tomorrow morning –'

When she had gone and he was alone with his pain, he thought suddenly, she will not come, she will be killed, she will be run over, I shall never see her again. However *this*, though it was somewhere and hurtful, was not the great pain which overcame him as he left the closed door and knelt down, and then prostrated himself on the floor. Why had he sent her away? Moreover, how had she ever come? But oh the pain, he was overtaken, constituted, it was this which made him into some other thing, some broken form of being. And yet he also knew that he could not even die, he had *thus* to live. I am ill, he thought as he lay on the floor, I am a different thing, I should lie quiet, but I cannot, will this last forever? Will there ever be *reason* again? The word 'reason' seemed to glow above him like a red-hot poker, so close it was to searing him. He could not later remember how long he lay there with his face upon the floor, or if his face were simply being burnt away by the pain of the heat or was it the heat of the pain.

He sat up at last, still sitting on the floor, and drawing his hands rapidly again and again over his face. He thought, and this perhaps was 'reason' at last, I cannot marry this girl! Tilting himself over he began to crawl, then to kneel, at last holding onto the edge of a chair, he stood up, then sat down upon the sofa. He spent some time simply breathing deeply. He found himself wishing that he might eat or drink, but it was impossible. Should he go to bed? Impossible. What time was it? Did that matter? His watch had come off somewhere. Was it not rather dark? He managed to stand up and stagger to the wall and put a light on. He walked back to the sofa and sat down again. He was aware of his more quiet breathing, some presence of reason, or was it reason itself. He wondered if he could eat and drink. He went out into the kitchen and sat down. An open bottle of wine and a wine-glass stood before him. Why was that there? Oh of course. He drank a little wine, then a lot of water. He returned to the other room where he found his watch which was lying on the sofa. It was eleven o'clock. What time had it been when he had sent her away?

Had she felt the beginning of his horror, and run away in fear? No, he concluded, he had been rational and loving when he sent her, and she had understood – but could she *really* understand? That could not be, she had gone away quietly just to please him.

He got up and went to his bedroom and looked at his bed. Had they been there, in that chaos? If only he could put his mind in order. He went back to the kitchen and sat down and drank some more wine, he could not eat. He thought, what does all that struggling and confusion amount to? It amounts to this. I cannot marry a woman who is not Jewish. My father did, but I cannot. Why is that? I know why but I cannot think or tell it at this time. Indeed I cannot marry any woman. My father's sufferings, my grandfather, my grandmother, the whole of that indelible sorrow, all that is *forever*, I must carry, not sharing it with any other being. Oh my God, my God –

The door bell rang. Tuan thought it is Rosalind, how *terrible*. He moved out into the sitting room and stood there trembling. The bell rang again. He thought, it is her, I must *not* go to the door. The bell rang a third time. He went to the door and opened it. Jackson came in.

NINE

Dearest Benet, do forgive me! You will, won't you? You *must*! I never really wanted to marry Edward, he was very reticent and awkward with me, sometimes it was as if he were just doing it to please you! I did care for Edward, but rather as a sister, no not really as a sister, I was sort of sorry for him, or perhaps it was really all because of Hatting! Anyway, I did not feel properly in place in the English country scene! It was all, what was happening to me, becoming increasingly unreal! I am so sorry, I keep on saying that, I prostrate myself (that's a saying of Cantor's!), I mean I am truly very sorry for the confusion which I brought about, not that it was very long, thank heavens! In the end it was Jackson who really helped us out (I don't know how much you know), I ran away from Edward in that *awful* way because I had become so sure that I did *not* want to marry him and I *did* want to marry Cantor, I was with Cantor in Australia, you know, all the reality was *with him*, and Edward was just make-believe, and then Cantor *turned up* before the wedding and he was so noble, he carried that message (you know) and carried it in his mouth like a dog and pushed it through the door at Penn at night, it was a real romantic rescue! Then there was a bit of confusion when I felt sort of guilty and I wanted to think and Cantor and I were apart, and I wanted to discuss things with Ros and Tuan and then

Jackson came and he brought me to Cantor, and Cantor and I fell into each other's arms, and it was suddenly *heaven*! Jackson was *wonderful*, Cantor now calls him his brother! We are going to be married very very soon, with a lovely wedding, we have bought a lovely house in Sydney, and we are often out on his brother's huge sheep farm, and we are to have a cottage out in the Bush! We go riding ever so often. His brother and wife are *angels* – the brother runs a very large business, not just farming, and Cantor helps (and I may be a secretary!). They are half Norwegian you know (well why should you know!) and Cantor is going to buy us a house in Norway too, and that will be easier for you to come and see us, and of course we'll visit England too. I have written to Ros, but got no reply, no doubt because I hadn't sent her my address! But I have sent her one now and you too can see the address above. By the way, Mamma is *thrilled* and may be coming over! Oh dearest Benet, you have been *so kind* to me during years – *forgive me* my trespasses! – Much much love from your devoted Marian.

Benet, now in the drawing room at Penndean, read Marian's letter through twice. It made him utterly miserable. This misery was, he was aware, totally selfish. He believed, did he not, that Marian would probably be happy, perhaps very happy, with her Norwegian-Australian. 'Visit England' – was that likely? There would be the house in Norway. Perhaps *he* might come on business! Surely Benet was glad for Marian, whom he had for so long treated as a much-loved daughter. Now he had meddled in her life, and she had shaken herself free. Well, she had always loved horses when she was a girl! But what also now disturbed him, paining him so, was Jackson. Perhaps he might have consoled himself by reflecting that Jackson had no right to interfere with the problems of others and might even, in doing so, make all sorts of serious mistakes. Jackson, a servant, should not, leaving his post, have run away to sort out chaotic love affairs, and in doing so dabble in impertinent deceptions! So, Rosalind and Marian, and even the upright Tuan, had deceived him! Why had not

Jackson come straight to him, Benet, when he had discovered Marian with Tuan? Were they all laughing about it, making a fool of everyone, making a fool of Benet? No wonder Jackson dared not now show his face. He would vanish – perhaps leave England, become a butler to Cantor, or else simply disappear in London, careful not at any point to touch the circle of Benet and his friends! Herein Benet was conscious of a particular painful 'loss of face' – *they* knew that we would never speak of Jackson now! Owen had already made a fool of him. But perhaps Owen was right, perhaps Jackson had killed himself out of pique, or of grief. This was conceivable, but surely not likely. He hates me now, Benet thought. Why, oh why, had I written that horrible letter! Everyone would now regard me with embarrassment, with politeness, with pity. They used to say, 'Where is Jackson?' Now they would avoid the subject, perhaps, avoid Benet. But even all this was not that which hurt him the most deeply. He felt as if he had ruthlessly shot down a beautiful incomparable bird, fatally wounded a gentle affectionate animal – no, not quite that. He had just wantonly missed a chance, and simply, carelessly, lost the affections of a most valuable friend.

It was morning. The sun was shining. He left the drawing room and wandered to his study. His work on Heidegger lay there neglected, unfinished, the sheets covered with his handwriting, piled in confusion. He thought, as he put the sheets roughly together, this is a sort of nemesis. Looking randomly at what he had written, he thought: I am indeed rushing in where angels fear to tread! Sitting down he scanned half a page. No good, *just no bloody good*! He sighed and picked up the poems of Hölderlin, which had always accompanied him upon his journey into Heidegger. '*Wo aber Gefahr ist, wächst das Rettende auch.*' 'But where danger is, rescue is ready too.' He closed the book quickly which he had opened at random. Not for me, he thought. And he thought then of late words of Heidegger: '*Nur ein Gott kann uns retten*'. 'Only a God can save us'. Was *he* not then in despair? Benet got up and went into the library. Who can be my companions, he thought, in the years to come? He felt the presence of Uncle Tim, and in a vivid picture recalled that scene, Tim at the door at Tara, and visible over his shoulder, Jackson. It was the first time he had seen Jackson clearly by daylight. Uncle Tim *knew* at once. But *what* did he know, and what was it now that Benet was yearning for? He recalled the tears which he and Jackson had shed when Tim was dying. Now near to tears again, he wandered around the library, caressing the books.

The telephone rang. Benet cursed. Of course he did not dare to switch it off in case there were some good news or some kind of *miracle*. He lifted the receiver.

'Oh Benet – hello!'

It was Edward.

'How kind of you to ring up.'

'I've got some news.'

'What?'

'I'm getting married!'

'Oh – good heavens – who – ?'

'You'll be surprised!'

'Oh – ?'

'I am marrying Anna Dunarven!'

'You – marrying Anna – oh Edward, how – how splendid – I – '

'Yes, you are surprised, but it is really so, and we are to be married very soon, just as soon as possible, not anything grand, just quickly in a Register Office, and a party of course soon after at Hatting – '

'Edward, I am so happy for you! And for Anna! What absolutely marvellous news – !'

'Listen, we're at Hatting now. I wonder if we could come over and see you?'

'You mean – '

'Now, immediately – is that possible? We'll drive over, we won't keep you long, we just want you to be the first to know – '

'Yes, yes, dear Edward, come over at once, of course!'

Benet put down the receiver. He sat down shuddering in the nearest chair. He leaned forward holding his head in his hands. His head was full of sudden clattering chaos. *Edward* marrying *Anna*? How could that be? Surely Edward had not seen

Anna for years, he had nothing to do with her, after all he was a child, was he not, when Anna left after Lewen died? No, not a child, but very young. Were there secret meetings in France, was he her lover there? Surely not. He took Marian instead, took her as a second best – perhaps Marian *found out* and that was what the last-minute message meant – but was she not already tied up with Cantor? Then Edward must have gone back to courting Anna – But when I talked to Anna when we met at the house she never mentioned Edward, nor did Edward ever mention her. Oh how *confusing*!

'But how wonderful!' said Benet.

They were sitting in the sunshine on the terrace, where the little plants which had so cheerfully pressed themselves up between the paving stones were now wilting in the perpetual sunshine. Edward and Anna were side by side on a old long teak seat, and Benet was sitting opposite to them, with his back to the sun, upon a wicker chair. In the distance Bran was capering between the Wellingtonias, perhaps hoping that his gaiety might be visible. Benet wondered – what does *he* think about it? Anna was wearing a green dress streaked with red and a big white straw hat. Edward had doffed his linen jacket and had laid it across his knees, and had opened the neck of his shirt. They were, it seemed, dazed in some sort of ecstasy, leaning their shoulders together, holding hands, frequently looking at each other and laughing. It was as if they could scarcely hear what Benet was saying! In fact, taken by surprise, Benet was finding it difficult to say anything suitable.

'So,' he said, 'were you meeting in France?'

'Oh sometimes,' said Edward, who was doing more of the talking, 'but in England too, and of course Anna was travelling – '

'Oh – where were you going to?'

'I used to go to Ireland.'

'Oh of course – and you saw Edward – '

'Oh in London,' said Edward, 'but also in other places – Anyway *now* – '

'Now, of course you know – '

'It has all worked out very well,' said Edward. 'Is it true Jackson has left you?'

'Yes.'

'I'm sorry. Why did he go?'

'I think he just got fed up and wanted to move on. I say, would you like something to drink or eat? It's quite late. Do stay for lunch!'

They looked at each other.

'We'd love to,' said Edward, 'but we've got to go to London. We've got to do the rounds there! We've so much wanted to see you, you've been such a friend – I hope you understand about the wedding.'

'Yes, of course. I shall expect to come to the party – perhaps it could happen here – '

'We'll send you a card,' said Anna.

They all stood up.

'Why, hello!' said Benet to Bran, who had materialised from the garden. 'But *you*'ll go to the wedding, won't you!'

Bran said nothing. Edward said, 'Of course! Come along then.'

Chatting about the heavenly weather they drifted into the house and out at the front door where Edward's red Jaguar was standing. Benet waved them goodbye.

When the Jaguar had stopped outside the front door of Hatting Hall, Bran, who had been silent in the back of the car during the journey, jumped out, announced that he was going 'to visit Spencer' and, running back towards the front gate, disappeared. In his presence Edward and Anna had exchanged a few remarks. 'How solitary Benet seems.' 'He's got his books.' 'He's sorry about Jackson.' 'Yes – I wonder what happened there?'

Now, after watching Bran's departure they mounted the

steps in silence. The door was partly open, letting in the sunshine. They entered the large hall, dark by contrast.

Montague appeared, smiling.

'Oh, Montague, *thanks* for arranging the flowers so beautifully!' said Anna. She had already made friends with the staff. She followed Edward into the drawing room, closing the door behind her. He was standing with his back to her, looking out on the garden. She put her arms round his waist and leaned her head against him. 'Edward, my dear love – do you still love me?'

'Don't be silly!' He turned round, and holding her as in a dance, propelled her to the enormous sofa which faced the fireplace. They fell down clasping each other onto the sofa.

As they adjusted themselves into a sitting position she said, 'Of course you are worrying about Bran and – '

'Bran is *thinking* again.'

'Good thoughts, happy thoughts – '

'I'm worrying about you.'

'What *they* think? *They* don't think!'

'I'm afraid you'll stop loving me, you know I bring catastrophe. I have already brought confusion.'

'Edward, *don't* – I shall cry – I love you – I'm so happy, you must not stop me from being happy, you must not stop Bran from being happy. It's what I've always wanted and he has always wanted.'

'I hope he'll like that school.'

'Your school. You liked it.'

'No I didn't.'

'Oh you, you've never liked anything!'

'Except you – and Bran – '

'And now you've got us. Oh Edward, darling, don't cry – you're thinking about – '

'I think about *that* every moment of my life.'

'You mean Randall – Oh my dear – '

'Don't say anything, I'm crying for you, for us – '

'It's a sort of prayer, you said that yesterday – It *is* a prayer, isn't it?'

'Yes. I do wish we were married. It's taking such a damned long time, I thought – '

'It's very soon now. And so is lunch. And I shall be the Mistress of Hatting! Come!'

Mildred was now beginning a little to wish that she had gone to India after all. Why had she so suddenly cancelled that journey, made void those tickets? She had held so attentively in her mind so many pictures of that future, she saw herself moving humbly among the barefoot poor, the starving, dressed in a stained and dusty sari. Women whom she had known were *out* there, Mildred had had no doubt that she would soon be among them and among innumerable others, Christians, Buddhists, Hindus, Muslims, servants of God or of gods. Was that not something ultimate? Not just busily, efficiently, to feed the poor, but to do so in humility, out of love, out of deep spiritual belief, as *servants*. Sitting, kneeling, upon the ground, in the dust. There where she had wished to be and now would never be. What *now* could she do, what great worthy thing, what profound humility could she achieve, which was not itself an act of pride and self-satisfaction? Well, do I want to be a *saint*, she thought. That way is a mystery, a long long servitude, a complete loss of self, an utterly new being, a cloud of unknowing.

Such a tumble of thoughts distracted Mildred as she sat, or more usually stood, in the crowded Underground train which in the morning (some mornings anyway) carried her from her tidy little town flat to the dirty miserable *dangerous* area of London where her Anglican priest lived, himself in a tiny shack, among his poor. His name was Lucas Begbrook. His parents were Methodists, but forgave his High Anglican curtsies and candles. Mildred knew of course that she belonged to Owen. Why then had she decided to go to India, was it to achieve an absolute severance? Because she had begun to disapprove of his drunkenness, and his chamber of Horrors or because she was just tired of him, or that she had realised that Elizabeth Loxon could look after him just as well? Actually all *that* was more likely to make her stay! More potent still, Mildred had now become aware of the fact that Lucas was, at any rate a little, in love with her. Was she in love with him? At least he came to her in her dreams.

Coming back in the afternoon in a less crowded train Mildred makes her way, as often, to the British Museum, going to the Indian Gallery. Here she goes first to the god Shiva to whom she bows, and to Parvati his wife who is also the river Ganges, how gently he turns to his dear wife with whom Mildred identifies. Now Shiva, a snake about one arm, dances, he has become Shiva Nataraja, four-armed dancer in a circle of fire. The god Krishna, also he dances, avatar of Vishnu, guide of Arjuna, yet still a cowherd god who plays the flute and dances with the milkmaids, his divine power convincing each one that she is the only object of his love. His flute he plays, this dark-skinned ancient being from the past of time. He saves his followers, an adolescent with a tiger-claw necklace, lifting up a mountain. He dances upon the opened hood of the royal cobra Nagas, Kala Nag. Mildred dreams of glowing birds flying in darkness, of cobras stretching out their hoods, and dear Ganesh, and dear Ganga, Ganges. Buddha incarnate in Vishnu. So Shiva with Parvati, Shiva dancing in a wheel of fire, Krishna with his milkmaids giving himself to each.

   She had not discussed 'worship of idols' with Lucas. She felt, emanating from the images, these live beings, a profound warmth of passion, of love, that of the gods themselves but also of their numberless worshippers. In India, at every street corner, the god with garlands round his neck. This was religion, the giving away of oneself, the realisation of how small, like to a grain of dust, one was in the vast misery of the world – and yet how vast the power of goodness, of love, like a great cloud, lifting one up out of the meanness, the deadliness, of the miserable ego. Worship. Ecstasy. These gods – and animals, Shiva with snakes about his neck. Snakes. Kala Nag. Worms, tiny creatures, she picks up off pavements and lays carefully in gardens. Innumerable beings. Shiva with his delicate uplifted hand, smiling upon Parvati, while round about them whirl creatures innumerable. The Ganges, the Thames, Mildred with tears in her eyes, turning away. What chaos, what suffering, such passion, such love, such infinity, she felt faint, she might fall to the ground. These gods – *and Christ upon His Cross.*

She left the room and instinctively made her laborious way to the front of the building where the cool Greeks lived. She went automatically towards the Parthenon Frieze. The huge room was almost empty, there was a visiting group at the far end, nearer two or three solitaries. Mildred stood, calming herself, breathing deeply, not looking at anything, her eyes glazing over as if by the sea. She stood still, her arms hanging by her sides. How *terribly* strange the past was. Another civilisation, another image. Then suddenly something else, a mystery, Jackson. Surely Jackson would come back – or would he? Was he not after all a very strange being, a wandering avatar, and as she thought of him there arose a dim line of high mountains. And suddenly she thought, surely such a being could easily destroy himself, and tears rose in her eyes.

Mildred quickly blinked. Near the door, standing near to the Frieze, one of the solitaries, was a boy, young, a schoolboy. The boy was looking at her. She thought, can he be Bran? – He *is* Bran! I saw him with Edward and Anna, only they rushed off so quickly. The boy stood still. Mildred moved. He was looking at her. She wondered if he would recognise her. She went towards him.

'Hello, Bran. Do you remember me? I'm Mildred.'

'Yes.'

'Your mother came round with Edward. They'll soon be married, won't they.'

'Yes.'

'That will be lovely.'

Bran looked at her silently. Then he said, 'I shall have a pony.' After that he turned to study the activities of the Frieze.

Mildred looked at them too. All this was so familiar to her. There was a boy, a thoughtful boy, about Bran's age, quietly helping a rider, perhaps his father, to adjust the length of his tunic, while the riderless horse moves on.

Bran said, 'There's a boy.'

'Yes, he is – '

As she looked at him she thought, just now he looks like *Edward*, how amusing! Of course he's *just* like Lewen. What a handsome child he is! Alas, that Lewen never lived to see him.

She said, 'You'll be going to school here in the autumn, won't you, you'll like that. They'll teach you Greek. I expect you already know some Latin.'

Bran, turning towards her, said, 'I know all Latin, and most Greek.' After which he returned his attention to the Frieze.

Mildred, disconcerted, said, 'Oh, that's good! How nice to meet you, of course we'll meet again, I'm sure you'll be happy here. Goodbye, Bran, *au revoir*.'

'*Au revoir*, Mildred.'

Mildred hurried away, immensely gratified by the farewell! She thought he sounds so like a French boy. That's charming! I expect he knows lots of languages! Oh I do hope he will be happy here – such a lovely child! And she wished that she had a child, and that that child was Bran.

Benet put down his pen. What was the use of going on like this? Innumerable others had done it better. His love-hate for Heidegger, and for Wittgenstein, was better kept to himself. He was not a scholar. He had really *done*, nothing. Long ago he had thought of writing a novel. He had begun one. It was put away somewhere. He had got nowhere with it anyhow. People, or some people, had once thought well of him. He had risen high in the Civil Service, he still studied, or at least read, philosophy. He had been a leader, an organiser. Or was all that really being done by Uncle Tim? Tim in his later years when he lived mostly at Penn, he had been the centre, the charmer, the star – far more interesting than Benet! Depression, thought Benet, as he rehearsed these thoughts. That's it. *Depression*.

He was living, for the present, at Tara, and doing his work, such as it was, there. The weather had changed. Cold winds were blowing over London. It had been a dark afternoon. Now it was beginning to rain. He thought, it's the end of the season. The game is finished. It's all over. I'd better go back to Penn. But he didn't want to do that either. Things were changing, the younger generation were taking over, *they* were now in charge. Well, he should have noticed that years ago! Of course Marian would never return, he would never go to Australia. Edward was marrying Anna, she would run Hatting Hall, the great parties would be there, the centre of gaiety, the centre of activity, the centre of power, would be there. Edward would be transformed, he *was* transformed, he was now the strong man, the Lord of the Manor as his father had been. Now everything would fall into the lap of Lewen's grandson. Benet was pained by his inability to communicate with Bran. He felt that Bran regarded him with hostility. Such a beautiful boy, Lewen's son, soon to be a tall youth, at last to inherit Hatting Hall. How amazing, who would have imagined it, that Anna should marry Edward! And who, Benet wondered, would inherit Penndean?

These were some of Benet's fleeting and painful thoughts. However now he had an even more piercing pain in his breast. Jackson was gone. 'Who is to blame him?' as Owen had exclaimed after Benet had, miserably, foolishly, divulged the contents of his letter of dismissal. Of course the others had been questioned, but had nothing to offer. They think ill of me now, Benet said to himself, adding that he deserved such a judgement. So the days went by and Benet began to feel that he was isolated, refusing invitations and now (he felt) ceasing to receive them! He had never, he thought, felt so unhappy, except when Tim died. And how close to me Jackson came *then* – only I thrust him away. What's the matter with me? Is it just that I am ashamed of having written such a hasty angry cruel letter? I might have uttered my reasonable displeasure in a cooler tone. Was I not rationally displeased when Jackson went about helping others? Many such considerations were produced as excuses for Benet's irritated outcry. But, as he well knew, a fiercer and more fiery anguish was burning in his heart, a helpless yearning for something lost forever. He loved Jackson, and he had killed him, or rather killed himself.

At that moment the front door bell rang. Benet hurried out into the hall. He opened the door. It was raining. Rosalind and Tuan were standing on the doorstep. Benet was for a moment confused. Surely these two did not go together. He said vaguely, 'Oh – hello – do come in – '

'May we come in?' said Tuan.

'Yes, of course, I'm so glad to see you, come into the drawing room. Why you're quite wet, do just drop your coats and umbrellas in the hall. Yes, yes, come in.'

They came in, dropping their gear, and followed Benet into the drawing room. He noticed that they were both smartly dressed. The trio now stood beside the fireplace. Benet murmured, 'It's so cold today, I might as well light a fire.' Then he said in a business-like manner, 'Well, tell me your problem!'

'Oh, Benet – ' said Rosalind. And suddenly her eyes were filling with tears.

'My dear – ' Benet thought, it's trouble, oh what a *nuisance*, some catastrophe, bad news about Marian, to be unloaded upon me, or something to do with Rosalind, why does he bring her here, they don't know each other –

Tuan put an arm round Rosalind's shoulders. She was now mopping her tears. She said, 'Benet, dear, listen, Tuan and I are going to get married!'

Then, holding each other, they both went into peals of joyous laughter.

Benet was so amazed that he stepped back with his mouth open. He was about to say 'Who are you both getting married to?' Then in the next instant he had seized upon Rosalind who was relinquishing Tuan, and kissed her ardently, and then came Benet and Tuan's embrace, and the laughing and the talking and the holding onto each other, and then they all sat on the sofa, one on each side of Benet and talking all at once.

'Oh I am so glad, *so glad*!' He was taking Tuan's hand.

'Oh thank you, thank you,' Tuan cried, then, 'Oh I mean, can I, Benet, I am so sorry, I am half mad, I can scarcely believe it's true – '

'It's true, it's true!' cried Rosalind. 'You are the first person we have told! Oh Benet, I love you so much, you have been a father to me, please now will you always be a father to us both, and we'll be just in the Register Office and you will be with us, you will won't you, oh if only Uncle Tim were here, you are great, and Tuan is great, and we are now and forever, and we thank you so much – '

'Thank you for telling me first,' said Benet. Turning to Tuan he thought, how young they are, and how tall and *noble* Tuan looks, like a Highland Chieftain, oh may they be happy! 'You will be so happy,' he said to them, 'I bless you – I won't tell anyone, I expect you would like to break the news yourselves.'

They had not thought about that, but said yes, they would like now to tell some of their friends, they would be having a little quiet secret wedding in a Register Office, and they would like him to come and perhaps just one or two others.

Benet was just wondering whether they knew about Edward and Anna when they cried out themselves about how wonder-ful *that* was. 'And of course Marian and Cantor are getting married,' said Rosalind, 'they are so happy, we have been talking to them on the telephone, and Mother is going over to see them, and then coming here to see us, and *she* is so pleased and she sends love to you by the way – '

Benet looked at them. He had gazed at Rosalind ever since she was a child. But Tuan, he realised, he scarcely knew at all. Now they were looking at each other and Benet thought, how handsome they are, and Ros with her soft golden hair cut above the shoulders and Tuan with his thick dark curly hair reaching down his neck, surely he is a *good* man, a lovely kind gentle man, she has chosen well – but what a surprise, and of course they would be penniless, Tuan has no proper job and Rosalind has no job at all! Her mother is a very uncertain quantity, she may be bankrupt by now! Of course I shall help them, I hope they will let me! He looked into Tuan's mysterious dark eyes and into Rosalind's pure blue eyes and wondered what their children would be like. Only after they had gone he realised he had not offered them a drink.

Benet did a lot of walking fast round the house and exclaiming and talking aloud to himself. What was to become of all these weddings? Nothing but surprises; he had expected Marian to marry Edward, then he had wondered if Rosalind might marry Edward, he had never expected Anna to appear from France, or Marian to go to Australia or young silent Tuan to seize hold of Ros. He had refrained from asking Tuan about his parentage, he must find that out. He was worried about Bran's hostility but hoped that it would pass. Would he, Benet, be invited to Australia? Would he become an intimate at Hatting Hall? Would Bran confide in him and love him? Would they all ask his advice? Or would he be quietly set aside? All these were instantaneous wandering pains. And now the most accusing of all. Rosalind had begun to say something about Jackson – but Tuan had somehow swiftly checked her. *He* must not be mentioned. Benet did not think that they had any news of Jackson – but they had intuited his, Benet's, shame, his helpless desire to recover what now would never be found again. *Remorse.*

Benet had considered returning to Penndean that evening but now it seemed to be too late. He went into the kitchen and ate some oddments standing up. He felt sick of himself and ready to weep. His pleasure in the forthcoming weddings had faded, they might even fill him with resentment. Pictures of his childhood began to rise up, how rude and unkind he had been to his father, how he had really not loved his parents at all. Things had gone wrong for him early in life, he had made them go wrong, he had even failed Uncle Tim, he had never really understood him, he had derided him and bossed him about. Such a great man – and Benet had ignored him. Now he, Benet, was suddenly useless and old. Had he ever enjoyed happiness, did he know what it was? The wind had gone down and the rain had ceased. He decided to leave the house and do his penitential walking outside. There was already a twilight over London. He put on a warm coat and a cap and began to walk at random, suddenly remembering a game he had played in childhood, *Getting Lost in London*. He had not played it, he recalled now, more than once or twice, since it was deemed to be dangerous! Benet was now ready for danger, for lostness. He set out from Tara, walking at first at random and attempting to lose himself. Soon however he found he was, after various circular wanderings, arriving at Earls Court station. He thought, this is no good, I'll go *right into the centre*. He took a train as far as Leicester Square, where he emerged, finding it raining again. By this time however he had discovered a new idea. He thought I must be in a *really different place* – somewhere like Brixton or Kennington or Clapham or Lambeth or Morden – places I have *never visited*, places unknown and far away, where I can *really* get lost. He went back down the escalator, and hurried along the corridor indicating Northern Line. As he reached the platform a train was coming in. The front of the train was marked MORDEN. He leapt on. His heart was beating fast. Getting Lost in London. He sat down and looked up at the railway map. Almost at once he saw EMBANKMENT. Next station but one. He had a brief period in which to reflect. Even then he hesitated, and rushed out just as the doors were closing.

Outside, Benet's crazy London game was over. It was not that he felt 'better'. He felt sick and frightened. He felt like a criminal who, prior to execution, is taken to the place of the crime. He began at first, leaving the station, to scuttle about, running away up Villiers Street towards the Strand. He reached the Strand, crossed the road, nearly being run over, and began to walk aimlessly along the pavement, looking into the windows of shops, in the direction of Waterloo Bridge. He paused for a while however outside the Adelphi Theatre and began slowly to make his way back. He stood still for a short while, then pressing through the crowds, crossed the road again. Here he walked cautiously down one of the streets parallel to Villiers Street, looking at the house where he used to live and where Jackson had first spoken to him. He felt a curious impulse to knock at the door. In fact he knocked, but

214

no one answered. He walked down as far as the garden which ran beside the river, then returned into the evening rush. He went back to Villiers Street, then stopped at the Arches and walked a little way in. He returned and stood upon the pavement, streams of men and women, hurrying, brushed past him. He stared a while at passing faces. Then he walked back down the hill toward the station. Underneath the railway bridge two men and a woman were standing. As he approached, the woman held out her hand to him. He fumbled in his pocket for a pound coin which he gave to her. He thought, why am I not like that too. And then, why do I think such thoughts, why am I here, oh God forgive me, except that I don't believe in God. He went into the station, intending to take a train, then stood looking out onto the Victoria Embankment. Just beyond was the Thames. He observed the thick stream of traffic and waited. Then he found himself standing at the foot of the steps leading up to the railway bridge; automatically he began to mount. Why was he doing this, he felt so tired and so senseless. At the top of the steps he paused. He thought, I am nobody now. He was the beginning of nobody. Now it was dark. The Thames below was full and quiet. It was dark on the bridge, a lit-up train rattled past. Benet turned to go down, then changed his mind and set off slowly toward the other side. Near the centre of the bridge a man was leaning upon the rail, looking down the river in the direction of Waterloo Bridge. Benet stopped, then moved on. The man turned to him.

Later Benet, looking back, wondered how he had remained upright. He also thought, or imagined, that Jackson's face was in some way lit up. He kept on walking until he was close to Jackson. Nearing, the hideous idea occurred to him of simply *passing by*, with a nod, or with a calm stare ahead. How this had occurred to him seemed later incredible – certainly it was not contempt or hatred – it was *fear*. He thought, suppose I speak to him and he just ignores me. He stopped a short distance away from Jackson, who had now turned towards him and certainly recognised him. Benet thought, I shall speak, then pass on. He came a little closer, then paused. He said,

'Jackson.' This alone, this alone perhaps, was all that would be expected of him, all he would be allowed to offer, before he passed by in silence. Stumbling, he went on however, 'I'm sorry.'

Jackson, turned now towards Benet and leaning against the railing of the bridge, said nothing. Very close to them another brightly lit train rushed by. Then silence against the hum of the city.

Benet, wanting, needing now, to say just one more thing, then slink away, said, 'You have been very kind to us – to me – I am very sorry.' He had by now noticed that Jackson was wearing shabby clothes such as he had worn when Benet first met him.

As Jackson still said nothing, Benet felt he was being dismissed, he could not simply stay there uttering feeble servile remarks, his misery in any case was making him speechless. He had now to decide whether he was to walk on, past Jackson, or walk back again the way he had come. He began to turn back, then decided to go forward.

Jackson said, 'Wait a minute.'

After this he turned from Benet and looked away down the river towards St Paul's.

Benet waited in silence.

Jackson, turning back, said, 'Why are you here?'

Benet said promptly, 'Looking for you.'

Jackson reflected on this, nodded his head, then turned away again towards the river.

Benet, wondering if this were a blunt dismissal, or seeking for something to keep the conversation alive, said, 'Have you got another job?'

Jackson, turning toward Benet, and now leaning with his back to the river, gazed at Benet and said nothing.

Benet, blundering on, said, 'Then I suppose you're here for – like when I first met you – ?' This was an even more tactless remark. Benet at that moment was overcome by something in Jackson's look, his stare, his untouchability. He wanted to say something about this, but of course it was impossible. Jackson was, naturally enough, trying to get rid of him. He thought of saying that he would be very glad to employ Jackson again, only this too was impossible! He said, 'I am sorry that I wrote that letter to you, I repented it very soon after – then I couldn't find you.'

'That's all right,' said Jackson. He continued to look at Benet but in what now seemed a rather bored or dreamy manner. He was waiting for Benet to go.

Benet, reduced to total misery, was finding himself unable to continue the conversation. He thought: I shall never see him again.

At that moment a burly man appeared suddenly beside them out of the dark. Benet thought: *this is his friend!* That *is* the end! Then it was clear that the man was asking for money. Benet instantly produced two pound coins and gave them to him. The man, who appeared to be grateful, murmured 'Thanks,' then disappeared. Benet wished he had given him more money. Jackson had not moved.

Benet said suddenly, 'How terrible. I wish Uncle Tim were here – '

The unexpected mention of Uncle Tim made a change of atmosphere. Why did I say that, Benet thought. Keep up your bright swords! Are we at war then – or what? He was suddenly conscious of being terribly hungry. He said, 'Look, let's go and have something to eat.' What a mad thing to say! He thought, of course he won't! He just wants to get rid of me. *Oh God, I won't ever see him ever again* – but it *can't* be like that. He said, 'Jackson, you *must not* be angry with me, please *forgive* me – after all – '

Jackson detached himself from the bridge. He said, 'Let us walk, anyway.' They began to walk back towards the station.

TEN

'So now all the weddings are over!' said Ada Fox, looking lovingly upon her daughter and her son-in-law.

'Yep!' said Cantor, who was leaning down over Marian's chair. Marian reached up a hand towards him. He kissed it. 'Ours was best though. They were sneaking into Register Offices. We had the real thing!'

'And you've bought the house near the Harbour?'

'Yes!' said Marian. 'There's a lovely tropical garden running down to the water! And kookaburras! We'll show you tomorrow.'

'Great! And what lovely in-laws – such a charming brother and sister-in-law, Cantor, and what an estate! I'm sorry I didn't see any sheep.'

'That's what our farms are like here,' said Cantor, now sitting down and putting his arm round his wife. 'Twenty acres to one sheep. Got to be big.'

'I'm in love with Australia already.'

They were sitting after breakfast in Cantor's present house in Sydney, from which they were soon to move to the larger new house with the kookaburras.

'I'll love to see your new house. Then I've got to take the plane to London. There'll be a lot to talk about up there too! Fancy Edward suddenly marrying Anna! She's much older, isn't she – and a little boy at a difficult age. I wonder if that will work. Edward is a bit of a rotter. He must have been making up

218

to Anna all the time! What an escape you've made, darling – of course you never intended to marry him, I know! You've got hold of just the best man in the world! And then there's Rosalind marrying Tuan, who never opens his mouth, and he wants to live in Scotland and he hasn't any money. And I gather Mildred, after all that fuss, hasn't gone to India at all, I expect she was afraid someone would pick up Owen when she was away – or hasn't she got hold of an Anglican priest as well? I don't think *she*'ll ever marry. And hasn't Benet got hold of his butler again? You see, I know everything – that letter I got from Owen. He's such a chatter-box, bless him!'

'But where will you stay?' said Cantor. 'You didn't say – '

'Oh, *everybody* has asked me – of course I shall stay with Mildred in London, I'm longing to see the priest! In the country, that's a problem – both Benet and Edward will want me – or shall I stay at the Sea Kings? Yes, perhaps I will, I'll do that, so I shall be free!'

'I adore your mother,' Cantor said later to his wife.

'Yes,' said Marian, 'she is really a good egg, she is very tough and brave. She's disposed of two husbands, as well as the one she didn't marry.'

'I gather the American has gone. Perhaps she'll steal Jackson.'

'I doubt *that*!' said Marian.

'I wish *we* could have stolen Jackson. Or – no – he might steal *you*!'

'Absolutely not, my darling! Oh Cantor, how wonderfully lucky it's all been. I might have been in hell, and now I'm in paradise. Oh my dear angel, let me kiss your hands, I worship you!'

'Well, thank the gods of the Aborigines who have made it so, that we have such bliss!'

'I'm sorry Mamma isn't staying long enough for us to take her to Ayers Rock.'

'Oh well, she'll come back. And what a horsewoman she is too, I was amazed!'

'Yes, I should have told you, she's been riding all her life.'

'And wasn't it smart of Jackson to get back your gold watch

from the stables and send it to you! I love that fellow. You know I positively fought with him when he suddenly appeared saying he was my brother – '

'I bet you won.'

'Well – um – Now I'm proud to have him as my brother – like Abos do – yes, I elect him as my brother! And now, little one, sweet one – what do you think – just between now and dinner?'

'We shall be too early,' said Mildred to Owen. 'You are driving too fast, as usual.'

'We've got to posh up at the Sea Kings,' said Owen.

'Well, I suppose it doesn't matter if we turn up a bit early at Penn. I can help Jackson, and you can chatter and get drunk with Benet. Benet is so much better, isn't he.'

'Well of course. Losing Jackson was a bitter penance. Getting him back was something he didn't deserve.'

'I can't think how he lost him. He didn't show us the letter. It must have been an awful letter.'

'It was awful.'

'You didn't see it?'

'No, but he mumbled a lot of it to me, like in church.'

'*Please* don't drive so fast. Thank heavens it's only us and the others. It's beautiful, like magic – Rosalind and Tuan, Edward and Anna, it's all so amazing! I think Benet imagined Rosalind was going to marry Edward!'

'I thought Tuan was gay! Well, perhaps he is gay too. Those two are living on nothing. Apparently her mother doesn't cough up any more. Tuan has given up the university, he just goes to that bookshop thing once a week. She's not going to the Courtauld, she's just teaching herself to paint, that costs money, and there isn't much evidence that she *can* paint!'

'Well, Benet can help them – so can Edward – so can we – '

'Who's we? You mean you and Lucas? Just tell me when you're leaving.'

'I've seen some of Rosalind's pictures – they're not bad.'

'All right. Probably better than mine. I'm going to give up painting. You'll have to support me, you and Lucas – till the kids arrive.'

'You know Ada Fox is coming next week, she's staying with me. Of course you know, we're old friends.'

'She must be mad.'

'I think Edward will *not* invite her!'

'Edward will not invite anybody.'

'Anna will run Hatting from now on. How extraordinary, it's all been happening so quickly, and working out so well!'

'If Edward is haughty and Tuan is penniless and Cantor is fed up with Marian – '

'Cantor and Marian are blissfully happy, they're deeply in love with each other.'

'Who says so?'

'She's written to me, and I believe it.'

'Ha ha. I think I'd get on well with Cantor, he's that sort of rogue and rotter type.'

'I do hope you won't get too drunk – '

'I wonder if Benet and Jackson have separate bedrooms.'

'It's amazing about Edward, it's so sudden – '

'He must have been living with Anna in France, while he was courting Marian in England. I daresay Anna put her foot down.'

'I wonder.'

'So he's not as shy as you think!'

'I feel sorry for little Bran. Edward is sure to want a son of his own.'

'Yes, and Bran will be shoved into the background, he's being carted off to boarding school in the autumn.'

'If only Lewen were still alive.'

'Who is Lewen? Never heard of the fellow.'

'So there'll be just us and Owen and Mildred and Edward and Anna,' said Rosalind to Tuan.

'So Benet said.'

'That will be a nice number. We can all talk to each other, like usual.'

'Benet called it a wedding feast.'

'And we are the juniors. The youngest newly-weds! I like that too!'

'What a pity Marian and Cantor couldn't be there, but that would be impossible of course!'

'Of course. I wonder if time will smooth any of that away. But not now. There would be a duel! When Mamma arrives next week she'll tell us – well, she'll tell us only the good things.'

'Let us hope – for the good things. It's strange that the weddings went so fast, Owen and Mildred were quite dazed, so was Benet.'

'At *that* time Benet was in a daze of misery.'

'Now, thank heavens – Anyway we had a good lunch with Owen and Mildred afterwards, and you kept taking your ring off and putting it on the table.'

'Yes, look at it, dear dear ring, all the same you must have spent too much – I *will* keep it on in bed tonight.'

'Benet has given us the grandest spare bedroom, all our own on the other side of the house.'

'I wonder if we shall always be allowed to be there, in *that* room. Mildred and Owen insist on the Sea Kings – And Jackson, now – we've never known where Jackson slept. I wonder when and how Jackson came back.'

'I expect he just walked in at the door and Benet had been expecting it, and they started up as before.'

'Like Jackson walked in on you. What did you talk about that night? About Benet, and what Jackson was to do? I've been so full of our joys I've never asked you that.'

'It wasn't about him, it was about me. He was there – and I was – recovering – '

'Recovering – well, yes, evidently – anyway you were all right the next morning. I was sick with terror, I could not sleep

222

– I thought you might have changed your mind, there were so many things against me – '

'Oh my darling girl – dear heart – you are not wishing – it was otherwise?'

'No, of course not, *silly* – there, my ring forgives you – don't drive so fast – watch out for the sign – I wish Bran were here this evening. Edward and Anna intimidate me a bit, they seem so much older and more experienced, it's wonderful how *they* have found each other. Edward must get on with the little boy. Poor boy, he must be a bit at sea, having lived in France so long.'

'Edward may have been in France a bit himself.'

'I'd like to explore France but all that costs money. Mamma travels but I can't think where she gets it, I'm not earning anything at present but I *will*, I've decided to give up painting – '

'*To give up painting* – are you *mad*? And what about the Courtauld?'

'Oh I don't want that, it's far too expensive. I suppose I may paint in the evenings, but you were talking about my going to an art school, that's out of the question, we have to be realistic – as it is we are nearly penniless – '

'Look, Rosalind, about our living in Edinburgh – '

'Oh, that's all right, that's all *settled*, I shall *love* living in Edinburgh, I shall love living with *you*, *anywhere*. Truly – whither thou goest I will go, and thy people shall be my people, and thy God my God!'

'Hmm, I'm not sure I have a God.'

'You can ask Jackson. Well, we shall miss him a lot I suppose. Anyway I shall get a job, and *you* can get a *proper* job, in a bookshop for instance – Come now, it will be fun looking for a flat and a job – I promise I'll paint a bit occasionally – What's the matter?'

'Rosalind – there is something I must tell you – '

'My dear dear love – you're so solemn – stop the car will you – there in that place – yes – now my dearest one, I will help you and tend you and be with you for ever and ever – I don't mind how poor we are – oh do not worry, do not grieve, you are mine and I am yours – now tell me what you want to tell me.'

'Well, it's something I've kept secret, from everybody really, and perhaps I shouldn't have done, only now – '

'My sweetheart, don't grieve, don't be sad at all, whatever it is, any sorrow, any distress or fear, you must share it with me – '

'Well, we've been talking about money, and – '

'Go on, I can bear it, please don't look like that, dear dear Tuan – we'll deal with money somehow – '

'You see, I've let you be, and you've been wondering how we can live, and how poor we shall be – '

'It *doesn't matter*, Tuan, we shall be together – '

'Well, I'm – about money – actually I'm not short of it – at all – I am really – well – really I am a millionaire.'

Later as they drove on Tuan explained how his great-great-grandfather had founded a paper-making firm in Germany. This firm had flourished and produced subsidiary firms in Edinburgh and Glasgow. Tuan's father had told Tuan how his father and grandfather had escaped to Scotland when the persecutions began. Tuan's father inherited the business which, after his death, became the property of Tuan. Still pursuing his philosophical studies Tuan, unknown to his London friends, began to spend a part of every week in Edinburgh. Now, since his deputy had retired, he had decided to spend more time in Edinburgh, and less in London. After all, he was head of the firm, and did not regret it. He was relieved now that he had informed Rosalind of this!

As he drove Tuan fell silent, allowing Rosalind to keep reassuring him how little she cared about leaving London, how much she looked forward to Edinburgh, and, quite frankly, she did not complain that there *was* some money! Now she could paint *and* try the Courtauld! Tuan was now finding himself even farther away, transported to the ghetto in Berlin and to Auschwitz. He wondered if he would not talk any more about such things to Rosalind. He recalled his doubts, the doubts he had first discovered, perhaps on that occasion round Benet's dinner table, just before the awful message came. Was it right for him to proceed down that road – down *this* road? Might he now continuously be attacked by black fits like those which

224

had come to him already, when he had bitterly driven Rosalind, who was now his wife, away from him. He thought, I wonder if Jackson hadn't come in that night, would I have broken it all up. Not that, as he remembered, Jackson had said very much to him – though he did certainly speak to him. Tuan thought then, and it occurred to him again now, that perhaps Jackson was Jewish. Yet it was impossible to ask him. He also thought – what am I doing, carrying away good sweet Rosalind? I shall go back to the Synagogue. Really, deep in my heart, I want to be a Rabbi!

At Edward and Anna's swift little Register Office wedding in London the following, besides the Registrar, were present: Montague, Millie, Elizabeth Loxon, Oliver Caxton and Bran. Edward and Anna and Elizabeth and Oliver and Bran had a celebration lunch in the Savoy, after which Edward, Anna and Bran returned to Edward's (now also Anna's and Bran's) house where the red Jaguar, housed in the garage, was taken out and conveyed the family back to Hatting Hall, where they were greeted by Montague and Millie who had already returned by train. On the following day Bran was led to the stables and introduced to a beautiful little brown and white pony called Rex. Fortunately Bran had quite often ridden ponies in France, and was deemed unlikely to fall off. Anna had never mounted a horse, and Edward had never mounted one since Randall's death.

After the tension of the marriage there was much relief, though of course other problems began at once to appear. Love-making was not one of these. From their second 'first day' as they called it, when Edward had so bravely and suddenly 'shown up', their passion for each other had remained fierce and tender, seeming, they were sure, likely to last forever and ever. However there were inevitable difficulties, one of these being their unavoidable incognito. After much discussion on this they had concluded that, for all their sakes (including Lewen's), it must remain intact. Edward was, concerning this, more anxious than Anna. The moment when Bran had thrown himself into Edward's arms had been, for them, a validation of how they were hence to live.

However Edward could not avoid the burden falling upon him. He was to protect them now – and forever. He was made anxious, for instance, by Anna's *insouciance*, how much had she told Bran and how much had Bran found out for himself? How long had Bran known and how? And how, if at all, was Jackson involved? He had been, rather guiltily, relieved when Jackson had vanished, and rather dismayed when he reappeared. However, about this particular he was now increasingly relieved. They had also of course endlessly discussed Bran's future. The fact that he was put down for Edward's old school was of course, had to be, a pleasant surprise for Edward and a token of Anna's, now glowing, optimism. However he was, on further reflection (and this he had not mentioned to Anna), uncertain about the wisdom of this choice. Of course they could if necessary remove him, but this would be a sad pity. Edward had been, for the boarding school in question, ardently groomed by a suitable British, also boarding, prep school. Bran, however, had hitherto spent his school life in French, excellent of course, day schools. Would he not regard cricket with contempt – even more the Wall Game? Suppose he simply refused and demanded to go back to France? Would they not all have to go? He knew that he loved Bran passionately, as much as he loved Anna. Bran had put his arms around him. Bran had withdrawn a little. He was indeed rather quiet and Edward felt it better not to disturb him. Still he felt quite certain of Bran's love.

Such were some of the problems which Edward now attempted to banish from his mind, as he and Anna climbed into the red Jaguar to drive across the valley to Benet's dinner party at Penndean. Bran and Rex and Millie and Montague all came to see them off. Are we late? I think so, but so much the better. The sun shone, everyone seemed to be, and perhaps was, for a time, very happy. Edward and Anna had been informed that it was to be a small party, all familiar faces, all three married couples and their host – and Jackson. Anna commented that they had not seen *him* since before his dreadful expulsion. They were both curious to see what Jackson might be like now – and also of course Benet! They laughed and speculated as the red car flew along.

ELEVEN

Benet's guests at Penndean arrived in this order. First Rosalind and Tuan, who were staying the night, and wanted to arrive early so that they could quietly change, murmuring to each other, and settle into their bedroom. Mildred and Owen came next from the Sea Kings, *almost* late, because of Owen's deliberate dallying, even though they had arrived at the Inn quite early. Edward and Anna, enjoying their privilege as locals, arrived late. Benet had welcomed his guests, leading the 'love birds' up the stairs to their room, greeting Owen and Mildred, who put down their coats in the hall, and then Edward and Anna, who had left their coats in the car. Owen and Mildred were first in the drawing room, followed by Rosalind and Tuan, with Edward and Anna last. Of course it had been for some time general knowledge that Jackson was back. Now Benet, mingling with his guests, disappeared at intervals into the kitchen from which Jackson appeared distantly two or three times, waving to the arrivals. 'Waiting for Jackson,' Anna murmured to Edward. The chat before dinner was a little briefer than usual because of Benet's anxiety. At dinner the *placement*, from host's right to left, was as follows: Benet, Anna, Owen, Tuan, Edward, Mildred, Jackson, Rosalind, Benet. One question at least having been silently answered, soon everyone was busily talking.

Benet had, since the announcement, seen Edward and Anna together, once in London when he had invited them to a little post-marital party, and once again at Hatting when he had tactfully invited himself 'just to say hello'. Anna was now very apologetic.

'Benet dear, we are so sorry, we've hardly seen you, usually it seems that we've been in London when you were here, and here when you are in London – we do love you, you know!'

Benet thought that her words, though awkward, were sincere. He recalled that first visit to her when she had returned to her London house, how pleased he had been to see her, and how little he had got on with Bran! For an instant he thought, yes, I think Anna and Edward do love me. But they will not tell me much. He said, 'So Bran has a pony called Rex!'

'Yes! How do you know?'

'Sylvia told us. And I'm afraid the village knows!'

'Of course! He adores Rex, but I think he loves Spencer even more.'

'So dear Spencer is still with us. Oh Anna, I'm so happy for you and Edward, it's a sort of miracle – '

'Yes, we've been so lucky, we've done it at last, Edward plucked up his courage!'

'So you've been meeting each other in France, and in London, well of course – and Bran will go to school, to Edward's old school you said! Is he looking forward to it?'

'Oh yes, he's delighted with everything – '

'I want to make friends with him.'

'Oh, surely you are friends already!'

'He gets more and more like Lewen every day.'

'Yes, doesn't he. Look at those love birds, aren't they sweet – they are so young – you must be pleased with them, they are like your children!'

'Yes, that was such a beautiful surprise. They're going to live partly in Scotland and partly in London.'

'How can they afford two places, poor things? Tuan hasn't any sort of job, has he? And Rosalind can hardly afford an art school. Ada is not so rich now, you know. We shall have to help them out, don't you think?'

'Yes, I have already thought of that.'

'Have you seen her paintings, are they good?'

'Oh yes, quite good I think, Owen sometimes helps her.'

229

'Dear Owen, he's just the same, isn't he. Aren't they staying at the Sea Kings? We could have put them up.'

'Well, so could I. They wanted to stay there.'

'No chance of *their* marrying I'm afraid! Mildred is still in love with an Indian god, isn't she?'

'With several, I think. *And* some pious priest in the East End! Oh Anna, Anna, I can't tell you how happy I am with you being here!'

'You're not upset about Marian? Well, you must be a bit.'

'I was a bit, but that's all gone. She seems to be very happy with her Australian.'

'Didn't Jackson have something to do with that?'

'Well, a very minor part. How did you find out?'

'Marian wrote to me! The mother is coming here, isn't she, Ada Fox? Someone said you were going to put her up.'

'How clever these someones are!'

'Sorry, you don't mind? By the way, thank you so much for that lovely cigarette case!'

'I'm glad you like it. Edward's looking so well, isn't he, so positively beautiful, so rapturously happy!'

Owen was pressing his right foot against Tuan's left foot under the table. Tuan, not turning, did not remove his foot. He smiled a gentle angelic smile.

'So that's it for you, my dear. I congratulate you and her. She is pure beauty and pure goodness. Am I surprised? Yes, but only in a mean selfish way, and almost that's gone too. Look, now she's talking to Jackson! May I paint a picture of the two of you together?'

'Dearest Owen, why not!'

'Thanks for the "dearest". I say, Benet, what splendid wine! Benet's cellars are famous. I know she loves me, I have known her far far longer than you, ever since she was a child. I think she's got the perfect man, I thought there wasn't one. But what's all this about going to Scotland, why on earth Scotland – to make your fortunes there?'

'Well, we'll be just as much in London too –'

'You must get a proper job, my boy. I don't want her to work except at painting, perhaps she'll soon be a painter, then she'll support you! Not that painters make much money, certainly not to begin with, and, God damn it, most of the time nothing at all! We used to sing like nightingales when Tim was here, but I think that was before your time, before you found us, that is, what a bit of luck, don't lose us, will you, don't lose *me* anyway – '

'Oh I won't!'

'I need you. When Mildred is up in the mountains squatting on her sari, I shall be in dire need.'

'Is she going?'

'I don't know. Fortunately she has discovered a bloody Anglican priest, name of Lucas, and my God, do you know she wants to be a priest herself! What is England coming to! But never mind her, let us feast our eyes upon your lovely bride, she's been talking to Jackson, look, she's seen us, I bet she knows what we're up to, she's laughing, she's waving, damn, now Benet's got her. By the way, what do you think about Jackson? All right, we can discuss this later. You know, I haven't really seen you since I kissed you in the grove underneath those big dark trees. You won't refuse my kisses now? Oh thank heavens, I knew you wouldn't! Now it's time for me to do my best with Anna, while you fence with Edward, who is now relinquishing Mildred to, dear me, Jackson!'

Edward, having steered off the subject of Lewen, had been arguing with Mildred about the future of the Anglican Church. 'My dear, it is done for. If there is any Christianity alive in the next century it will be the Church of Rome. Rome has always held ruthlessly together, discipline, discipline, that is what is attractive. All the same, I doubt if that will last much longer either. The Anglicans are a catastrophe, jaunting along in all sorts like a circus, there is nothing deep there, and they know it! What might be decently preached is the *truth* that there is no God, no life after death, and Jesus is not divine. Perhaps something decent might follow – not just money and technology and success – I wonder – *we* shall never know. As for pure survival, my bet is on your Hindu and Buddhist friends – and Judaism, ask Tuan sometime – well, I'll ask him myself now he's escaped from Owen.'

Mildred had been longing for this move, it was the moment she was waiting for; just as Anna was turning to Owen and

Benet to Rosalind, Mildred found herself turning towards Jackson. She trembled, she shuddered, she thought he is different, he is more, even more, handsome, his dark eyes are larger, so calm and glowing, his lips are gentle, his expression is loving, he is secure because Benet has forgiven him, no no, *he* has forgiven *Benet*! But it isn't that, he has changed, like in suffering, like a sea-change, that is in Shakespeare isn't it, his skin is different, darker and more glowing, when he went away it was for another incarnation, he belongs with people who go on and on living, perhaps it is Tibet or somewhere else, how old is he, a hundred years, a thousand years, they come like guardian angels, they *are* guardian angels, now he is talking to me in a strange language, yet I understand, I reach out my hand and touch his hand, and his hand is burning. I am speaking to him and he is speaking to me, he has the stigmata, he was beaten like Christ was beaten, he is damaged, like the Fisher King in disguise, he is afraid of being caught up with by those who know his shame, and how he was found in a cardboard box in the rushes beside the river. Uncle Tim found him and nursed him like a wounded bird, like Prospero on his island with his secret sin, suffering agonies of remorse, and he said 'this thing of darkness I acknowledge mine', of course Caliban was his son by Sycorax, Jackson is Caliban, he is the one who knows the island and the animals and the plants and strange sounds, Jackson is really Benet's illegitimate son, Shakespeare too felt remorse, his great soul was filled with remorse, like Macbeth, like Othello, 'Keep up your bright swords, for the dew will rust them', and the Indian Rope Trick, and Kim running over the housetops, and the Angel of the Annunciation, and yes, I shall hold the Chalice, I mean the Holy Grail.

But now she begins to hear Owen's loud voice coming through, 'Where are our great leaders now, where are our great thinkers, are we to take orders from elsewhere from invisible bureaucrats, Marx saw that poverty could and must be removed, nobody listened, everything is ruthless now in our so-called democracies, we must smash up our senseless, cruel capitalism, as it is no wonder Alexander has gone to Japan – '

The table was beginning to disintegrate. Anna, next to Owen, was murmuring, 'Yes, yes, yes indeed,' and trying to engage the attention of Edward, Rosalind was gazing at Tuan, Benet, who had been scanning the table, at last stood up. Everyone began to rise.

Owen, abandoning his speech, now exclaimed, 'To the garden, to the garden!' Everyone, laughing and jumbling, were now up on their feet, when Benet cried, 'Wait! We must have a toast to Uncle Tim!'

All glasses were lifted and clinked and the cry was 'Uncle Tim!', followed in some cases by murmurs of 'God rest him!' or 'Dear old Tim, bless him!' Those who had known him well had tears in their eyes.

After that there was a stampede through the drawing room and out into the garden where, following tradition, the guests scattered into the dark. The stars, since it was already later in the season, were less brilliantly milky, more like a very dim carpet upon which formations more familiarly appeared. The dewy grass was wetter, the bats were fewer, the weird cries of owls came less often from the huge Wellingtonias, toward which Owen looked sadly as he saw Tuan propelling Rosalind in that direction. Edward and Anna strolled away arm-in-arm towards the rose garden, its little fountain now audible in the darkness. Owen, foiled, took charge of Mildred, who now was quietly weeping. They sat down at the far end of the terrace. Benet looked round for Jackson: but Jackson was not to be seen. Benet, breathing deeply in the moist air, walked slowly on towards the end of the lawn, alone.

TWELVE

Rosalind and Tuan were locked together in the big four-poster in the 'old part' of Penndean. After coming in from the garden they had hurried to their bed, avoiding the others. Now it was like being in a warm very quietly moving sea, or like very slow dancers in a slow sleepy waltz. Or like world class skating, as Tuan had remarked, except that it was all in the same place. She had skated when she was younger. Could Tuan skate? She had never asked him! How lovely, if they could skate together in Kensington Gardens! As it was, everything that should have happened between them had happened between them. It was like a fairy tale or a miracle or some absolute spiritual formation of new being, like entering a huge beautiful holy house. Before they went out to the Register Office they had both instinctively knelt down, as in some holy chivalry. They had by then passed the stage of 'are you sure', wherein each one, quite sure, was anxiously testing the strength of the other. Tuan was indeed so absolutely a knight, Rosalind found herself positively seeing, in and out of her dreams, his glowing silver armour and his noble helmeted head. I have found him, she thought, I have *found* him! He held her so gently and so firmly, he so pure in heart, somehow like a child, but so courageous and so loving. The future, ahead, yes, so much of future to come, and children, wonderful children whom we both have made. All this, she herself, whom she had fought for and won, continuously bathing his wounds. And she had fought for him too, when suddenly, in a flash of lightning, she saw, and was then afraid that it was too late. So many strange things had brought them together, so many divine accidents. Really Marian had brought her to him, and he saying he would call Rosalind, and how Marian and I slept, and how Tuan looked at me in my sleep, and Marian ran away, and then Tuan and I held hands and kissed, and then Tuan said he had so much darkness and I must go away and then he told me his dreadful story about the dog when everything else was nightmare, and he was weeping, and he sent me away and I went away and I came back and he said more things about how Marian had gone and I was free to move into a space really my own and he meant I was free to marry Edward, and he threw me out and I came again and he said at last, 'You have won, dear child,' and we went to bed together, and we lay down as we are lying down now. But I know that he has still strange pains which he tries to conceal from me, and I have heard him murmuring Hebrew in his sleep and I think that pain will never altogether go away, and I shall bind my love closer and closer about him, as I am binding it now, and holding him closer and closer with my love.

And Tuan, lying so closely bound beside her was thinking, whatever sort of girl I have married, I have married the right one, that I absolutely love, and who loves me and can understand my tears, and of course the pains will go on and in time may be different but will not go – and oh my dear dear parents – And more and more I shall devote myself to holy things, my Maimonides, my Spinoza, my Scholem – hmmm, I wonder if Rosalind will inherit Penndean, or will Benet give it to Marian or to Jackson or the Quakers?

It was indeed late when Edward and Anna got back to Hatting. They had not spoken to each other upon the short drive, but at one point Edward's left hand sought Anna's right. Then there

235

was the quiet entry through the front door of the silent house, and the tip-toe mounting of the soft-carpeted stairs and along the corridor to their bedroom. Montague and Millie slept downstairs. Bran slept, at his own wish, at the farther end of the house. Reaching their bedroom they dropped their light coats upon the floor and sat upon the huge bed embracing each other. After that, sitting cross-legged, they discoursed, as Anna observed, in slow tones, like Indian gods. Beneath their soft loving voices their thoughts ran to and fro like mice. Anna thrust Edward away a little, gazing at him as if with a fresh amazement. They talked at first about Jackson, about his *situation*, how did Benet get him back, or did he come, and so on, and then about Benet, was he happy, was he frightened? And how utterly happy Rosalind looked, fainting with happiness, and how handsome Tuan was but probably penniless, something must be done, and how serious Mildred looked when she was talking and listening to Jackson about India and no doubt Jackson had an Indian streak himself. Anna, stroking her hand gently down Edward's pale hawkish face, thought how noble and how tragic he looked and how difficult of access even now, he could look so far away. He is counting up the problems. He had talked a little to her about Randall, she had waited anxiously and silently for that. Of course she had known, as others had, about Randall, but without details. What Edward now had to say to her was little more than what she had known before, and then perhaps forever nothing, maybe it was better so. Edward talked to Bran now more than she did. How strange, she thought, I believed that I would have to go through life deceiving my son. Will there be new deceptions? Surely not she prayed. All those photos and letters, even a letter from the doctor, she had burnt some of them but not all – she had left them for Bran to discover. And then Bran threw the stone through the window, and did not that begin everything. Oh now let them all be happiness – happiness and ponies – but also Edward's school – they would have to see – how much I wished I could believe in God! Mistress of Hatting, yes – yes! My love for Edward increases, it burns, I love him with all my heart, I would fight for him like a tiger. But I shall have as the years go by to be

236

silent, to be discreet, even before him, even before Bran. Oh Lewen, Lewen, from the grave, you must forgive us – I know that you will.

As they undressed and lay down, turning out the light and seeking each other in the dark, Edward's thoughts, less orderly than those of his wife, wandered about. He thought of course about Randall, perhaps she was thinking about Randall too. Now she is asleep. I can hear the waves as they were – and again when I went the *second* time. I shall not go there again ever. I have not told her about *that*, I have told no one about *that*, as if I were to drown myself at last – but now I have her – thank heavens I came to them, oh thank God, tears, tears – and now I am back as it were at the start when I had her in my arms and she lied to me and said she was already pregnant with Lewen's child, and I understood all the lies and all about her and about everything and I had to give it all up – and I felt terrible grief but also I felt noble and how I must do what was right for her and for Lewen – oh Lewen, where are you now, wise and good Lewen, you must pardon us for Bran's sake too – Oh Bran, may he love me, may he not ever hate me. He will grow to be a man – oh what then? – but now for their sake and for my own – How lovely it was in the garden at Penn after dinner when we walked arm-in-arm and saw the little fountain and heard it so softly in the night and sighed so deeply and kissed each other and were alone – how's Bran now, he must be asleep – I must sleep too – it is nearly morning – oh God have mercy upon us.

Meanwhile, at the Sea Kings, Mildred was sitting upon Owen's bed, while Owen, wearing only pants and a shirt, was sitting beside the dressing table, pouring more whisky into his glass. His sturdy nose was red, his pale blue eyes were watery, his cupid lips were pouting, his fine untidy hair, sweeping across his brow, was chaotically visible in the mirror behind him. Still filled with the evening's exaltations and feeling that the night would never end they had of course been arguing. How extremely handsome he is, Mildred was thinking.

Returning to an earlier topic, Owen was saying, 'You *were* talking to Jackson, you were chatting away to him, your mouth was opening and closing – '

'Now look here,' said Mildred, 'I'm sure I said nothing, or almost nothing – He poured it all into my ears, he was talking about remorse and forgiveness and – he has such beautiful eyes and – '

'Confound the blighter,' said Owen, 'I suspect he can make himself invisible, he is something out of Kafka. I had to forgive him for vanishing. You are rather beautiful tonight. I think I said that before. I suspect if you pulled back the curtains you would see the dawn.'

'I am sure it is already with us,' said Mildred, shaking out her skirt. For ordinary everyday life she wore longish brown skirts, for rare special evenings she wore an old familiar very long dark blue real silk dress, with a lapis-lazuli brooch holding a glimpse of white lace. Now for Owen alone she had undone her long dark brown hair, taking out the tortoiseshell combs one by one and letting her hair fall down on either side of her pale thin face. She thought, as usual, of the Lady of Shalott. She thought I really must go off to bed, I can't go on sitting here looking at this dear big animal!

Owen, picking up her thought, said, 'Don't go, have some more whisky.'

'I've had some more whisky. And you should stop. You won't be able to drive.'

'Of course I will. As for that fellow, he is bewitching you. As for you, you play the mouse while filled with passion, and you talk too. I wish he would bewitch me. The gods of India will scoop you up in the end.'

Mildred stood up, then stooped to pick up her combs which had fallen to the floor. Her thick long glossy brown hair fell down past her shoulders to her waist. She began to gather it together and toss it behind her.

'Well, goodnight – Do stop drinking.'

'Wait, wait, pale maiden. Let me see if I can get up. Yes, I can. Let me blunder across the space between us.' Only a little taller, he kissed her, upon her closed eyelids, then on her mouth.

'Oh my darling, do go to bed.'

'You love me.'

'I love you. Goodnight, dear beast. If you can fall onto the bed, I can turn off the light.'

'No, no, first I go to the loo, then I get into the bed, then I turn out the light, I promise you.'

Mildred padded away, softly closing the door and gliding quietly down the corridor. She entered her bedroom, turned on all the lights, and began to undress. She undid the old brooch, extracted the lace, and pulled her long dress over her head and dropped it to the floor and stepped out of it, then removed her petticoat, shoes, stockings, knickers and vest. Then she put on an old long-faded cotton nightdress, white but covered by very pale pink flowers. The curtains were closed. She went to the window and cautiously drew the curtains a little apart. Yes, it was certainly dawn! The sudden sight, in mist, of nearby woodland and far hills, startled her, and she hastily closed the curtains. She thought, how strange, Owen and I are together, like quite different furry animals, well at least we are both furry. How long, how very long, we have known each other. Oh how I love him, I love him so much.

Pulling the sheet and blankets back she sat on the bed. She was suddenly trying to remember what Jackson had said. *Jackson*. And what had *she* said, had she said anything? It was already fading, of course she was so tired, she would think it out tomorrow. Only it is tomorrow. She put her hand on her heart. Was it really true at last, that she might be a woman priest, and hold the Chalice in her hands? How sleepy she felt now and how happy. Lucas would ordain her. They would live among the poor. And the Indian gods would come to her too, indeed they were already with her, the beautiful powerful ones whom she knew so well, whose feet she kissed. Krishna dances and the cobra stretches his hood and the little boy shall be among the Greek gods too. Oh all pure and loving ones be with me and forgive me for my sins, and I shall hold the Chalice which is the Grail. She slipped down, kneeling beside the bed, her hands clasped, her eyes filling with tears, and she found that words were coming to her, holy words, all mixed up, repeated again and again, oh Christ, my lord and my god, God is love, let me be worthy, *dominus et deus*.

Owen staggered out of the bathroom, swinging the door, and made his way to bed. He gazed at the bed, frowning, then sat down heavily upon it. He had turned the light off in the bathroom but the light was still on upon the dressing table. He staggered across and put it out, now finding himself in complete darkness. He moved cautiously toward the bed and fell upon it, as suggested by Mildred. More turning and fumbling found him a light switch beside the bed. He edged the blankets out from under him and struggled with the top sheet, humping himself up and pulling it. He managed to get his legs between the sheets and blankets and wriggled himself down inside. One of the pillows fell upon the floor. Reaching down unsuccessfully to find it he somehow put out the bedside light. He squirmed back, discovering another pillow in the dark, and rolled himself at last into the centre of the bed where he could put his head down. He felt a bit ashamed of being quite so drunk in front of Mildred. Well, why bother. Would she be off one day, perhaps soon, with her gods or rotten Lucas? Tuan had been snaffled by Rosalind. Jackson had wrapped himself in a cloak of mystery, was it worth trying to unwrap him. How strange that he had had him in his house and shown him things he had shown to no one else. Jackson had been in his kitchen inventing eggs and things – how exactly did he escape? Owen could not remember. He simply vanished. I shall flounder back, thought Owen, I'll get hold of him again. How could I be so taken by that weirdo, that snake in the reeds? Benet does not deserve him, I'll get hold of him, I'll hold him down and teach him to paint – Christ – so *he*'s got into the scene as well – Christ, I must paint, I must try to be worthy of being a painter, I must invent, I must create, I must kneel, I must start as if from the beginning. Owen adjusted his head and then went quietly to sleep. He dreamt that he was a slug crawling slowly along the ground, and Piero and Titian and Velázquez and Carpaccio and Turner were standing round him and looking down at him with faintly puzzled frowns, and he was shouting up at them, but his voice was so miserably tiny, he was sure they could not hear him, and when he tried to wave his horns at them he suddenly realised that *slugs do not have horns*. Not even *that*, he thought in his dream.

THIRTEEN

Usually now Jackson did not allow Benet into the kitchen except, and that very briefly, as a spectator. On this occasion he allowed Benet to assist him a little before the 'wedding' feast, but Benet was not to rise from the table, and Jackson, though pressed by some of the guests, was the only person to move about, bringing and removing the items. When the stampede into the garden occurred Jackson was not seen, and it was assumed, rightly, that Jackson, smilingly, rejecting help, such as had been proffered by less well-trained visitors, had disappeared to deal personally with the washing up. Benet, after seeing off all the departing guests, the young lovers being already in bed in the 'old part', listened to the still continuous sound of crockery in the kitchen, and of course did not interrupt it. Later there would be silence, when Jackson retired to copious ground floor quarters beyond, while Benet went to his big usual first-floor bedroom with the view of the garden.

However, though he undressed, he did not go to sleep, but sat upon his undisturbed bed in his pyjamas with socks and slippers. His thoughts continually returned to Jackson and the meeting on the bridge. This surprising evening continued with their walking all the way through the night from the river to Tara. Benet was all the time in terror of Jackson suddenly disappearing and never being seen again, he was also very afraid of *annoying* Jackson. Jackson however was relaxed as if it were just a stroll through London after a pleasant evening.

Benet's suggestion of food, not repeated, was not picked up. In any case Benet was all the time absorbed in Jackson's presence and also his conversation. The presence alone flustered Benet, who felt that he must inform Jackson of what was going on in his absence, for instance that Edward had married Anna, and Tuan had married Rosalind. Or did perhaps Jackson *already know* – perhaps indeed more than Benet – of these happenings? There was also, now seeming far in the past, the news of Marian, that she was alive, also married, and in Australia. Benet also recalled, though with no intention of revealing it, his visit to Owen, who had entered so profoundly into his sorrow, suggesting even that by now Jackson had killed himself with grief! Benet had then summoned up his dream, that Uncle Tim was looking at him, and then looking down at the floor, where there was a long black shadow. These horrors, were they to be divulged also? Afterwards Benet did not know for sure *what* he had said on that night – he had certainly rambled on with his confessions. But what had Jackson said to him? He could scarcely remember anything except for the very last bit, which had caused Benet considerable anguish. They were now very close to Tara. What would happen? Benet thought – the worst. They stopped at Tara, at the bottom of the steps. Who would speak first? Benet said hastily, 'Listen, *please*, do come in – let's have a drink – I mean – I am asking you to forgive me – will you please come back again to stay, and be with me – as a friend you know – *please*, Jackson?' Jackson had stood, looking at Benet with, as Benet thought, a rather dreamy look. He said, 'I'm sorry, I must go. As for what you say, I think you should consider it. I shall come back here, if I may, between twelve and one, in a week, or let us say about two weeks, and see how we both feel.' After this he turned and walked away.

Benet waited for two weeks. Jackson returned after two weeks and a day. Benet had waited in anguish, distracted if he did not come, if he *never* came – and also wondering what on earth he was to say to him. What he decided on, and what he said, when Jackson appeared, was uttered at once, 'Listen, I want you to stay with me, to be with me now *as a friend, not* as a servant.

243

Of course that's so now, isn't it? I want that you should live with me permanently – *please*. Of course you'll be perfectly free – '

These were Benet's first words, standing opposite Jackson in the drawing room. Benet trembled.

Jackson, smiling faintly, looked at him, then said, 'Such an arrangement, if attempted, must of course be between equals.'

Benet said, 'I am sorry, *of course* I take that for granted.'

'And I cannot guarantee that I will stay here or indeed anywhere permanently.'

'Well, of course. I just want you to be here as my friend – '

Jackson looked pensively away, then said, 'Well, all right, let us give it a try.'

'Thank you! Then what about a drink to celebrate? Here is a bottle and two glasses – '

'I have noticed them. A glass of water please, then I shall go. I shall be back in three days.'

'Let me drive you over in the car?'

'No, thank you.'

'So now you will live in the house – '

'If you don't mind I would rather stay in the Lodge.'

When Jackson left, Benet felt a sudden outburst of joy. He put his hand to his heart and sat down in the drawing room on a chair near to the door. Then he sat there for some time, beginning to wonder whether these 'arrangements' might not in the end break his heart.

Now all was silent in Penndean, and Benet, as he sat upon his bed, was rehearsing what had happened since the great day of the re-entry of Jackson into Tara. 'Benet's friends' were all pleased to hear of Jackson's return and of his new status and even came over formally to greet him, though many, especially the love-birds, were more concerned with their own immediate lives, and the phenomenon, now time had passed, was settling down into ordinary. Jackson, now visible much more than Benet, might be spoken of (by some perhaps ambiguously) as 'Benet's friend'. He was promptly made famous as a cook, and urged to write a cookery book. He still worked in gardens, Benet's and those of others, did shopping, was an electrician, a carpenter, a maker of things, a mender of things, a man of all trades. Indeed he was revered as such. Life at Penn and at Tara went on almost as usual. Benet was now at least confident that he was the person closest to Jackson. With this, he held silently to his heart the final pronouncement concerning the Lodge.

Jackson now read a great deal, perhaps he had done so before, he was often in the library when Benet was in his study. They sat together in the evenings in the drawing room and talked, 'yarned' as Benet said, Benet recalling his parents, his childhood, his first memories of Uncle Tim, how his father derided Tim, how Benet came to love him. Benet also chatted of his various travels, but had not yet ventured to mention Venice. Of Jackson's past nothing was said. 'A strange kind of human being,' Owen had called him. Jackson read, having read many of them already, all Tim's books, those about India and the East, also Tim's favourite novels. Benet had noticed earlier, and remembered now from a repartee at dinner, that Jackson had probably read Tolstoy, at least he had been able to defend Sonya. He had certainly read Shakespeare. Benet had talked freely about his own work, as it concerned Heidegger and Hölderlin, these interested Jackson and he encouraged Benet to go on, indeed insisted that he should. Of course the talk often returned to Uncle Tim, and Benet had only lately remembered, he did not recall when or why, that Uncle Tim had told him once that Jackson knew some oriental languages. Of this nothing was said. The close observers, such as Owen and Mildred, and Edward who sometimes came over by himself, agreed that the pair were 'getting on very well together'. Benet knew however that there was a border over which he could not take a step. That 'stoppage' at first distressed Benet, but in time he took to it, finding in it a kind of tender vibration. More ultimate was Jackson's throwaway remark, 'I cannot guarantee that I will stay here or anywhere permanently'.

245

After a while visitors became less inquisitively frequent. Ordinary life went on. Rosalind Berran, now Abelson, was to have a baby. (Never mentioned by Tuan except once passionately to Benet: 'Oh let it be a boy!') Marian Bjerke was also about to have a baby, she and Rosalind kept up a constant correspondence. Priscilla Conti (Priscilla was a professional singer) came and talked a lot with Jackson and they sang together. Benet had never heard Jackson sing. 'A wonderful voice,' Priscilla said, as she dashed back to Italy. Jackson had occasional private conversations with Oliver Caxton, these took place in the Lodge at Tara. Jackson more often, and regularly, visited Owen, with whom he often stayed for a long time. So things were changing. Most profoundly disturbing to Benet was that Mildred had introduced Jackson to Lucas Begbrook, and that they were probably generating 'holiness' between them! All these private visitations Jackson of course mentioned to Benet but did not discuss.

The dawn was now perceptibly present, introducing a transparent curtain of pale blue. The rising sun was gently making his presence felt. The revellers of the previous night were still asleep, Edward and Anna were asleep, Owen and Mildred were asleep, Tuan and Rosalind were asleep, Benet was asleep. Bran was not asleep. He made his way cautiously down the big stairway and tip-toed towards the back of the house, here he unlocked a small door which led out into the garden. As he hurried across the grass his shoes and socks were wet with dew. The pale gravelled path was also damp, waiting for the sun to warm it. Bran, taking another key from his pocket, unlocked a green slatted wooden door, carefully locking it behind him. He was making for the stables. His nearness was already now being announced, as his feet crunched more gravel and again more paving. He heard a faint little cry, almost like that of a cat. He hurried on to where Rex's head was visible, over the lower door of the stable. Bran ran forward and threw his arms round Rex's neck. The pony whinnied again as Bran rubbed his brow gently against the warm fur, then standing back and drawing his hands down Rex's nose and over his wet black nostrils. They looked at each other, the boy and the pony, with their wild eyes, both young, both passionate, they looked at each other with amazement, and with passion and with love. Bran said, 'Not yet, my pretty one, my dear, goodbye for a little, I shall come back soon.' In an instant then he turned and ran, listening to the high whinny of the little pony, he ran zig-zag avoiding the front of the house, darting along an alley of yellow privet and crossing another gravel path and slithering down a grassy slope towards a well-kept brick wall. He climbed over the wall at his particular place, falling, then stumbling into the long grasses and dashing across the tarmac road. He climbed over a five-barred gate and ran upwards now, panting, across a field, then through another gate. He stood a while breathing deeply by a hedge, then walked on, slipping through another hedge into another field. Here he stood, breathing hard, looking anxiously about. Then in the still slight hazy morning light he saw the big hunter coming slowly towards him. He called softly, 'Spencer, Spencer,' as he walked now to meet him, and in a sudden clumsy embrace they met, Bran clutching at the great neck and seeking for the great head, as the horse leant down towards the boy. Bran felt a strange feeling on his bare arms where a big strong tongue was licking him. Clumsily he reached to get an offering, a carrot, out of his pocket, but Spencer was not interested, and had now removed his tongue to Bran's face. Bran then began to walk slowly across the field, the horse following, and stopped again reaching up his arms to the horse's neck, stroking his huge face, looking into his beautiful eyes, and tears came to Bran as he said his name and felt with his hands the warm smooth tense skin; and it was as if he were holding up all the world. He had been thus to the field more than once, but this visitation had something very special, painful, a burning sensation, as if there were flames licking them both, lifting up their faces to the heat of the risen sun. Bran found himself sobbing. He lay against the horse's side, pressing up against the shoulder, thrusting his hand into the mane, as if by Spencer's gentle movement, the horse and he were one. At last the ecstasy was passing, and Bran said to Spencer, 'I am sorry, oh I am so sorry,' apologising for not being able to be, with and for the other, something perfect. He detached himself, kissing the warm fur, murmuring, 'I'll be back again,' and turned away and ran back across the field. Before he reached the hedge he fell, his ankles tangled by thick bindweed. He hurried on, the way he had come, down the hill. Spencer followed him slowly as far as he could. He was very old and tired. Bending his elegant legs he lay down in the long grass.

Jackson, who had also got up early, had had his interview with Spencer and was beginning to walk down towards the river when, looking back, he saw Bran appearing. Unobserved, he sat down in the grass and watched the boy and the horse, both his friends. He was also, he observed, now the companion of a very large spider who was busy completing a web between the tall grasses. The spider ran hurriedly over to see what was happening, but there was only a minor disturbance. Now Bran had gone, but Jackson continued to sit motionless in the grass. He breathed deeply. Sometimes he had a sudden loss of breath, together with a momentary loss, or shift, of memory. So he was to wait, once more, forgetfulness, his and theirs. He thought, my power has left me, will it ever return, will the *indications* return? No assignment. But punishment? Madness of course always now at hand. He had forgotten where he had to go, and what he had to do. To the mountains. If he went to the mountains now he would find no one there. Stay with Benet – among the rich – seeking the poor? How strange just now that he was able to sing. Assigned? He remembered now that he could sing. But he had come to the wrong turning. With Benet, had he finally made a mistake? Have I simply come to the end of my tasks? I wish I could say – 'I have only to wait.' How much did Uncle Tim understand, I wonder. Or, how much now will I understand. My powers have left me, will they return – have I simply misunderstood? At least I had called Benet to the bridge. Is it all a *dream*, yes, perhaps a dream – yet my strength remains, and I can destroy myself at any moment. Death, its closeness. Do I after all fear those who seek me? I have forgotten them and no one calls. Was I in prison once? I cannot remember. At the end of what is necessary, I have come to a place where there is no road.

As, casting off all this, he began to rise, he felt something strange. The spider had discovered his hand and was now walking upon it. Gently he assisted the creature back into its web. He walked down towards the river and crossed the bridge. As he came nearer now to Penndean he began to smile.